CW01151855

# THE QUASIMODO KILLINGS

VANCE AND SHEPHERD MYSTERIES BOOK 1

JOHN BROUGHTON

Copyright (C) 2022 John Broughton

Layout design and Copyright (C) 2022 by Next Chapter

Published 2022 by Next Chapter

Edited by Fading Street Services

Cover art by CoverMint

This book is a work of fiction. Names, characters, places, and incidents are the product of the author's imagination or are used fictitiously. Any resemblance to actual events, locales, or persons, living or dead, is purely coincidental.

All rights reserved. No part of this book may be reproduced or transmitted in any form or by any means, electronic or mechanical, including photocopying, recording, or by any information storage and retrieval system, without the author's permission.

# ACKNOWLEDGMENTS

My sincere thanks go to the CEO of Next Chapter Publishing, Miika Hannila, and to expert author, Brian L. Porter, without whose encouragement I would not have embarked on what was a new genre for me in The Quasimodo Killings.

# FOREWORD

## BY BESTSELLING AUTHOR BRIAN L PORTER

John Broughton is an established and accomplished author of historical fiction with over a score of published works to his name. I was therefore flattered to receive a request to write the foreword to *The Quasimodo Killings,* his first venture into the mystery/thriller genre. Having spoken to John, I knew he was a little apprehensive about taking this big step, departing from the familiar and embarking on a new literary journey into what was, for him, new and uncharted territory.

*The Quasimodo Killings* introduces the reader to Detective Inspector Jacob Vance and his assistant, Detective Sergeant Brittany Shepherd, who are called upon to try to prevent a series of murders, after the new Chief of the Metropolitan Police receives a threatening letter after making a speech promising to 'get tough' with the criminal underclass that she perceives as the biggest threat to law and order in the capital. Unless she publishes a public retraction of her speech, the writer of the letter promises to exact revenge by committing a series of nine murders across London, all in the name of the mysterious Lord Robert. Thus, the scene is set, and Mr Broughton takes us into the heart of the investigation as Vance and Shepherd attempt to prevent the deaths of a number of innocent members of the population without any way of identifying them in advance, and with no clue to the identity of the would-be killer.

Usually at home in the world of Anglo-Saxons and first millennium Viking raiders, it's safe to say that John Broughton has successfully made the transition from historical fiction to the world of present-day crime and its detection. It's a perfect illustration of the old adage that, 'you can't keep a good man down' as he does a great job of keeping his readers guessing as his first mystery / thriller is engaging and entertaining and will, I'm sure be the first of more to come in his latest venture into this new genre. It's certainly a brave step to leave behind all he has previously achieved in order to try his hand at something he'd never considered until recently. I'm sure, like his historical novels, *The Quasimodo Killings* will bring him more success and may even bring about the birth of a whole new series featuring Vance and Shepherd…who can tell?

Brian L Porter

Bestselling author of the highly successful Mersey Mystery Series and the Family of Rescue Dogs series of award-winning nonfiction.

# CHAPTER 1

## NEW SCOTLAND YARD, VICTORIA EMBANKMENT, LONDON, UK, 2021 AD

The new commissioner of the Metropolitan Police had every reason to feel satisfied. As only the second female in her position, following the early retirement of her illustrious groundbreaking predecessor and the first from a BAME background, Aalia Phadkar chose this press conference to impact not only on the general public but also the powers that be.

Even those most unconvinced by her appointment had to admit that she had considerable merits, not least, her striking looks. Some opted to call her statuesque, which her severest critics declared apt because she was, they grumbled, as hard and unfeeling as an ancient Greek bronze effigy dredged from the bed of the Ionian Sea. Instead, her ardent supporters pointed to her undoubted intellect and profound cultural preparation but mainly indicated her crusade to pilot the Met into the vanguard of modern policing techniques.

The occasion of the press conference called to bring to a conclusion the capture of Angus McBain, the so-called Glasgow Slasher, whose chain of razor attacks on innocent young women had terrorised the nighttime streets of central London for over a year, provided Phadkar with the platform she desired to outline her vision of the Met's future.

"Ladies and gentlemen of the Press," she began in a clear voice in perfect received English—

"Strewth, she sounds like the Queen," muttered a Fleet Street hack to his colleague, a petite redhead from a rival tabloid.

"She might as well be, with all the power she wields, but let's hear what she has to say." She tapped her roller ball pen on her notepad to demonstrate *her* concentration to him.

"I would like to begin by congratulating my colleagues in the Metropolitan Police from the assistant commissioner down to the most recent recruit among our constables and all the support staff whose magnificent work has led to the arrest of the so-called Glasgow Slasher, thus bringing to an end the disfigurement of solitary pedestrian women whose lives have been ruined by this species of lowlife. Regarding which, I wish to take advantage of this auspicious occasion to send a message to the disreputable specimens who, unfortunately, live in our midst." Her voice took on a clarity that would have resounded in the crowded room without the aid of the microphones ranged before her.

Determination sounded in her every word. "It is my declared intention to propel the Metropolitan Police to the avant-garde of Western policing. I intend to press the Government for greater investment in technology so that our American cousins and Chinese counterparts will only be able to stare and attempt to imitate us. So, I address my next comments to the criminal fraternity of which Angus McBain is an all-too-typical exemplar. Today's criminal hardly possesses the intellect of the fictional Moriarty. Scum like McBain have zero culture, an ignorance bred of disdain for the educational opportunities provided by society and wilfully spurned by their underdeveloped brains. This type of squalid individual had better beware since our intention at the Met is to clean the capital of such *vermin* using every means possible. Indeed, the modern police force intends to demonstrate the merits of an educational system second to none, which enables the force to draw upon the smartest brains the country has to offer." She paused to beam triumphantly around the assembled denizens of the English Press.

Her pause was well calculated and allowed her philosophy to penetrate the minds of her audience. Now was the moment to strike. "To make the streets of our metropolis safe for the law-abiding citizen at every hour of the day, I unashamedly use this platform to address the Prime Minister himself—he has declared several times that he is the most public-spirited member of his party. As such, he will consider my appeal for an increase in staffing for our overstretched personnel. I refer not only to our old-fashioned constables on the beat in some of the more degraded parts of this fine city but also to the motorised elements and the invaluable deskbound members of our policing community. Thank you for your attention. May I end with a motto? *Altiora etiam petamus,* which is not the Met precept, but would do surprisingly well, as I am sure you will all appreciate. She beamed around at the shuffling embarrassed figures in the body of the room, many of whom felt like the uncultured criminals she had berated moments earlier.

"Let us reach yet higher," murmured the redhead to her unkempt colleague.

"Yeah, whatever," was his ungracious acknowledgement of her learning.

The commissioner provided them with a superior smile, her perfect white teeth transforming the cold, stern image of the speech into an irresistibly attractive portrait for the press photographers. Gliding from the platform like a black swan on a lake, she took the congratulations of the Met Press Liaison Officer and the high-ranking members of her force with gracious aplomb.

*All in all,* she reflected, gratefully sipping an espresso coffee dispensed by the top-of-the-range machine in her office as she sank into the plush leather swivel chair behind her desk, *I couldn't have asked for a better start for my inaugural speech. It'll be interesting to read the daily papers in the morning.*

She could not know that the most captivating literature the

following day would arrive in the form of a letter. That particular communication, postmarked London WC1, she now laid on the green leather surface of her desk. Seething, she dialled an internal number and, her tone icy, said, "I want you in my office without delay, Detective Chief Inspector. I hardly need add that it is a matter of urgency."

Malcolm Ridgeway closed a report he was reading on an armed robbery at a jeweller in Harrow, frowned, stared at the receiver on his desk, and dwelt on the unusual nature of the call he had just taken. The standard procedure would have been to use an intermediary, for example, the Chief Superintendent contacting him on behalf of the commissioner. Direct contact from the great chief herself and in such a brusque tone surely meant trouble of the kind he could do without. He glanced in the wall mirror, adjusted his tie by a millimetre, checked under his chin to make sure his morning shave had been immaculate, and smiled at the reflection of a fifty-four-year-old that stared back at him. *Not bad for my age. I'd give myself ten years less.* He hoped that he would meet with the same approval from the Ice Maiden herself. He knew perfectly well that she was born and bred in the United Kingdom, but he couldn't entirely rid himself of certain preconceptions even if he considered himself a paragon of liberal acceptance. She had used his formal title, Detective Chief Inspector, not his name, which suggested she was in a bad mood. Once, she had addressed him as Mal, just like his other colleagues, who called him *Big Mal,* as much for his stature as his facial resemblance to a famous football coach of yesteryear. *Oh well, I'd better shoot upstairs and not give her an excuse to lay into me.*

Curious and full of trepidation, he knocked on her door. He had not enjoyed the privilege of entering the sanctum reserved for the top brass and didn't know what to expect. The faint scent of perfume, mixed with the aroma of freshly ground coffee, wasn't among the sensations he might have anticipated. Nor was the fleeting smile of welcome instantly transformed into an expression bordering on glacial. Yet, her voice was kind and gentle,

"Good morning, Malcolm. How are you? Well, I hope, and Ruth? How's she doing?"

He cleared his throat, wondering how much information was appropriate. "Oh, she's thriving. She signed another contract yesterday, you know, for those Regency romances she writes. Soon she'll be making a name for herself. I wouldn't give them shelf space if it weren't for her being my wife. Not my type of thing."

"I'm sure they're outstanding, Mal. I must read one—I love that period, Jane Austen, Lizzie Bennett and all."

"I'll bring you a signed copy, ma'am."

She almost purred, "Would you, Mal? That would be so kind. Now, then on to less pleasurable matters." She opened a desk drawer and tossed him a pair of latex gloves. Needing no prompting, he wriggled his hands into them but couldn't control his puzzled expression.

"You probably wondered why I called you directly?" Not giving him time to confirm, she hurried on. "It was because I want you to deal with this matter with the utmost discretion. For the moment, I don't want the upper echelons of our force to know about it. Clear?"

"Abundantly, ma'am."

"Good, here, this letter arrived this morning. As you can see, it's addressed to me and was posted in the city centre yesterday afternoon after my press conference." Ridgeway scrutinised the unremarkable white envelope with its typed address before withdrawing the plain, triple-folded sheet of A4 paper. Unfolding it, he read:

*Dear Aalia Phadkar,*

*Or I'm sure you'd prefer Madam Commissioner, given your pompous love of titles and qualifications. Consider this carefully: Lord Robert*

*instructed me to inform you that unless you publicly retract your calumnious diatribe against the criminal classes with a handsome apology, there will be dire consequences. Lord Robert wishes to inform you that many of his fraternity have an extensive cultural preparation, worthy of Conan Doyle's arch-villain. Furthermore, he firmly believes that nobody in the Metropolitan Police, not even your exalted self, can aspire to his unsurpassed intellect and therefore, he has issued this challenge through his humble servant, yours truly, viz. if the said public apology is not forthcoming by the first day of the next month, to be circulated as a press release, the dire consequences will assume the form of a series of executions—eight, to be precise, which will only cease if the Metropolitan Police has the wit and cultural preparation to explain the theme underlying the killings in the minutest detail. If, and only if, by the eighth murder (how I dislike that term) your minions have not reached a solution, the ninth—the master killing will reveal all to even the dimmest of your detectives. May I suggest, Madam Commissioner, that you swallow your inordinate pride and issue the most grovelling apology that your arrogant nature is capable of?*

*I remain, your, and Lord Robert's humble servitor,*
*One whose name is writ in blood.*

Unsurprisingly, there was no signature.

Aalia Phadkar indicated a seat, its padded surface inviting Mal to sink into its softness.

"Before you take that down to forensics, Mal, I'd like to discuss the contents. Let me begin by saying that I have no intention of succumbing to the writer's threat. What sort of an impression of police competence would a grovelling apology to the criminal fraternity convey?"

"Of course, ma'am, it's out of the question. And there's no guarantee that this is other than a crank getting himself off on threatening the most high-ranking police officer in the UK."

"Strictly speaking, Mal, all chief constables are my peers."

"Not for modesty, I wouldn't think." He further ingratiated himself with his schoolboy smile.

"What are your impressions of the writer and their threat, and what makes you think the sender is male?"

"The whole tone of the thing. The writer's thrown in a few long words to make us think he's educated, maybe to graduate level and added the last line to highlight that he's a cultured fellow. You'll recognise the allusion, ma'am."

"Yes, indeed, a twist on John Keats's epitaph."

"Quite so. Clever really, substituting blood for water. In that way, he gets two messages across simultaneously."

"Yes, he wants to underline that he's cultured. But what do you make of this reference to Lord Robert?"

"Not a lot, ma'am. It may simply be a red herring. He wishes to insinuate that he works for a peer of the realm."

"We'll leave no stone unturned. There can't be that many Lord Roberts."

"That's as good a starting point as any. But, you know, many people love to christen their kids Prince, Duke et cetera, so this Lord Robert might be a black guy from Brixton, say?"

"I can see that you're already thinking laterally, Mal, that's why I wanted you on the case. But what about a DI—do you have anyone in mind?"

Ridgeway scratched the short hair at his greying temple with his forefinger. "Given the delicacy of the case, ma'am, I think the best call is DI Vance."

"Jacob Vance. Jake the Rake?"

"He did have a bit of a reputation as a lady's man, ma'am, when he was a young constable but there's no truth in it. He's been happily married to Helena for sixteen years. It was his manner whenever he was near skirt that gave him his unwanted fame. He's moved on, I've always found him a perfect gent."

"Mmm, I see. I had wondered." She smiled ambiguously.

"He works with DS Shepherd. They have an almost telepathic understanding—a good team."

"Smart girl, Shepherd. I've followed some of their cases. I'd say she's in line for a promotion but, as you say, shame to break up a good team. Use the phone, Mal," she pointed, "and get them up here, smartish!"

Brittany Shepherd was first through the door, Vance hard on her heels. Aalia Phadkar had an eye for tiny, apparently inconsequential details. That Brittany had preceded Jake meant either that she was confident or that, as she suspected, Jacob had played the gentleman, holding the door for his DS. The third possibility was that Jake was scared witless and every second gained outside the dreaded room counted. She smiled secretly at this thought. Yet, of the two, Shepherd's oval face was paler, contrasting notably with her short dark hair, cut in a 1920s straight bob. Her sapphire blue eyes, turned-up nose, and full lips made her the force's sweetheart. Her lithe figure contributed to a certain bygone actress appeal.

"Good morning, ma'am." Vance almost bowed but limited himself to an unshowy raising of the right hand, enough to convey friendliness but with respect. Aalia matched his warm smile with her own.

"Inspector, Sergeant, take a seat." She waved a casual hand and, sitting, set the example. The desk seemed an intimidating barrier to the two officers, a sensation eased only by the presence of their immediate superior, who, at a nod from Phadkar, began to outline the need for discretion in this case. When he had read the contents of the letter, ostentatiously displaying his latex gloves, Jacob Vance asked. "Excuse me, sir, how can we keep the lid on this one? We're going to have to involve Max." He referred to Max Wright, the resident computer geek. If anyone needed to find out information about a person, Max was the turn-to guy. The problem was, Max worked in an open space filled with the desks of other curious detectives and computer specialists. Max's workstation was the latter's envy since, as they complained, he inevitably got the first-class equipment from his superiors, no matter the expense.

Before Ridgeway could reply, Aalia Phadkar intervened, "It's a question of discretion, Jake. All I ask is that you do your best to avoid the usual speculation that accompanies a case when we try to keep it mum."

"Of course, we'll do our best, ma'am."

Shepherd, with some colour returned to her cheeks, asked, "How seriously are we to take these threats? Do you envisage a killing spree based on the writer's objection to criminals being labelled individuals of inferior intelligence?"

Phadkar formed her lips into a pout. "We don't know who we're dealing with, Sergeant, the man who wrote the letter, if it was a man, may be a psychopath."

"That occurred to me, ma'am," Brittany said. "This Lord Robert might not even exist but might be a voice inside the head of a delusional psychotic."

"Good thinking, Brittany, and if that is the case, we may have to consider the threat of nine murders more than hot air."

"In that case, ma'am, might not a cleverly couched apology save innocent lives?"

"To hell with that, Jake! I'm not taking back a single word of what I said in my speech. We can't cut the kind of figure that will satisfy this troll! Meeting over! Get to work and collar this individual. Ah, Mal, I want the forensic report on the letter and envelope on my desk as soon as possible. We might get a lucky break. See to it!"

The three detectives left the room with their hearts in their boots. The case seemed intractable, and worse, impossible to keep under wraps.

"Surely, nine human lives are worth more than a pathetic apology," Brittany murmured.

Jake Vance heard her and said, "C'mon, Brit, it's not a simple sergeant who has to apologise, is it? If Her Ladyship made a public apology, it'd make headlines in *The Washington Post*. She's right about that."

"Bollocks! There's nothing simple about this, Sergeant. Look out for a laxative in your coffee! Only joking, boss!"

"I wouldn't put it past you, Brittany Shepherd, the Lucrezia Borgia of the Met!"

"Lucrezia—? Oh yeah, right! She got a bad press, you know. Talking about the bloody press—some historians say she never did anyone in."

"Well, I'll be inspecting my coffee from now on. Can't trust female sergeants!"

They laughed their way back to his office, turning a few heads in the busy room.

"Coffee, boss?"

"Bloody hell, no!" he bellowed and since the door was ajar, more heads turned to stare in their direction.

"Well, go on, then, make us one. I'll get onto Max after you've poisoned me!"

They exchanged a conspiratorial grin and Brittany winked. Had they known how many espressos they would consume during this case they might not have been so cheerful.

# CHAPTER 2

## RIVERSIDE APARTMENTS, FULHAM, LONDON

THE OCCUPANT STARED OVER THE BALCONY RAIL, LOOKING DOWN TO the Thames, admiring the view, and watching the steady progress of a cargo barge sending a regular wave from its bows. A few pleasure craft, their owners taking advantage of the calm, sunny weather, cruised past the more cumbersome vessel. Time to go indoors and make a coffee, the observer decided, padding in soft moccasins over the polished parquet floor. Soaking in the ultra-modern surroundings, he blessed Aunty Amy's bequest.

Never in his wildest dreams would he, a simple, comprehensive school statistic— and nothing else of academic note—from Southwark, have imagined owning a luxury £860,000 riverside apartment in Fulham. Not that he lacked intelligence, far from it. Concerning education, he had deemed the state GCSE examinations pointless and, even before this great stroke of good fortune, he had believed in his unique destiny that did not comprehend tests or university study. He alone knew what his brain was capable of. Years of isolation and a solitary diet of periodicals and encyclopaedias had, in his opinion, furnished him with a store of knowledge at the postgraduate level that included astrophysics, genetic engineering, and forensic science. When once, out of ridiculous and unfounded insecurity, he had done a series of IQ tests, without cheating, of course, he had scored a more than satisfactory 168. A pointless exercise since he knew he was MENSA standard.

He lovingly stroked the stone worktop in the kitchen and clicked the switch at the power point to set his coffee machine working. First, he ground the beans in a receptacle at the top, dispensed the freshly-ground powder into the holder, flicked another switch on the steel exterior of the machine, and listened to the hiss of the steaming hot water pass through the grounds to produce a delicious espresso that he sweetened with a level teaspoon of cane sugar. He raised the tiny cup in a silent toast to the apartment—he had only moved in two days before. The flat still seemed to hold a magical quality that he promised to maintain by keeping it fanatically tidy and clean. Apart from his obsessive nature, it was the least he could do in memory of Amy, whose house-pride was legendary in the family. His aunt had lived in a modest flat in the more elegant quarter of Clapham from where she made her fortune playing the stock market, trading in futures. He had understood broking techniques in a flash. He might do the same if ever her vast endowment ran low, which he doubted after his prudent investments. Amy was an astute woman, avoiding all the many pitfalls her chosen activity threw up daily. She worked with lower spreads, regulating them carefully, fully aware that 72% of retail CFD accounts lose money. He rinsed and dried his cup, putting it in line with the other four on the coffee machine hotplate, positioning the cup so that its handle matched the angle of the others perfectly.

It was time to do some planning. The resident shuffled over to his desk, only delivered from the warehouse yesterday afternoon. The delivery men had complained about its weight. So they should because it was a solid walnut, two-columned Victorian-style piece. He had wondered whether it would be out of keeping with the modern surroundings, but he needn't have worried. The contrast pleased him enormously, as did the matching Kimberly-style chair in the same wood with green leather upholstery. He chuckled as he sank into it—oh yes, he had taste, which was easy to indulge when money was no object.

He glanced at the monthly calendar—the only clutter along with the antique pure copper pen holder he could tolerate on his flawless desktop—counted the days and smirked, only ten to the deadline he had set.

Turning the key in the top drawer on the right, he took out an A4-sized print of an abstract painting. He withdrew a pack of clear acetate sheets of the type used for overhead projection from deeper in the same drawer. Carefully, he laid the transparent plastic over the print, took a set of acrylic paint pens, selected the colours to match the painting, nine colours in all, then began to shade over the acetate with a delicacy and accuracy of touch worthy of a calligrapher.

One of the advantages of a solitary existence is that one's mobile phone rarely rings. To make sure, he had put it on silent mode. Therefore, he was able to concentrate for the twenty minutes it took him to complete his matrix. With a flourish, he removed it from the original, held it up to the picture window, ignored the splendid view of the river and grunted in satisfaction. Next, to be sure, he took a sheet of white paper from a ream and placed the transparency over it with immense care. The reproduction of the abstract pleased him. The question that now tormented him was one of scale. He selected three maps of central London, each to a different scale. Deliberately choosing one he knew to be too large, he snorted and replaced it in its drawer. The second map might work, but it did not take him far enough to the north of the Thames, so it joined the first in the drawer. The third, as he suspected, was ideal. All he needed now was to position the transparency carefully and, with the point of a pair of dividers, prick through the plastic film to outline the boundaries of each colour. That would take him a long time of monastic-style dedication. He chuckled at the idea of a monk poring over an illuminated manuscript. Having selected yellow, he realised that it would take him an hour to circumnavigate just the one colour.

When he finished, he removed the transparency, rolled his neck to ease his tense muscles and drew back his elbows to relieve the pain in his upper back that was his constant accursed companion. Directing the light from an anglepoise lamp, the only other item he could abide on his desk, onto the map's surface, he took a black pen and dipped the fine tip repetitively into the series of holes created by the divider. Brilliant! He now had a clear outline in the abstract shape of one of part London E2. He sighed heavily at the thought of having to repeat the procedure for eight other colours. Maybe he should do one a day, but no! The white area was so small that he could do two on that day, which would mean a week of pricking out, and he had ten days. There would be three days to spare, then he would fit in other vital preparations.

The next essential stage of his planning involved consulting the AZ of London for the street names in the yellow demarcation zone. *Demarcation!* He chortled. How apt to use a military term! He just hoped that the Met bitch wouldn't apologise—no chance of that, surely?

It took him another hour of careful sifting through street names, in which he couldn't find what he wanted, and he snarled with frustration until he had a brainwave—but then *he* would, wouldn't he? In a new notebook, bought especially for the occasion, he inscribed 1) and next to it wrote Allenbury Lane, E2. That would give the police a hard time!

Thoroughly pleased with his ingenuity, he put everything away until the desk was clear, tilted the anglepoise back to its starting position, checking it out from different places in the room until satisfied. Replacing the desk seat with similar millimetric precision, he then took to an armchair, positioned by the window so that he could gaze at the river meandering past his apartment complex. He rolled his neck again before settling to consider the efficacy of his chosen method of execution. In truth, he had already decided on a technique that met his exacting criteria. Prime among them was cleanliness. Even murder had to be executed to meet his demanding standards: no mess, maximum speed and efficiency, and above all no traces left behind. Aalia Phadkar needed to know who she had to reckon with.

Ten days, from one point of view, seemed an eternity, but from the other, he needed to cram in a great deal of preparation. Moving home had cost him valuable time, but he did not regret it. In some respects, his choice of accommodation might prove another red herring for the police. The first action he had to take was testing the murder weapon in real life. It had overcome every obstacle in his fervid imagination, but you couldn't beat a *live* experiment. Or should that be a dead experiment? He sneered at his joke—a pity the world could not appreciate him. But it soon would!

Standing slowly, to avoid a dizziness that plagued him, he drew his elbows back to ease the ache in his upper spine, walked over to the hall, unhooked a black hoodie jacket, slipped it on, and returned to his desk. Unlocking the second drawer on the right, he withdrew the murder weapon, already loaded that morning, and guided it into his pocket, handling it with all the respect something so lethal (he hoped) deserved.

As he descended in the lift, the question troubling him was where to commit the crime, not to mention the choice of victim. Much as he would like to murder a person, it would impinge on his overall plan. No, it would have to be an animal. A large dog would be perfect. Again, ideally, he would strike outside his preferred area. No need to alert the coppers in advance. Where did dog lovers tend to congregate? A public park would be suitable; plenty of confusion there to make his getaway. With this in mind, he took the underground as far as Green Park, crossed the busy road, followed the railings as far as an entrance, slipped into the park, kept strictly to the path, muttering that other people shouldn't stroll on the grass—so unnecessary.

At last, he spotted an empty bench, where he sat to survey for a potential victim. A somewhat obese gentleman wearing an inappropriate pair of red shorts offended his eye, but his gaze lingered. Holding his attention was the retractable leash, on the end of which romped a black Labrador. As a potential victim, it was ideal. A young animal in prime health belonging to an aesthetically unpleasing owner seduced him.

There were no CCTV cameras in the park, so he needn't pull up his hood until he wished to exit the recreation area. He concentrated, recognising that he must not draw attention to himself, especially after the deed. Somehow, he had to approach the dog while it was far from its owner. Waiting until the frisky Labrador's perambulations brought it in his direction, he rose slowly, strolled casually towards the dog, went down on his haunches, took a striped humbug from his mouth between forefinger and thumb and held the boiled sweet out for the dog to sniff. Delicately, the animal took it into his mouth, wagging its tail. Its false benefactor made a show of ruffling the dog's fur as it crunched the humbug before quickly and furtively extracting the weapon. The Labrador yipped and ran off, looking back accusingly, for the moment intent on resuming its sniffing. But only for a moment, just long enough for the murderer to resume his place on the bench to watch intently as the hound staggered, keeled over to lie twitching, and expire. *Two minutes at the outside!* The killer smiled smugly and rose to walk at a natural pace along the footpath to the gate he had used to enter. Just before reaching it, he looked back at the bereaved owner attempting to bend over his defunct pet.

Raising the hood despite the warm weather, the assassin, head bowed, left the park to stride along the pavement towards a bus stop. He would use his Oyster Card to take him as far as another underground station. It was good practice to mix up the transport as if he was under surveillance, which, of course, he was, just like the rest of the metropolis's inhabitants, not that the ignorant masses, on the whole, knew or cared about that. He gazed across the aisle at a youth whose hair was shaved trendily at the sides and the back. Why did people ever follow fashion? He never would. Didn't they realise that their desire to shake off a nondescript image had precisely the opposite effect by aggregating themselves in a stereotypical mould? For a fleeting moment, a yearning to stalk this individual to make him one of the select nine gripped him. Lowering his hood, he shook his head, deciding that he could not afford to waste time on a nonentity. Taking another humbug from its bag, he popped it into his mouth and rolled it around his tongue. He snorted, what a contradiction! It was because the youth was a nonentity conforming to fashion that made him want to kill. As usual, his planning overview took precedence. How could he imagine that the random killing of an adolescent on this bus would achieve anything worthwhile?

By the time he rose to alight opposite a tube station, his mind was at peace for once. Of course, when he got home, he would report to Lord Robert on the undoubted success of the method. Lord Robert was a busy man, so it was understandable that he tended to speak with him late in the day, often even after his servant had retired for the night. He felt sure that his patron would be delighted with the progress made on their grandiose scheme.

Back home, he carefully replaced the weapon, sat in his armchair, and smiled at the river. He had only gazed upon it for two days but already considered it an old friend. He admired the stately way it flowed past his home. The thought that the river could be relied on to continue what it had been doing for centuries pleased him. The waterway was permanent, not like futile humanity that could snuff from one day to the next, just like that dog. True, he had helped it on its way, but one minute it was romping in the sunny park, the next—

Well, he had a mission, and that made his life worthwhile. Maybe he should celebrate. A slap-up meal in the restaurant down in the complex reception area would be ideal. He loved the way the architects had designed the tree-lined boulevard to welcome visitors to the development. The precise topiary of the trees in their large vases, the fruit-laden orange trees in the entrance hall, and he would be able to enjoy the restaurant's riverside terrace. Today's work deserved as much.

# CHAPTER 3

## NEW SCOTLAND YARD, LONDON

Ridgeway drummed his fingers on the desk, leant back in his leather chair, tilted back his head on its comfortable rest and stared at the ceiling. At certain times of the day the sunlight spotlighted the one small area that the decorator had missed when passing his roller over the surface. Small things like this no more than two-inch aberration irritated Mal beyond belief. Not that he would ever take steps to remedy the slight defect that nobody else would ever notice. Pragmatically, he preferred an excuse for irritation from a non-human source to doing anything about it except sighing whenever he focused on it.

The reason for his bad mood and boredom could be summed up in two words—unnecessary pressure. There was no point in the commissioner pressing him for a breakthrough, and on what basis? he asked himself. Why should a crank letter have an experienced professional policewoman so agitated? On reflection, the first days in a job of such enormous responsibility would test anyone's nerves, he reasoned. More so if that person had to overcome the scepticism and prejudices that he had come so close to expressing. The more he thought about his attitude to Aalia Phadkar, the more he was ashamed of himself. *Political correctness? I'm not a male chauvinist, nor am I racist. My Rachel would tear me apart if I confessed any doubts about Aalia.* He glanced back up at the ceiling where, thankfully, the sun had moved a little to the right, no longer highlighting his fixation. *Besides, she's proved herself an exceptional detective. Not everyone would have pinned sufficient damning proof on the Talarico clan to dismantle it and break its stranglehold on the narcotics trade in London. She's a damned good copper.*

A knock on his door snapped him out of his trance.

"Come!"

Another woman he admired slipped into the room. Dr Sabrina Markham, head of forensic science, whose competence was second to none.

"Good morning, Mal. I thought I'd bring this myself since I'm the bearer of bad news."

She probably was because he could detect her Manchester accent, only perceptible when tense or shocked.

"Regarding the big chief's letter, Sabrina?"

She smiled very slightly in recognition of his sharpness.

"Well, yes. *No news is good news* except in my sector. I've put the letter and envelope through every test known to science—but nothing. Your troll is extremely careful. Everything about this communication screams caution. The sheet is standard white printing paper available at every supermarket in the city. The ink is standard and authentic HP black. Even the individual's conservative choice of font, Calibri, suggests a desire to hide their personality. Whoever this person is, they have used every precaution. The envelope was sealed with a moist cloth impregnated with London tap water, so no saliva for a DNA sample, I'm afraid. No trace of a fingerprint, so they've worn latex gloves. This crank did not want to give you anything to work on, Mal." She uttered this last sentence with a definite Lancashire accent.

"Don't stress, Sabrina! I swear I wouldn't have mistreated any of your colleagues had you chosen to send a messenger. It seems to be a lot of fuss over nothing. After all, threats are two a penny in this day and age. It doesn't mean that the nutter who wrote the message has any real homicidal intentions. There's a difference between dashing off a threatening letter and committing murder."

Doctor Markham did not like speculation, as her profession required certainties. This worried her. "I'm sorry to say, Mal, but the care this person took not to leave traces suggests otherwise. If it was a desire to make a throwaway statement, why take the trouble to ensure the letter was squeaky clean?" She looked apologetic, almost embarrassed.

"Thanks, Sabrina, you're spot on, of course. I'm not thinking straight. I suppose what worries me is who the recipient was."

"As far as that goes, it should be me who's worried, not you. Here's my report, just lines of nothingness. Maybe the commissioner will think I'm useless at my job."

"Don't worry, Doc. Everyone knows you're the best! And that includes the big chief herself."

"You're too kind." She smiled, and her brown eyes twinkled, reminding him that the forensic scientist, for all her brilliance, was a beautiful woman in her forties. Not for the first time, he marvelled that she had remained single. Still, he recognised many advantages to that state, not that he would ever contemplate life without his Rachel. What was it about scientifically orientated women that appealed to him? He smiled warmly and winked at Sabrina when he took the plain manila folder containing the report. She beamed at him and retreated from the room, glad to have imparted her news with so little fuss and discussion. One thing she could say for Ridgeway, he was always fair and considerate. *His molecular biologist wife, Rachel, was a lucky woman,* she thought, as she pressed the button to summon the lift to make her way over to Lambeth and her kingdom of microscopes and sophisticated ultra-violet gadgets.

As for Ridgeway, he could see no point in putting off revealing this lack of progress. Aalia Phadkar had impressed on him that she wanted the forensic report on her desk as soon as possible. So, he strode along the corridor to call the lift from the floor where Sabrina had exited. Upstairs, he knocked on the commissioner's door to deliver the folder.

"Ma'am, Dr Markham is scrupulous to a fault, and she found nothing, which is significant in itself."

This comment did not disconcert Phadkar, who remained impassive, limiting herself to saying, "Indeed, it is. We must take the sender even more seriously. The contents of the letter assume greater importance. Has DI Vance made any progress regarding the mysterious Lord Robert?"

"I know that he put Max Wright to work on that score."

"Well, lean on them a little, Malcolm, would you?"

"At once, ma'am."

He returned to the floor below, this time taking the stairs two at a time, and strode across to Sergeant Wright's computer, where he found another sergeant bending over the technician's shoulder. Arriving just in time to hear an expletive, he coughed discreetly to gain their attention. "Anything to report, Sergeants?"

"Yes, sir," Max Wright replied, his hand massaging the nape of his neck, his green eyes peering up from his tilted head. "I've checked the House of Lords, both sitting and non-sitting members. Among the Hectors, Ruperts, and Ambroses, I've found fifteen bona fide Lord Roberts. That is, excluding the famous Lord Roberts himself as his given names are John Roger, quite apart from the fact that he is the most upright of men."

"What else?"

"Well, another seven have Robert as their second name, but I've been unable to discover whether they use it in preference to their first name."

"So, there's a starting point, at least, for you, Sergeant Shepherd. You can get over to the Lords. Elimination is going to be important in this affair. I hardly need to tell you to pussyfoot on this. I doubt anyone will object to revealing the name they use. List the seven, Sergeant Wright, and you get along to Westminster and find out what you can, Brittany. Report to Vance and take him with you, and remember, softly, softly."

The sapphire eyes made contact. "Will do, sir."

She knocked on Vance's door and, without waiting for the usual abrupt "Come!" barged in.

"Isn't it normal practice to wait for a reply, Brittany?"

"Eh? Oh, yeah. I thought I might catch you with your pants down!"

He glared, but seeing her cheeky grin, relaxed, and grinned back. "I'm hoping you mean figuratively and not literally, Sergeant."

"What? Well, it would hardly be literally, I hope. I'm probably the only person in the Met who ignores that Rake name you somehow got tagged with. I know you'd never betray Helena."

"Keep that to yourself—I don't want my reputation in tatters. Anyway, what brings you bursting into my privacy? You know, I might have a sensor fitted to the door controlled by a remote device. People not waiting for permission after knocking could receive a mild electric shock from the knob."

Shepherd laughed. "That'd do wonders for your career! Imagine giving the commissioner or Big Mal a sizzle!"

"Mmm. I had in mind a *lowly* sergeant. But I take your point. I'd need a monitor, too."

Brittany Shepherd smirked. "I hope you're feeling *lowly* today, boss. They've ordered both of us to hobnob with the peers of the realm."

"I beg your pardon?"

She giggled. "Yeah, you seem humble enough, begging! We have to make *discreet* inquiries as to nomenclature." She shook the list of seven names under his nose. For example, is the Baron of Tankerness known to all and sundry as James or Robert?"

"Oh, I see. James Robert Wallace. Wasn't he the Deputy First Minister for Scotland a little while ago?"

"The very same. And if he's known as James, Jim, Jamie, or

Jimmy, he's in the clear, but if he goes by Robert, Bobby, or Robbie, he remains firmly among the suspects."

"What? A right honourable gentleman like JR Wallace?"

"C'mon, sir, they're all right honourables, aren't they? The thing is, we want to eliminate them from our inquiries without anyone getting wind of what's going on."

"Nothing's bloody going on, Brit! That's the trouble. All this fuss over a crappy crank letter! I can hardly credit it."

"Well, I have my directions from above, and they include taking you with me. So, are you coming, or disobeying orders, sir?"

Vance reached for his warrant card and slipped it into his pocket, put his hat under his arm and said, "What, are you still here?" To which he received a snort, but he smiled inwardly. He couldn't invent a better colleague or sergeant even if he wanted to, which he didn't. "You're driving, by the way."

"Don't be daft."

"Eh?"

"It's only five minutes on foot. It'll take longer to drive at this time. Come on, fight the flab, Jake."

"That would be Jacob to you, and what flab? There ain't any!"

"Well, I wouldn't want to see you in a swimming costume!"

He breathed in and pulled his stomach under his ribs. "See, there's not an ounce."

She laughed. "Now let your breath out! See, look at that overhang! Bet you've got love handles, too."

"You won't be finding out any time soon, but you might be back on the beat or directing traffic at Marble Arch if you're not careful, young lady."

By now, they were walking briskly along the Victoria Embankment, oblivious to the intense automobile traffic running parallel to the Thames. Vance was determined to force the pace to see whether his sergeant could keep up with him with her shorter legs. Flab, indeed! He'd show her! She didn't know that her immediate superior officer rose every morning when there wasn't a case to occupy him to go for a run in Hyde Park. Also, she'd be surprised to know that he was getting faster, having cut twelve minutes off his time. She wouldn't be so surprised to see that he flatly refused to give up the occasional pints of London Pride, his favourite tipple. Brittany expected him to drag her into a pub whenever work allowed. Yet, he knew that every pint of ale went straight to his waistline. Still, he would not renounce either his masculine pride or his pint of Pride.

Big Ben loomed in front of them but failed to chime the hour. Jacob sighed and checked his watch; he missed the regular bongs. Restoration work had silenced the bell since 2017, and it wasn't due to resume until the New Year. The Great Bell had marked the hours since 1859 without fail. He especially missed the midday bell with its prolonged sonority.

"Sir?" Brittany tugged at his sleeve. "How are we going about this?" He noticed she wasn't out of breath. "I mean, we can't just barge into the chamber and interrupt proceedings, can we?"

"First, we'll show our credentials to get into the palace and then we'll make our way to the Lords' Bar. Much better an informal setting for this operation, besides someone might offer us a drink."

"On duty? Not on your life!"

Shut up, Brit!"

They managed to persuade the armed police to admit them, but not without difficulty. Indeed, Vance had to convince the guards that they'd be in trouble with the commissioner of the Metropolitan Police herself if they did not oblige. That, a phone call to New Scotland Yard, and their warrant cards did the trick. Getting into the Lords' Bar proved even more challenging. Understandably, security was high, but as the police inspector pointed out to the burly guards, his job to make inquiries took precedence over the procedure, where a threat to national interests was concerned. So eloquent was his argument that Shepherd hardly recognised him. Duly admitted, DI Jacob Vance continued in this vein, approaching a dignified personage, and identifying himself with authority and politeness that obtained the cooperation of the peer of the realm who waved him over to a low table surrounded by five comfortable armchairs.

"Now, what can I do for you, officer?"

"Sir, we wish to eliminate some gentlemen from our inquiries. The matter is delicate, but we feel confident that none of the seven gentlemen is in any way involved in…" he cleared his throat, discreetly, "…anything unseemly."

"I see, and who are these gentlemen you refer to?"

"Firstly, Baron Wallace of Tankerness. Do you know him, my Lord?"

The white, bushy eyebrows rose, and the peer's expression clouded. "Jamie Wallace? Good heavens, yes. But he'd not perform an improper action to save his life."

"I thought not, my Lord, and I'm more than happy to take your word for it."

"Good man! I say, won't your charming sergeant join us? Come on, Sergeant, take the weight off your feet. Although there's not that much weight, eh, what!"

Of the other six, all life peers and entitled *Baron,* this particular Lord, by coincidence himself named Robert—Vance made no mention of police interest in the name—a retired civil servant, circumstantially cleared them all by referring to each by a name other than Robert when quizzed. "Dear Geoffrey," he said of one, "he would be appalled to know you had mentioned his name, even to clear it. Do you know, we have Lords Spiritual in our House, but I doubt that any one of them is saintlier than Geoffrey. I say, won't you have a little snifter whilst you're here, dear upholders of the law?"

"On duty, my Lord," Brittany replied primly.

"Me too, but what harm could a single malt do? I hardly think Lord Robert will report us, will you, sir?"

Good heavens, no! I dare say Hitler would have won the war,

but for the wee drams that kept us going. Ha-ha! Come on, Sergeant, a G&T, eh, what?"

"Well, perhaps not too stiff, my Lord."

"Good gal, that's the spirit! No pun intended, by the way! You'll join me with a drop of Glenfarclas, won't you, Inspector? Cask strength, be warned!"

It was the first time Vance had tasted this dark golden scotch. Although he was someone who prided himself on his knowledge of whiskies, he wasn't quite ready for the pungent malt with its ripe, rounded aroma. He detected a hint of caramel and enjoyed the delicious aftertaste. Playing up to his host, but in all sincerity, he said, "By Jove, Milord, this isn't a malt for the faint-hearted!"

"Ha-ha! I did warn you, old boy! Sixty per cent, I believe. But we have to celebrate, do we not?"

"Milord?"

"Haven't we cleared the names of seven peers between us?"

"Oh, I see. Why, yes, we have. About which, forgive us, duty calls!" In reality, another measure of the superb Glenfarclas would have ended any efficiency in Vance's working day. With profuse thanks, they left Westminster in a buoyant mood.

"You can't resist, can you, Inspector?" the sergeant teased.

"I can resist anything but temptation, Sarge."

"Oh, come on, your wit's no match for Oscar Wilde!"

"No, but the great author wouldn't have treated that peer with so much respect. At the least, he'd have had him sweating over his birth name."

"Why, is he a Lord Robert, too?"

"Didn't you catch that? You knocked back a suspect's gin and tonic, Sergeant. But I'll tell you what, the old boy has exceptional taste in whisky. I'm inclined to remove him from our list of suspects on those grounds alone, but, of course, my professionalism will prevail."

"Do you think it extends to buying some extra strong mints, sir?"

"What are you talking about, Detective Sergeant?"

"I don't think it advisable to report to DCI Ridgeway exhaling Glenfarclas fumes in his face, do you?"

"Good thinking, Sarge, you're not a pretty face."

"I think you mean not *just* a pretty face, sir."

"No, I always choose my words carefully, Brit."

She gave him the benefit of the doubt. There might have been a compliment in there—tucked away. In any case, they made a detour for the strongest mints he could find. Then, the time came to report back that their list of suspect accomplices had shortened by seven.

"Max did say there were fifteen lords called Robert, didn't he? Just how are we going to eliminate them?" Vance asked reasonably enough.

"Especially since the only crime we have to investigate is a threatening letter to the commissioner."

"Aye, but only three days to the deadline, Sergeant."

"Let's report to Big Mal, sir."

"He'll want it in writing, Brit. That's your job to type it up. No mention of whisky and gin, mind. Oh, you might include the conscientiousness of the lads on the gates. They gave us a hard time, as they should."

"Will do, sir. It won't take long. I'm a sixty words per minute lass, me."

He knew that was the least of her talents. *Wasted as a sergeant,* he thought as he wandered over to Max to check out on his progress.

"We can exclude those seven, Max. But that still leaves fifteen lords, doesn't it?"

Choosing not to remark on the minty breath that assailed him, Max smiled up at his likeable superior officer. "Not exactly, sir, I think we can eliminate at least five. Unless, of course, you wish to consider the Bishop of Exeter as a likely criminal?" He grinned up at Vance, who was considering the possibility of a prelate involved in delinquency.

"I guess we can discount him," he conceded, "so, he's a Robert, then?"

"We're only looking at Roberts, sir."

"Print me off the ones you think we can and can't exclude. Two columns of full names and titles, okay? Oh, and Max, well done!"

Vance strolled into his room and thought it wise to suck on two extra strong mints before following up with an espresso coffee. He felt better for having accomplished something positive regarding one of the strangest beginnings to a case he could recall. But if the letter weren't a hoax, the situation would become serious within three days.

# CHAPTER 4

## LONDON E2 (THREE DAYS LATER)

The blonde, Bethany, changed down to the second gear of her Harley-Davidson Sportster Iron 883, slipped into neutral, and cruised down Allenbury Road until the purring machine reached the end where Allenbury Lane led nowhere. Switching off the lights, she killed the motor and braked, putting the bike onto its kick stand. She dismounted, patted the saddle, running her hand appreciatively over the corrugated leather seat. Her eye lingered on the mustard-coloured petrol tank, which with the front and rear matching mudguards were the only parts of the machine that were not black. Even the number plates were black because she'd covered them by taping them over with pieces of plastic bin liner.

She removed her crash helmet, shook free her long, straight, blonde hair, and looked around. Satisfied that the streetlight was sufficient for her purposes, she laid the helmet on the seat, felt in her pocket for the deadly object and, reassured, she sidled across the pavement to stand out of sight behind one of the brick uprights that acted as pilasters to support the overhanging balconies built in series along the facades of the upmarket terraced houses.

Her reconnaissance work earlier in the week paid off handsomely when at precisely eleven o'clock, as expected, a young woman, also with long, straight, blonde hair walked into the lane and, as anticipated, paused, full of curiosity. She admired the powerful motorcycle parked outside her house. Bethany crept out noiselessly, her soft-soled trainers chosen for the job, pulled out her weapon, reached her unsuspecting victim and asked, "Do you like my bike, miss?"

Startled, the young woman spun around in time to see another blonde female smiling at her. Off-guard, she had no time to react when the needle plunged into her throat. Her eyes bulged and her knees buckled. Bethany took her under her armpits to haul the dying woman into the patio of her own house, sheltered by the balcony, before gazing around to ensure that nobody in the quiet lane had seen anything. Removing a can of black spray paint from her leather jacket, she sprayed it onto the red brick wall: **9-1 = 8.** The round plastic top clicked into position on the spray can, so she thrust it back into her deep pocket.

Unfeelingly, Bethany bent over the dead woman, whose only motion had been a couple of final twitches of the legs and placed two united fingers on her throat to ensure there was no pulse. Satisfied, she took out a small square of paper prepared at home, quickly re-read the nine words, unbuttoned the top of her victim's blouse, no easy feat in latex gloves, and slipped the note into the woman's cleavage. *What a shame,* thought Bethany, *she's a pretty one, but as Lord Robert says, there's no room for compassion.* Next, she took an artist's brush from her inside pocket. She had sharpened the top end of the wooden handle to a point so that driving it into the woman's ear channel, rupturing the tympanum and forcing it up into the brain was not as difficult as feared. One last thing, she rifled through her victim's handbag, found what she was hoping for and stuffed it into her pocket. Her work completed, she strolled back to her vehicle, pulled the helmet on, clipped the chinstrap, removing the bike from its stand and wheeled it, still in neutral, along the lane for fifty yards before springing lightly onto the saddle, kickstarting the bike and roaring off through the gears, shattering the silence of the quiet residential area.

Before long, she was heading towards Tilbury port, reassured by the banality of the late evening traffic, where she had rented an eight-by-six-foot container for two months. The thief-proof container was equipped with a padlock, which she opened to release a lever. The front of the metal box swung open on well-oiled hinges so that she could push the Harley-Davidson inside with no trouble. She unclipped her helmet and tossed it onto the floor of the container where her leather gauntlets, syringe, can of black spray paint, and, almost, the latex gloves joined it, but then she thought again and replaced them on her hands before picking up the shoulder bag she had left in preparation in the container days before, then she shut the metal box—one could not be too careful. She took off the gloves and stuffed them in her pocket before walking casually out of the container warehouse, smiling brightly at the watchman, who called a cheery greeting.

Bethany strolled out of the terminal to Tilbury Town station. Before crossing the road to approach the station, she tied up her hair, piled it on her head and pulled a black beanie over it so that there was no trace of blonde. She checked her appearance in a compact mirror and satisfied, felt it didn't matter if the station CCTV captured her image. She glanced at her watch—perfect! The last train for central London was at 23:44, which would take her to Fenchurch Street station for twenty-four minutes after midnight. From there, she would take a taxi home. The journey was complex enough to throw a bloodhound off her scent—she smiled at the image and gratefully accepted Lord Robert's congratulations. She slipped her smartphone into the back pocket of her jeans, opened her shoulder bag and, unzipping the internal compartment, took out her Oyster Card to pass through the automatic gate. She reminded herself to top up the prepaid card when she arrived at

Fenchurch Street. She didn't have time here with just four minutes to departure.

There were few passengers at this hour on the train, which had come from Southend via Benfleet. Bethany judged them to be shift workers heading home to bed. Nobody bothered her, although she had to look away when a middle-aged fellow smiled at her, having caught her eye. She was relieved when he stood to get off at the next stop. Grays. She didn't need anything to complicate what was proving to be a perfect operation. Forty-five minutes after departure, she sauntered out of Fenchurch Street station, having recharged £20 into her card.

The seven-mile journey to her flat in Fulham passed uneventfully as the taxi driver was obligingly taciturn. She let him keep the change out of gratitude for leaving her in peace. No other residents crossed her path as she took the lift to her apartment. The simple action of slipping inside and closing the door with a sigh of relief sealed the success of her mission. Lord Robert would be delighted.

In an act of supreme irony, Bethany went over to her Bose sound system, selected Lou Reed and played *Walk on the Wild Side,* humming along with the tune as she took off her blonde wig to reveal short light-brown hair. She went into the bedroom, stripped, removing the bra with its padding to expose a flat hairy chest. He stared at his reflection in the full-length mirror and grinned. There was nothing in the slightest feminine about his less than perfect but undoubtedly male physique. He sang along: *Candy came from out on the island…* and hummed in tune with the coloured girls that go *Do, da, do, da do, do, do, do.* Oh, yes, he had taken a walk on the wild side, alright! He dressed and wondered whether Lord Robert might want updating, but he never decided when to contact him—it was always, and inevitably, the other way around.

The question now was, he speculated as he sat by his window to admire the twinkling lights reflecting in the river, should he wait or contact the police at once. Surely, they would find the body tomorrow and see his warning. What would they make of the Jack Kerouac quote? Nothing probably—the commissioner bitch couldn't hope to match his intellect. Besides, he had taken so many precautions. They'd be chasing red herrings for days. Yet, the urge to contact them was so impelling. Maybe just a short letter to reiterate his conditions was in order. Mind you, he couldn't waste much time because he had to set up the second murder on Satchwell Road. That would need extra careful planning. Luckily, there was no need to rush. This evening, the woman, entirely taken by surprise, hadn't been in a state to resist, so the police would find no incriminating DNA. Reconnaissance took rather a lot of his time, but as tonight had proved, its dividends were indisputable. Wincing, he massaged the top of his spine with four fingertips, scowled, and mumbled a complaint against his ill-luck before padding into the kitchen in his soft slippers to take two strong painkillers with a glass of still water. Back in the lounge, he smirked at the loudspeakers as Lou Reed assured him it was a *Perfect Day*. It was late and time to retire, so he switched off the sound system, picked up his mobile and by now in bed, he reassured the suave voice of Lord Robert that plans were well in hand to ensure the successful continuation of their project.

Sometimes, Lord Robert, despite his undoubted pedigree, was insensitive. It was late, and his faithful servant was tired, wanting only to sleep, but the voice nagged him for details and questioned why the killing had to be so clean. He left his minion in no doubt that he would appreciate butchery, maybe by knife, Jack the Ripper-style, giving it more impact. It was hard to defy the demanding aristocratic voice. Its insistence, along with weariness, was giving him a headache, despite the painkillers. However, at the end of their conversation, the peer accepted the need for efficiency and cleanliness. He also reluctantly concurred that the complexity of the case for the police would ensure maximum effect without unnecessary carnage.

# CHAPTER 5

## ALLENBURY LANE AND NEW SCOTLAND YARD, LONDON

DETECTIVE CONSTABLE MARK ALLEN SWEPT INTO VANCE'S OFFICE, his expression one of a man bursting to inform.

"What is it, Constable?" Jacob rose slowly from his seat to seem less intimidating and more receptive to the young detective.

"One of our mobile units called in, sir. It appears there's been a murder in Allenbury Lane in the Bethnal Green patch. Dr Tremethyk is already on the scene and has requested a forensics team. The victim is a white female in her thirties. A neighbour found her at eight o'clock this morning, lying in front of her house."

"DC Allen, on your way downstairs, find DS Shepherd and send her up to me, there's a good lad."

Allen grinned at the popular inspector. "Will do, sir."

A few minutes later, Shepherd appeared. "Is it true there's a murder for us to investigate?"

"Get the car, Brittany. I'll explain on the way."

As she navigated towards Allenbury Lane, Shepherd asked, "Do you think the perpetrator is the sender of the letter? I mean, the date's right, isn't it? Wasn't last night the deadline? If they found her at eight o'clock, I'd presume they killed her yesterday."

"We'll know soon enough, Brit. You know what I think about coincidences."

"Yeah, you don't believe in them—I know," she murmured, more to herself.

A police car, several uniformed constables, and the usual blue and white crime scene tape draped across the entrance to one of the terraced houses awaited them in Allenbury Lane.

A policewoman stepped forward to prevent them from approaching until Vance flashed his warrant card.

"Scotland Yard, sir? You'll be taking over the case, I expect. This way please."

"Where are you from, Sergeant?" he asked as he pulled on the white disposable suit she handed him.

"Bethnal Green, sir. The woman over there, with Constable Harris, called 999. We came straight over. We're the nearest station." She lifted the tape to allow the two detectives to pass.

"You were right, boss." Shepherd nudged Vance and pointed to the black paint on the brick wall. **9-1=8.**

"Nine minus one equals eight. It has to be the sender of the commissioner's letter."

Vance, who had eyes only for the white-clad figures bending over a woman's body, hadn't noticed the sprayed message.

"Yes, that confirms that this is their handiwork, Brit. Our job is to make their arithmetic stretch no further." His tone was bleak.

"Greetings, DI Vance," a voice with a melodic Cornish accent called. Jacob grinned at the Chief Medical Examiner of the Metropolitan Police, Dr Francis Tremethyk. They had worked many cases together in the past, and while Jacob was delighted that he was on the case, one thing grated—Tremethyk's propensity for calling him *me-dear* and *boy,* terms of affection common to the most southwestern of the English counties. Right on cue came, "Rum business, this, me-dear. At first glance, it looked like a straightforward heart attack, but if you tread carefully over here—don't want to be upsetting the remarkable Markham, do we, boy? —you'll see a puncture wound to the neck. Here, look, see it? No, this is a case of murder with substance or substances unknown. And yes, before you say it, I'll get the results to you as soon as I've completed the post-mortem. All I can tell you, for now, is that she died sometime last night, I'd say between ten and twelve hours ago. The body was moved, by the way, boy. Look at her high heels, they've been dragged along the pavement, like, see the abrasions. I'll bet forensics will find traces nearby, me-dear.

Tremethyk turned to his photographer and held out a hand. Even without a word of communication, the other white-clad figure with telepathic understanding handed a plastic evidence bag to the doctor, who passed it to Jacob. "Found it between her breasts, poor lassie. Whether she put it there herself or your killer placed it belongs to your field of investigation, not mine, me-dear."

Vance slipped the bag into his pocket, silently pointing to the victim's left ear.

"Ah, yes." The Cornishman said and nodded. "Odd business that." His accent became more marked when he was disturbed by something—a tendency Jacob had picked up on— "Inserted post-mortem. I'll be certain when I examine the body back in the lab. It would have been the cause of death if the poor lassie had still been alive, but at first glance, this was done after her demise. God knows why!"

"Mind if I take a look around the area, sir?" Shepherd asked.

"You do that, Brit. Oh, see what the neighbour woman who called in the crime has to say."

While Shepherd scouted around, noting the installation of a CCTV camera on the corner house of the row pointing back along the terrace, the forensics team arrived, shooing Tremethyk, his photographer and Vance away from the body.

"Sir, Mrs Wilson—the neighbour who found the body—is

still in shock. The usual stuff. Spoke well of Gillian Coombs, an estate agent, it seems, and didn't see or hear anything. But regarding that, take a look over here." She led him a few paces down the lane and pointed to the camera. "If it's working, we could be in luck."

"Come on, the car! There's nothing else we can do here. Let's get back, report to Commissioner Phadkar and get a warrant for the CCTV."

"Shouldn't you give that note to Dr Markham, sir?"

"All in due course, Sergeant. We need a head start in this case. Don't worry, I won't pollute it." Even as he said this, with Shepherd driving along Allenbury Road, he pulled on his latex gloves, opened the evidence bag, unfolded the note, and read aloud:

*"The low yellow*
*moon above the*
*Quiet lamplit house."*

"What the Devil? Mean anything to you, Sarge?"

Shepherd frowned and clicked her tongue. "Unless—"

"What?"

"It's not one of those Japanese poems, is it? Aren't they usually just three phrases?"

"A haiku? Good thinking. Could be, but let's see, how many syllables? The haiku should have seventeen. He counted. Nope, thirteen."

"It just means it isn't classic Japanese, that's all. But what's the point they're making? There must be something hidden that we're missing."

"As I see it, it's just confirming the nighttime murder." Vance folded the paper carefully, replacing it in the evidence back and returning it to his pocket. "But remember the commissioner's letter. He quoted from memory: the murders *will only cease if the Metropolitan Police has the wit and cultural preparation to explain the theme underlying the killings in the minutest detail.* So, it's a test of our collective intellect. If you remember, Brit, they underlined *minutest*. It means, hey! Bloody white van drivers! They're the worst of road hogs. Did you see how he cut in?"

"If I hadn't, sir, we'd have crashed. Soddin' London traffic! I should be the one grumbling. Anyway, you were saying?"

"Ah, yes, they want us to explain who wrote this haiku, if that's what it is, and why they left it on the body. So, as soon as we get back, I'll pass it on to Wrighty. He'll find out who the poet is, at the very least."

The series of traffic lights began to annoy Shepherd. "I reckon we should spray this car with holy water, then we might get a few green lights!"

Still, as they turned into New Scotland Yard, Vance realised they had made good time despite the traffic.

"You'd better come with me to report to Big Mal. He'll know best how to get the warrant out of the commissioner."

As it turned out, Aalia Phadkar was only too eager to oblige the three detectives lined up before her.

"I imagine you are judging me for not issuing an apology now a young woman is dead, but consider this, either way, I suspect our killer would have struck. These people are depraved. They will take any excuse to sate their evil appetites. Remember, we cannot descend to making a pact with the Devil. What we *can* do is bring them to justice as soon as possible, so, yes, you can have a warrant for the closed-circuit film."

She scribbled a signature on the document and stamped it. She looked up with a curious smile. "Normally you'd have to go through a court, but as part of my remit, I'm authorised to bypass procedure. Time appears to be as valuable as ever." She handed the warrant to the grateful Vance, who folded it neatly and slipped it into his breast pocket.

"Much appreciated, ma'am. With your permission, we'll be on our way."

"Pull out all the stops, Jake. I want to look this murderer in the eye as soon as possible."

"Bloody liberty, calling me Jake," he grumbled to his sergeant as they took the lift to the floor below.

"The commissioner is just trying to be friendly and approachable, sir."

"Trust women to stick together!"

Shepherd treated him to her most infuriating grin, which elicited, "If Big Mal hadn't stayed to discuss the case with her, he'd have backed me up."

"Meaning you can't deal with your lowly sergeant alone, eh, boss?" She repeated the smirk, and he snorted and strode out of the lift, where in other circumstances, he would have gestured for her to step out first. As if to reinforce his disapproval, he marched ahead to Max Wright's computer. The sergeant was busy working on another case and, since he was in a bad mood, Vance did not wait politely for the technician's attention as he might otherwise have done.

"Max, we're off to fetch a CCTV tape. Top priority when we get back, meanwhile, as a matter of urgency, find out where this poem, or whatever it is, comes from. And for God's sake, wear gloves. When you've copied the words, get it across to forensics in Lambeth ."

"Anything else, Detective Inspector?" Max knew a bad mood when he saw one, so he made sure not to make his question sound sarcastic.

"Yes. I want you to find out whatever you can about a certain Gillian Coombs, estate agent in her thirties, resident in Allenbury Lane. Everything you can, mind, for when we get back. Come on, you!"

Brittany Shepherd rolled her eyes at Max Wright behind his back, winked and trotted after her inspector. In the car, he forgave her for her cheeky grins. It didn't take much because he knew that they had a splendid working relationship. He made peace by saying, "Well done, by the way, Brit."

"Eh?"

"For spotting the CCTV camera. Not everyone would have noticed."

"Sorry to contradict you, sir. I think anyone on our floor would have—but thanks, anyway." She took her eye off the road for a fleeting moment, long enough to smile at him.

He grunted and smiled inwardly.

When they arrived, forensics were still combing every square inch of the crime scene. Dr Markham waved Vance over. "We don't seem to be of much help these days, Inspector. All I can tell you with any certainty is that the victim was probably killed about here." She pointed to the road in front of Ms Coombs's house. "There are micro-traces of red leather that begin here. It's from the victim's shoe heels. She was dragged to the position where she was found, perhaps to conceal the body until the morning. Nothing else, I'm afraid, but if you look over there, you'll see there's a CCTV camera. If it's working, it might tell you more than we can. Your killer left no traces, just like their letter."

"I'm on to the closed circuit. I've got a warrant in my pocket."

"Splendid! In that case, I'll call off my team. There's nothing to find here."

"Thanks, anyway, Doc. I have a feeling you'll contribute a lot to this case, all in good time. If you'll excuse me—"

The detectives strolled to the corner house of the row. Vance glanced at his watch. "They might be at work, Brit. In that case, be prepared to assist with an illegal operation."

"You're not seriously contemplating a forced entry, I hope?"

"Well, if it comes to it. Look, we have a callous murderer on the loose, and I have a warrant to back me up."

"It doesn't provide for breaking and entry, though. You could get yourself suspended."

"If a woman answers the door, you do the talking otherwise I'll deal with it."

Vance pressed the doorbell and heard a brief version of a

Brandenburg concerto chime. Behind the fluted glass of the front door panel, the distorted figure of someone dressed in pink appeared.

"Over to you, Sarge." Vance stepped back.

A woman, maybe in her fifties, wearing a pink cashmere cardigan and a calf-length denim skirt, peered at Shepherd, who was flashing her reassuring smile.

"Good morning, madam. Police." Brittany held up her warrant card for scrutiny. "I'm Sergeant Shepherd, and this is Detective Inspector Vance." He displayed his warrant card.

"You'll be here about poor Gillian, I suppose. What a terrible, terrible thing. This neighbourhood is so quiet."

"May we come in for a few minutes, ma'am?" Vance asked.

"Oh yes, of course." She opened the door wider to admit them into a hall leading into a tidy lounge off to the right. Please take a seat, officers. Will you have a cup of tea?" She hurried into the kitchen, followed by Brittany, who asked, "Do you live alone, Ms—erm—"

"Jackson. Debbie Jackson, and it's Mrs. My Fred's at work. He's a straddle driver at Tilbury Container Port. I think his job title is Container Terminal Operative. He's been there for over twenty years." She tossed teabags in a pot and clicked down a switch.

"I wonder, did you know the victim?"

Debbie Jackson shuddered visibly and pulled her open cardigan across her chest with crossed wrists in a defensive gesture. "Not really, she kept to herself. Always had a ready smile and a polite greeting," her voice caught, and she wiped an eye. "Sorry, it's such a shame. That young policeman said—but wasn't she too young for a heart attack?"

Shepherd considered the situation before saying as gently as possible, "Gillian didn't die of natural causes."

Luckily, the kettle took on a life of its own as it began vibrating and sending out a cloud of steam. With a loud click, it switched itself off so that Mrs Jackson bustled about pouring boiling water into the teapot and stirring the bags with a spoon to extract the maximum flavour.

"I'll just let it brew a few minutes. Do you like your tea strong, Sergeant?"

Brittany agreed that she did and, scrutinising the woman's face, saw realisation dawn.

"Do you mean Miss Coombs was murdered?"

"I'm afraid so. Do you know if she'd been receiving visitors or whether she was in a relationship?"

"I'm not a nosey parker, Sergeant!"

"I didn't mean—but at the moment we're clutching at straws, anything you can tell us, even the smallest detail, might be important."

"Well, let me see." She found three cups and saucers and arranged them on a tray. The cups looked to be made of fine bone china to Brittany, who smiled her approval when they were joined by a matching milk jug and sugar basin. They were all patterned with a delicate blue wildflower. "I'd like to help, but as I told that nice young constable earlier, Gillian was no trouble. No men coming and going and never any loud music or anything of the sort. She'd sometimes wash her car on the road on a Sunday morning, which annoyed my Frank. He always said she should take it to a car wash. But I saw no harm in it. *It's not as if she uses the bloody thing,* he'd say. Oh, excuse my language, officer, just quoting Frank. You see, she only seemed to drive it on Sundays, and she keeps – er- *kept* it in a garage on Allenbury Road. Well, I suppose, better to pay rental than leave it parked here on the road at all hours. Would you mind carrying the tray? I'll bring the biscuit barrel and the teapot."

They sipped their tea, Shepherd commenting on the wallpaper to relax their agitated host. Suddenly, the inspector said, "I noticed you've got a camera on the outside, madam."

"Please call me Debbie, Inspector. Yes, it was Frank's idea. A few years ago, there was a spate of burglaries. We had a break-in once, but they didn't take much, just a gold bracelet, but the police got it back for me. They caught lads from the council estate, ne'er-do-wells, the lot of them. Since then, thank goodness, we've been trouble-free, but Frank insists on keeping it running. I never look at it, mind you, no reason. Frank called me once to look at a badger prowling around—lovely! Frank sees to it. It's on a forty-eight-hour loop, but he'd be able to tell you more about that. He regularly cleans the lens at weekends."

"Debbie, do you mind showing me the installation? Has my sergeant told you that this is a murder investigation?"

"Do you want me to ring Frank? He might be able to get time off. I don't understand a thing about it. All I know is what he said—it's connected to the computer."

"That won't be necessary, Debbie. I know my way around these things."

"Frank was thinking of changing the system. He says that you can link up with smartphones these days. He says in that case he'd be able to check our house from work. Isn't it marvellous what they can do nowadays?"

"The computer, Debbie?"

"In the backroom, Inspector, I'll show you through."

Vance, on seeing the set-up, breathed a sigh of relief. It was an NVR system with a Power over Ethernet extender for cables over a long distance while maintaining high image quality. They were in luck since Frank had taken good advice. Bless him! The Network Video Recorder was connected to the same IP network. That was why Frank was on a forty-eight-hour loop so as not to use too much memory on his hard disk. Vance turned to Debbie Jackson.

"Here's my card, Debbie. It has my number. Tell Frank to ring me, and I'll explain why I've taken his computer to Scotland Yard. Oh, and call me if anything comes to mind about that poor woman. Any unusual sounds last night, or if you remember anyone behaving suspiciously in the street of late—that sort of thing."

She looked stricken. "I don't think I can let you take Frank's computer, Inspector. He'll be furious."

"Need I remind you that this is a murder inquiry, madam?" Vance used his most formal tone. "The computer footage might have captured the murderer. Anyway, look at this. It's a warrant signed and stamped by the commissioner of the Metropolitan Police. There's no arguing with that! I don't think Mr Jackson will want to get on the wrong side of the highest-ranking police officer in London, do you?"

He didn't wait for a reply but began unplugging cables and removing plugs from sockets. At last, the desktop computer was in his arms. Shepherd gently retrieved the warrant and folded it, putting it in a pocket. "Don't worry, Debbie, you'll have your computer back in a day or two. It could be a big breakthrough in the case, and it'll be down to you and Frank."

Relieved to settle into the car and drive away, the detectives sighed simultaneously, then laughed about their synchronised reaction.

"Nice lady but transmits anxiety. Max will make the most of this for us," Jacob said, jerking a thumb towards the back of the car. He'll be able to get close-ups of the killer, I'm sure of it. Did you see the angle of the camera? Our Mr Jackson has it pointing right along the road. It'll have captured all movements in the street over the last forty-eight hours until I pulled the plug. Didn't his wife say it picked up a nighttime badger? And that he kept the lens regularly cleaned? You see, there are some sensible citizens, after all."

"I hope you're right about him, boss. She seemed terrified of his reaction to us taking his blessed computer."

"Which is why you'll be the one returning it. If you find so much as a scratch on Debbie Jackson, I want to know. Then we'll see how big a man our straddle driver is!"

"Do you think this closed-circuit works?"

"Judging by the cabling, I think it will give us good images. It might not be the latest technology, but then, neither is my trusty old Leica camera, but it beats your iPhone pictures any day."

"I just pray that Max can work his usual magic."

"Bear in mind that it was dark, and the streetlamps are designed for a quiet lane, not a motorway turnoff. The badger gives me hope, but we'll have to keep our fingers crossed.

# CHAPTER 6

## NEW SCOTLAND YARD, LONDON.

VANCE ADDRESSED THE CONSTABLE ON DESK DUTY AS HE PLACED THE computer on the counter. Since very few members of the public ever wandered into the reception area, this task was considered *a cushy number* by the lower ranks.

"Constable Whiting, isn't it?"

The young officer smiled and nodded, pleased the inspector had remembered his name.

"Be a good lad, and take this computer up to Sergeant Wright, will you? We'll hold the fort till you get back."

"Yes, sir, right away." Glad to have something to do other than keep a check on surveillance monitors, PC Whiting gathered up the device and hurried over to the lift.

"Didn't I tell you, you're unfit?"

"You've been getting too big for your boots, recently, Detective Sergeant, soon to be demoted."

"You couldn't do without me, boss."

Their banter continued until Whiting reappeared, looking pleased with himself.

"What are you looking so smug about, Constable? Vance asked.

"Sorry, sir, it's just that I've taken the lead in the team's fantasy football, and Sergeant Wright is in second place! I'm still chuckling at his expression. Better get back to work, suppose." He dashed behind the counter and kept his head down.

"How much do you win at that caper?"

"Five hundred pounds, sir. There are twenty of us in the pool, see."

"No wonder you're chuffed. Good luck with that!"

"I'll need it, sir, long way to go, yet."

They took the lift where Vance said, "I haven't the patience for fantasy football. The real thing's bad enough."

"I thought you were an Arsenal fan."

"Yeah, that's what I mean!"

She didn't risk a smile, knowing that he suffered when his team lost. He'd been suffering a lot recently. She just hoped that Max Wright had something for them.

The detective-technician was already attaching cables to Frank Jackson's computer. He looked up and smiled. I take it this beauty has the CC film on its hard disk, sir?"

"Right, Max, but did you get anything from that note?"

"I did, yes. It's entitled *Haiku*. It's a poem by the American writer Jack Kerouac, one of a collection of his poems."

"Jack Kerouac? Wasn't he one of the beat generation?"

"That's the fellow."

Vance grunted and frowned. The significance escaped him, but he said, "At least we can go some way to explaining the killing in the *minutest* detail. Did you take it over to forensics, my lad?"

"I did, Sabrina—*er*—Dr Markham, in person, rang five minutes ago to say that there were no traces again. This killer is *scrupulous*, she said."

Vance and Shepherd exchanged a knowing smile. It was common knowledge that Max Wright was sweet on the Head of Forensics. He hadn't finished, either. "Doctor Markham confirmed what I already knew. She recognised the poem was by Kerouac and knew the title. Cultured lady, our doctor."

"I believe she knows a lot about fine wines, too," Shepherd said mischievously.

"Does she?" Max pondered this information as the sergeant winked at her inspector behind his back.

"What about Gillian Coombs?" Vance brought their attention back to the case.

"Not much to report. She left grammar school with average grades, then obtained her Level 2 and 3 CPD Certified Estate Agent Diplomas, as far as I can tell, working online from home. Until her death, she ran a branch of a chain of estate agencies in Bethnal Green. She was on £25000 a year. Her father, a lawyer, is deceased whilst her mother lives in Sussex. I have all the addresses. She was an only child."

"Shame. Brit, check out her office. See if you can find anything useful. I'll arrange for a woman officer to break the news to her mother. I presume the Bethnal Green mob checked out Gillian's home. I'll give them a ring to see if they turned up anything of interest. Now, Max, before we set about all that, see what you can dazzle us with on Frank Jackson's computer.

"Blast! Naturally, it's password-protected, sir."

"Try *Debbie.* You never know."

"Should I phone her, sir?" Shepherd volunteered. "She might know the password."

"Aye, do that. She can call her husband if she doesn't."

"I'll give Deborah a go," Max said.

That didn't work either, so he tried spelling variations of the same name without success.

Ten minutes passed before Shepherd reappeared, clutching a torn piece of paper.

"Got it, boss!" she said. "Frank's blazing about his computer, but since it's a murder inquiry—"

"I should bloody well hope so!" Vance growled. "Well?"

"Type in Gantry Crane 72, Max, capitals G and C, no space between the words and numbers."

DS Wright sat back with a triumphant grin. "We're in! Why seventy-two?"

"Probably 1972, the year of Frank's birth?" Shepherd suggested.

A rapid calculation and Vance agreed, "That would make him forty-nine, about right, I'd say. What about the CCTV?"

Wright studied the on-screen desktop crowded with icons over a photograph of a young-looking Debbie. The technician clicked on a simple graphic icon of a blue wall-mounted camera.

"We're in, Inspector. Look, the day before yesterday's date, and it's daylight. Sixteen-nineteen on the clock."

"Can you take me fast forward, Max? We need the evening. Say ten o'clock?" The image zigzagged, and the clock raced until the technician stopped it at 22:00. Vance's sigh of relief was audible to the other two detectives.

"What, sir?"

"We got lucky, Brittany, see, it's dark, but the picture of the street is very clear. There's nobody on the lane at ten o'clock. That house there." He pointed. "That's Gillian's. Can you zoom in, Max?"

"Sure, like this?"

"No, too much. We'll need to see the road in front. Ah, good. That's perfect. Now take me forward in fifteen-minute intervals. At the third advance, Vance stopped him, let it run at a slow speed now—just a bit faster. Stop!"

All three stared at the screen. A motorcycle came to a halt opposite Gillian's house.

It's a Harley-Davidson, sir!" Brittany cried excitedly.

"The plates are covered," said the pragmatic inspector, his tone flat.

"Is that the Kerouac connection?" the sergeant insisted.

"Eh?" Vance was having difficulty detaching his attention from the screen. "Freeze it, Max. What do you mean, Brit?"

"Well, wasn't it him who wrote 'On the Road'? You know, she quoted, *"Nothing behind me, everything ahead of me, as is ever so on the road*." It was Kerouac who inspired the music and films, sir, you know, Peter Fonda in *Easy Rider*—his bike was a Harley-Davidson—"

"I'm old enough to remember that film, Sergeant. You have a point. There's a definite connection between this motorcycle and the haiku. Max, I want to know the model, the year and by the way, do you have some sort of program that can convert this black and white film to colour?"

The technician stopped humming *Born to be Wild* and said, "I might be able to get hold of one through my contacts. It might take a few hours, though."

"See if you can, look, the splash guards are a different colour from the rest of the bike. Move it along, Sergeant."

"Good God, it's a woman!" Vance exclaimed as the motorcyclist removed her crash helmet, shook free her long, straight, blonde hair and looked around. "Look how she's gazing around, almost as if she wants to be seen. Can you get a close up of her face? We'll get screenshot to print off and circulate. I'll call a photofit artist to make an improved image. Good. Hold it there. Print that off!" He snatched up the phone and barked orders. Moments later, a female officer arrived with a sketch pad and pencil. The inspector knew her. He made a point of learning as many names and details about his colleagues as possible. This attention explained why he was so popular even outside his immediate circle of staff. "Ah, Lizzie, how are you? Still dating that doctor?"

She blushed with pleasure and replied, Edward and I are engaged now, sir. We should tie the knot next summer, all being well."

"Good for you, Sergeant. Nice ring, by the way. You can tell doctors are better paid than us miserable coppers." He turned the screen towards her. "This is our killer. Make the sketch as close as you can, Lizzie, you know the score."

In an amazingly short time, the expert artist had the face on paper, reproducing the lineaments precisely.

"Usual procedure, Lizzie. Bang out enough copies for every station in London, plus run it past our Press Liaison people. We need all the help we can get."

The young woman smiled and nodded before hurrying off.

"Nice lass," Jacob acknowledged to no one in particular.

"Jake the Rake!" Brittany whispered to Max, who sniggered.

"I heard that, DC Shepherd," Vance snarled.

"What, eh? Detective Constable? I'm a sergeant."

"Not for much longer if you keep winding me up."

"Sorry, sir. I admit to being overexuberant sometimes when a case has a breakthrough."

"Breakthrough? We haven't got her yet. But we will!" he said through clenched teeth.

Max set the film running again and they watched the motorcyclist lay her helmet on the seat.

"It looks like we're after a blonde with long hair," the technician stated the obvious.

"Except that women can change their hair in the blink of an eye, old chap. She could be a redhead or a brunette by now—and with short hair." The inspector gazed at the monitor. "Look. She hid behind the brick column supporting the balcony, relying on the victim thinking the lane was empty apart from the swanky bike, of course."

They watched Gillian bend over to study the Harley-Davidson, and the other woman creep up behind her, take something from her pocket, speak with the victim, and then strike with stunning rapidity. "Freeze!" Vance ordered, and the film stopped with Gillian Coombs's knees buckled and a look of horror on her face. "Time of murder eleven-oh-three. Zoom in on the killer's right hand, Max. That's as good as we'll get. It looks like a syringe to me."

"It's a syringe," Shepherd agreed. "If you look carefully, there's the glint of a needle. Rewind it ever so slightly, Max. There, see!"

"There's very little else to glean from this. She'll drag the body over there where the camera can't include the body. Shame, we've lost visibility for let's see—mmm, she's going back to the bike, pulling it off its stand. It's eleven-sixteen now. In those ten minutes or so, she'll have done the black spray, her ritual with the paintbrush and placed the haiku on the body. And look at her now, cunning bitch, she's pushing the motorbike away so as not to wake up the residents."

"That doesn't quite add up, boss," Shepherd said. "Why bother when she's looked straight up at the CCTV camera more than once? She could have hopped on the bike and roared away. Even if someone had peered out of a window, by then she'd covered her head." She frowned and looked puzzled. "I don't know. My instinct tells me there's something that doesn't quite tie up here."

"Can you make a copy of the film, Max?" Vance asked, not commenting on his sergeant's remark but weighing up her words. He had come to trust Brittany's instincts.

"I can do that in five minutes. The quality is good enough for a copy, sir."

"Good, but don't forget my earlier request, Max, you know? Colour?"

"Will do. No promises, though."

"Brit, you hang around. As soon as our expert here has finished with the computer, take it to Debbie and check on her wellbeing."

"Whilst I'm in the area, I'll drive over to the estate agency in Bethnal Green to see if there's any gossip or evidence in Gillian's desk."

"Good. I'll send a woman officer down to Sussex to break the news to the poor girl's mother. Oh, and I should ring Bethnal Green to see about Gillian's house. I wonder if Dr Tremethyk has finished. I'll go down to the morgue after that."

"Don't forget your Vicks, sir." Brittany grinned cheekily.

It was always a good idea to create a medicinal barrier in the nostrils when visiting Dr Tremethyk's realm. The mortuary emanated a mixture of odours that turned even the hardiest stomachs. His Bethnal Green colleagues were friendly but could not help. An inspector told Vance, "The lass seems to have been a loner—something of a nun. No sign of men in her life. No diary, nothing compromising of any kind. If I might express an opinion—" he waited politely for consent.

"Please do."

"I'd say this was a random killing. Maybe opportunist. If anyone didn't deserve such a fate it was MS Gillian Coombs. A model citizen, I'd say."

"I'll bear that in mind, Inspector. Thanks for your help." Jacob Vance stared at the receiver for a few moments and thought, *Well, it wasn't opportunist, that's for sure. Our killer planned this well ahead.* He snapped out of his reflections, except for a vague unease about something his sergeant had said. Ten minutes later, he had finished giving instructions to PC Stephanie Williams, arranged a car and driver for her and apologised for saddling her with that most unpleasant of tasks—breaking the news of a child's death to a parent.

He took Shepherd's advice and, unlocking his desk, withdrew a small jar of Vicks VapoRub. It was time for his mortuary visit. How he hated staring at previously unblemished bodies sliced open and now stitched closed. Tremethyk stared at him with something approaching compassion. "You never get used to it, me-dear. Your report is ready in that folder, boy. Except for the most important part." His marked accent told Vance that Francis Tremethyk was particularly upset on this occasion.

"And what would that be, Doctor?"

"I've sent one of my assistants post-haste to the Toxicology Department of Imperial College. We should have the results sometime tomorrow morning. Best I can do, I'm afraid." His accent had subsided since he wasn't talking about the victim.

"So, they poisoned the poor woman, Doc."

"Oh, aye, and I have an idea what was used, and if I'm right, me-dear, we have a rare killer on our hands. But I'll not pronounce on it until we have our results. All I can say is that the young lady didn't suffer too much, death would have taken her in a matter of seconds. It's all in there, in your little light reading." He pulled a white sheet over the corpse that Jacob had studiously avoided looking at.

"Can I see the paintbrush?"

"If you can be bothered to go over to the remarkable Markham, boy. Your killer had sharpened the handle to a point. Well, it's all in there." He waved a hand airily at the folder. "Tell me, Detective, what's the use of me writing it all up if you boys want everything straight from the horse's mouth?"

"You're quite right, Doctor. I'll go and read it thoroughly. If it's too technical, I'll ring you."

"All right with that, boy. Happy reading, poor soul."

Vance wondered as he walked out to fresher air whether that last remark was intended for the victim or himself. He sat down in his office with a strong coffee and turned to a photograph of the paintbrush, noting how the killer had sharpened it to a wicked point. Finding the relevant passage in the report, he discovered that insertion had, indeed, been after death. The wooden point had penetrated the temporal lobe of the victim's brain.

Consoling himself with a fix of caffeine, he wondered why. What point was the killer trying to make? Culture! That was at the basis of the grudge against the police. Paintbrush? Was it a message that involved a painting? What about colour? The only clue regarding that was the black spray paint on the wall. No, it wasn't! He thought of the haiku. Didn't it mention yellow? He looked it up. Yes,

*"The low yellow*
*moon above the*
*Quiet lamplit house."*

So, if his speculation was right, black and yellow had to be considered, but which? And why? He swore and went over to the percolator. Another cup of coffee wouldn't help his blood pressure, but the only cure for that would be an arrest. He returned to read the pathologist's report from the beginning. All he gained from that was an impression of the efficiency of the murderer. Further progress had to wait on Imperial College. The report was not too long, owing to the vagueness regarding the murder substance. Gillian Coombs enjoyed perfect health until she met her nemesis.

Vance had just finished reading when a knock came at the door.

"Come!"

In walked Shepherd with her usual grin. "I waited this time, sir."

"So, you did, Brittany. It won't harm your chances of remaining my favourite sergeant."

They relaxed, and Vance indicated a seat, offering, "Coffee, Sarge?" He let her drink before asking, "Is Mrs Jackson all right?"

"Relieved to have the computer back. Debbie inspected it as carefully as I inspected her!"

"No sign of bruises or weals?"

"No, it seems our Frank Jackson was shocked at Gillian's death and can't do enough to help the police. Maybe we misjudged him. I reckon that his wife transmits anxiety. They're probably all lovey-dovey."

"I'm sure you're right. Now about Gillian's office?"

"I drew a blank there. The latest appointments are all vouched for by her colleagues. There was no mention of any sinister visitor nor any notes to help us. The other agents all speak of her in glowing terms. Our Gillian was a complete professional according to them."

"So, another dead end. It's increasingly likely that the murderer was unknown to Gillian Coombs, which makes our task harder."

"There's one thing that strikes me as odd, sir?"

Vance's antennae pricked up. "Go on."

Shepherd ran the tip of her tongue along her upper lip, something she did when in thought.

"When I spoke with Debbie Jackson, she told me that Gillian had a car in a rental garage nearby. She only used her car on Sundays. That makes sense with her home near to work. She could walk there in ten minutes. On my way across town, I popped into forensics to have a rummage inside Gillian's handbag. I thought she might have a pocket notebook or something, and I wanted to check out her recent calls."

"And?"

She bit her lower lip this time. "Nothing in the calls. Some to her mother, a call to her office, one to her dentist's. But what I didn't find that surprised me."

Vance fairly growled, "Out with it!"

"Well, sir, as I said, she had a car, but there was no driving licence among the contents of her handbag."

"Well spotted, Brit. I'll ring the inspector at Bethnal Green again. Let's see if they found it at her home. We'd better get forensics to give Gillian's car the once over, you never know. What kind of car is it?"

"Debbie Jackson said it was blue. We should ask her husband. He'll know."

"No need. The garage will only have one Gillian Coombs on their books. This case is becoming rather tiresome, Sergeant. As I see it, there are too many blind alleys. I'm afraid we need another murder to make progress. But that's the last thing we want, isn't it?"

# CHAPTER 7

## RIVERSIDE DEVELOPMENT, FULHAM, LONDON

Bethany entered the flat and kicked off the shoes nipping her toes before sitting in her favourite armchair to massage them. Seated there, she sighed with relief and gazed at the lights reflected like multi-coloured rippling snakes in the river. She smiled. Dear Aunty Amy would not recognise her if she walked into the flat as a ghost right now. If she did, she would be distraught. Without a doubt, she would never have left her fortune to a transvestite murderer. Amy was a good soul, everything Bethany wasn't, although, that wasn't true either. But for accursed misfortune, she might have been a pillar of society by now. Amy had seen past the adversity, bless her! Probably owing to the tribulations Bethany had endured, Amy had decided to make her the sole heir—not that there were other suitable candidates.

Bethany tossed the blonde wig on the coffee table and scratched at her short male hair, patting it into something like order. The second murder had gone as smoothly as she had planned it, without a hitch. Next time, though, she would change the approach if not the method. Travel was proving too risky. Returning the car to the airport rental returns was anonymous enough, but the late evening underground trip back from

Heathrow had stressed her. But enough of this negativity! What about the positives?

*There are plenty of those,* she thought, ticking them off on her fingers. *First, they'll be looking for a blonde female; second, they'll think the killings are confined to London E2—surprise; third, there's the Japanese connection—that was a masterstroke; fourth, there's the red herring of the street; fifth, they'll search for a relationship between victims—that's why I chose a man this time; and sixth—there must be a sixth, but I can't think of it! I'm tired. I'd better get some shuteye.*

---

Vance snatched up the receiver.

"Bethnal Green Station, sir, Inspector Preston wants me to put him through to you," DC Mark Allen's voice came over the line sounding breathless and curious.

Vance decided there was no point in asking Allen what was going on so early in the day. "Well, put him through, then." The line went silent for a moment as the young policeman on the Yard switchboard made the connection.

"Hello, Jacob, it's Will Preston. We've got another death on our patch for you. According to the Cornish fellow, it's a white male, aged twenty-five or thereabouts—the same modality—a puncture wound to the neck. He's at the SOC now, waiting for forensics. You'd better get your skates on, pal! The body is in an open passageway at the end of Satchwell Road, just off Bethnal Green Road, that's the A1209, by the way. Satchwell Road is a narrow street with a Japanese restaurant on the corner. Easy to find."

"OK, Will, I'm on my way, and thanks." He hurried across the room to Malcolm Ridgeway's room, responding to the invitation to enter.

"Sir, we have a second killing in the Bethnal Green area. I'm on my way, I just thought you should know." He trotted out the few details he knew.

"Thanks, Jacob. I want an update as soon as you get back. I'll inform the commissioner."

Pausing only to locate Shepherd, he explained the situation, established that she knew the quickest route through the London streets to Satchwell Road. Brittany knew the restaurant as she'd eaten there more than once.

"It's the Issho-ni, sir. Excellent food and reasonable prices. I'm not sure that the chef is Japanese, but he knows how to prepare delicious sushi."

"Raw fish, Sergeant, *raw fish*? You'll do yourself in with an intoxication one of these days."

"You're more at risk, Inspector. What, with your Cockney love of shellfish. I'll bet some of the cockles and mussels you eat come straight from the docks with them creatures sucking in all the filth from ships' bilges."

It was too early in the working day for their usual banter. They lapsed into silence. After a while, Vance asked, "Isn't that the restaurant down there? Why are you turning right?"

"Trust me, sir, I've been here before. Look, first left and left again and there's loads of parking. Taking Satchwell Road would have meant we had nowhere to park. Look, there are our lads over there." She pointed them out before tugging the handbrake.

"Well done, Brit. All the activity seems to be over by those railings." He led the way with a hurried stride. Hastily pulling on the white protective gear, he saw Dr Francis Tremethyk raising his head from over the body to rebuke him. "What kept you, *me-dear?* It's the same fiend as with that poor young woman. This time the victim is male. See here, the same *modus operandi*. Puncture to the throat and the very poison that did for the lass, I'll wager, boy. The earlier results should be through sometime this morning."

"I see the murderer has chosen a nostril and not an ear this time."

Jacob Vance stared at the two inches of a paintbrush that

protruded from the victim's nose. "Will that have reached the brain, too, Doc?"

"That it will, me-dear, but your killer will have had to use more force to breach the nasal cavity than a mere tympanum." The Cornish accent came over melodic and robust. The doctor was upset.

"But would a young woman have the necessary strength?"

"Is it a woman you're after? That surprises me! But, aye, with a well-sharpened shaft, a determined woman could do that. You'll be interested in the note, too, I expect."

"Another note?"

"'Fraid so, tightly rolled and pushed into the left ear. I couldn't miss it. It's in the evidence bag, here." He handed over the square plastic envelope. "Curious there's a Japanese restaurant a few yards away."

"Is that of any bearing, Doc?"

"It might be. We'll see what Imperial College has to say. Ignore me for now, just a hunch, me-dear."

"Time of death, Doctor?"

"It seems to have been between ten and eleven yesterday evening, at first glance. As ever, I'll be more precise when I've done the autopsy."

"Rather you than me. Thanks anyway. Ah, here comes Sabrina and her team. She'll be telling us to shift in a minute. Come on, let's save her the trouble."

After hailing Dr Markham, he stripped off his white forensic overall and recognising the Bethnal Green sergeant, wandered over to her.

"Good morning, we meet again under tragic circumstances."

She gave him a weak smile. "Good morning, Inspector. It looks like the same killer, sir. The night shift took the call at the station just before midnight. A customer from the restaurant on the corner said he stumbled over the body. The streetlamp over the cut-through is dead, unfortunately. The couple who reported the body had parked at the back of the restaurant—most people do. There's no real room on Satchwell Road."

"Do you have a contact number for the couple, Sergeant? It's possible that our killer ate in the same restaurant before committing the crime. She may have chosen her victim from among the diners."

"*She,* sir?"

"Ah, a slip of the tongue, but our preliminary inquiries point in that direction. Did you not see the photofit?"

"I haven't been into the station so far. I suppose if it's poison, as they're saying, it could well be a woman. As to the contact number, she flipped open a notebook, copied a mobile number, ripped out the page, and handed it to Vance. "Marcus Welsby and his fiancée, Deidre Walsh—nice couple on a pleasant evening out. We let them go home after taking their statement as it was late. Then we sealed off that snicket."

"Snicket?"

"Passageway, sir. Don't you call it that?"

"I will from now on." He grinned.

They were interrupted by a discreet cough and a polite voice, "Sir," one of the forensics team addressed the inspector, "there's something that might interest you. I was poking around the general scene and drifted into the road itself at the top end of the passageway—"

"The snicket?"

"Eh? Ah, yes, exactly. This way, sir. See the steel corrugated shutter under Flats One and Two, painted blue. Well, it's covered in white graffiti, except if you look closely, there are the black numbers, just like in Allenbury Lane." The white-clad figure pointed at the black-sprayed **9-2=7.**

Jacob Vance swore under his breath. The murderer was beginning to prey on his nerves quite as much as on Doctor Tremethyk's. Remembering himself, he said, "Well done, young man. Can we get a photo of this? One can't be too careful. I feel sure it's the same hand, but you never know."

Having decided to spend no more time at the crime scene, Vance, wearing latex gloves again, stared wordlessly at the note in his hand. The silence lasted long enough for Shepherd to comment, "Everything alright, boss?"

"No, it isn't Brit. To be honest, I'm pig-sick of this case. We have a perpetrator on the loose playing around with the police. It's obscene. She's killed twice and intends to kill seven more innocent people. We haven't got a clue where to start, which proves her theory that the police are a witless, culture-shunning bunch of twerps."

"Sounds like you've decided our killer is a woman, sir."

"True, based on the motorcyclist captured on film and that poisoners tend to be female, Sarge, but I'm not closing my mind to anything. Listen carefully, what do you make of this?" He read from the note:

*"I won't be happy*

*with the first one I pick*
*but will try different ones*
*until I know you. How*
*will I know you?*

*You'll feel warm*
*between my palms*
*and I'll cup you like*
*a handful of holy water."*

"Jeez!" Shepherd exploded, *"the first one I pick* sounds like her victim—Gillian Coombs, in fact— *but will try different ones.* But what does she mean *until I know you?* It's not a threat to the commissioner, surely? Nobody could be that mad!"

"We can't rule anything out, Brittany. We have to capture this murderer before she strikes again. Ah, here we are, Yard, sweet Yard!"

He slammed the car door and patted his pocket, where he'd slipped the evidence bag with the threatening note. It was time to report to his superiors about the bloody killer.

The perpetrator in question was working on a strangely shaded map on his desk. After careful reflection, because he faced a selection of one from three scattered locations for his next murder, he made his choice and consulted with the AZ of street names in the chosen sector, which was no longer E2, but N1. He turned to the correct starting letter of the colour and found that he did not have the same problem as the first two murders. One name struck him as particularly suitable as well as attractive. Time to go out on reconnaissance. Today, he would not change gender and maybe not even for the next murder.

His mind was racing back over the last killing, as he laced up a pair of stout walking shoes. He'd been over the first murder thousands of times, but the last one contained the matter of the hire car. Oh yes, he'd been saucy, all right! *I just hope I didn't overdo it! Let's see. I grinned at the Heathrow camera, I wore gloves in the car, and kept a hat on. They won't find anything.* Reassured, he double locked his flat and set off for Parsons Green station. At the underground station, he consulted the large wall map. He knew where to start because hundreds of thousands of fingernails, over time, had worn away the station name where he was standing by indicating their starting point. *People are so stupid. Why can't they simply use their eyes?* Using his, he traced the green line as far around as Embankment. He'd have to change there, continuing on the black, the Northern line, as far as the closest station to his destination. He laughed out loud, gaining himself some odd looks from a small group of Koreans. He couldn't help it—the nearest station was Angel. How appropriate for the Angel of Death!

Vance had reported to his superiors, displaying the evidence without contamination—they knew the procedure well enough.

Aalia Phadkar surprised him. "I know that poem from when I was younger. It's a lady poet called Roisin Kelly. I remember because I like her work. I'm afraid I can't recall the title offhand, but you'll find it through her name, Jake. It must mean something deeper to your killer. I can't believe it's a threat to my person."

"That was DC Shepherd's idea, ma'am. I can't say that I go along with her theory. But it never harms to take extra care, does it?"

"You'd better solve the case as quickly as possible if I'm to be victim number nine, Detective Inspector. We've already lost two. It's a hell of a high price to pay for an apology," she said bitterly.

"We're well beyond that now, ma'am," Ridgeway said in the same tone.

"I've set Shepherd onto talking with the couple who found the body, although I don't hold out much hope. Will you give me another warrant for CCTV if the owners won't cooperate, ma'am? I'm going back to the SOC in case there are any cameras operational."

Before leaving, he deposited the evidence bag with Max Wright, issuing the usual stern warning about contamination. "I want the title of the poem. He snatched up a pen and wrote Roisin Kelly on a scrap of paper—the author," he explained before dashing off, calling over his shoulders, "and then take it over to forensics, Max!"

He left the premises with the precious search warrant safely tucked away, requisitioned a car to drive himself to the murder scene, and swore at the traffic until arriving behind the Japanese restaurant. He wondered why he and Shepherd hadn't thought of the CCTV. After all, it was their only lead on the previous case. Their high standards were slipping. This murderer was getting under their skins. A police officer had to be unemotional, he told himself. The callous assassinations of two young people made his blood boil—other than being unemotional. He pulled up more or less where Brittany had earlier, got out the car, and stared around the almost square area, his eyes passing over satellite dishes, burglar alarms, and minor fixtures, but not a trace of a CCTV camera. *A case of out of sight out of mind, maybe,* he justified himself. He had nearly given up when he thought of the snicket. There were parking bays outlined in white on this side of the black iron railings. There was also a sizeable violet rubbish skip, but it did not block the view of those spaces as it was nearer to him. It was a slim possibility. *If only*—he strode to the passageway and heaved a sigh of relief. Set back along a path running perpendicular to it and blocked off from the passageway by a sturdy padlocked gate, was a brick-built construction named *Alliston House* on whose wall was a yellow enamel rectangle bearing the black graphic form of a wall-mounted camera. CCTV! He had to find another way into the building and persuade the owners to let him see the film.

By walking out of Satchwell Road, turning first right, walking around the block, he came to a narrow street called Gibraltar Walk. By exploring it, he was able to find the entrance to the apartment complex loftily named Alliston House. He entered unchallenged—so much for security—found a resident and extracted from the helpful middle-aged man the name of the custodian in charge of the CCTV. The person responsible for filming was a retired storekeeper named Griffiths, who seemed to grow agitated at the sight of Vance's warrant card.

"Did you know that there was a murder last night across the way, sir?"

The flustered elderly fellow confessed that he did not, insisting he steered clear of gossip but was more forthcoming about his monitor.

"Of course, I'll show you, Detective Inspector, we had it installed a few years ago. Most break-ins came along the back passageway that leads onto where your murder took place—bad business!" Tut-tutting, he shook his grey head, slowly turning to white at the temples. "When my Alice was alive—she passed four years ago—she was so worried that she persuaded me to raise funds to pay for installation. I've taken over running it but will confess that I don't check the blessed thing unless something untoward has happened. Last time, it was a break-in to one of the residents' cars down there. The police used it to apprehend the culprit I'm pleased to say."

"Excellent, sir. Is this the room?"

It took Vance a good half hour to get his fussy host organised sufficiently to replay the footage from the previous evening, but the delay was worthwhile. At 22.25 the evening before, a sparkling car pulled up parallel and close to the iron railings. He cursed because he couldn't see the number plate. He recognised the model as a Hyundai Tucson. It was probably grey, but then, everything on the CCTV film was some shade of grey or another. He caught his breath when a blonde with long hair got out, looked carefully around, walked into the passageway, waited suspiciously—unsurprised, he recognised her as Gillian Coombs's killer. He sucked in breath through his front teeth. What was she doing? He squinted. It looked like she was fumbling with an open purse. Suddenly, she dropped it so that the coins fell out. That was her game! The friendly young fellow, having now entered the scene was bending to help retrieve the cash and the purse. The killer repaid his kindness by stabbing him in the throat with her syringe when he straightened up. She stood there callously watching him die, only a matter of seconds, before gazing furtively around. The image wasn't incredibly clear because, unlike Frank's lane, there was no functioning streetlight, just the moon. He must remember to ring the Council Offices. A strong lamp might have deterred the murderer. Satisfied, the woman dashed to the steel shutter and rapidly sprayed her message before striding quickly back to the car.

He watched the exhaust fumes rise from the diesel, then, to his satisfaction, she reversed, turned the car, and he memorised the plate—KVI62KK. He'd made another breakthrough! He wrote it on the back of his hand.

"Mr Griffiths, I'm afraid I'll need to take your computer to New Scotland Yard."

The elderly gentleman, who had watched the horrific scene act out, couldn't have been more obliging.

"You take it, Inspector, and I hope you catch the witch! That poor young man! He only wanted to help."

Detective Inspector Vance drove back to base without swearing at the traffic even once. Instead, he was deep in thought. There were so many loose ends to tie up, but he felt that soon he would neaten up the wayward threads.

# CHAPTER 8

## NEW SCOTLAND YARD AND ANGEL ISLINGTON, LONDON

Inspector Vance radioed ahead to dictate the number plate of the Tucson. The radio operator relayed the message to Max Wright, who routinely had no trouble tracing the owners. So, when several minutes later, Vance rushed up to his desk, he beamed cockily at the flustered detective.

"The Tucson is a hire car, sir. It's part of a fleet at Heathrow."

"Get on to them and block new rental until forensics have given it the once-over."

"Already done! Forensics are on their way. But wait for the real news."

"What?"

The technician smirked and said, "Guess who rented the vehicle?"

"I know who hired it—I saw her on CCTV."

"Sure, but in what name?"

"Don't mess with me, Max. I'm not in the mood!"

Wright saw the dangerous glint in the inspector's eye and changed his tone.

"Sorry, sir, it's just that it was rented in the name of Gillian Coombs, our first victim."

"The gall of it! Cheeky bitch! How did she get away with that? There's a photo on the licence."

"I asked myself the same question, but, you know, let's say you've got a busy assistant on the desk, maybe taking phone calls whilst dealing with the customer—and what if our killer was wearing the regulation anti-covid face mask? She has long, straight, blonde hair like Gillian, after all. Also, it would all have been normal for the clerk: sign here; initial a waiver clause there; maybe receive a cash payment, no questions asked."

"Yeah, yeah, I get the picture. Talking about which, I'll ring the forensics people and have them check out all available CCTV images at Heathrow. The place is crawling with surveillance. Don't forget that colour program, by the way."

"I've put feelers out, but no joy, yet."

No sooner had he returned to his room than he received a call from Doctor Tremethyk.

"I have news for you, me-dear. The toxicology report has come through from Imperial College. It's just as I suspected. Will you come down to my office, or will I come up to you, boy?"

Vance thought for a moment. The pathologist's office was not as revolting to the senses as the mortuary. As a matter of courtesy, he decided. "I'll be down straightaway, Doc."

The Chief Medical Officer's room was spacious enough to be practical. Still, Dr Tremethyk had done everything possible to shrink it by cluttering all available surfaces with manuals, bags, charts, and sundry objects unidentifiable to Vance. On the positive side, the visitor's chair was sumptuously upholstered in soft brown leather. Its padding would have served to accommodate a man three times heavier than the inspector, who shuffled comfortably against the backrest.

"That Japanese restaurant at our latest SOC was probably a coincidence, me-dear," began the pathologist, "but, as I supposed, the poison was TTX."

Used to the roundabout methods of breaking news at the Met, Vance waited patiently.

"Aye, TTX—that would be tetrodotoxin to me. It occurs in nature but can be manufactured synthetically, which would require a sophisticated laboratory."

"Where does it occur naturally, Doc?"

The pathologist smiled, ah, that's where our restaurant comes in. More of that later. It's found in a fish, the fugu, which you might know as the pufferfish," he raised an eyebrow, and the inspector nodded, "but also in frogs, flatworms, newts, and, oh, the blue-ringed octopus."

"Which all raises more questions than answers, unfortunately. How does the poison work on humans?"

"That's what I like about you, me-dear. You have a curious mind. Well, normally, it's ingested—not our case since it was injected—the victim feels a tingling on the tongue or numbness that spreads to the rest of the face, swiftly spreading to other parts of the body. More and more nerves are paralysed until the unfortunate fatality is unable to move and dies of asphyxiation. In our two victims, the killer must have injected a strong dose since death was so rapid. Bear in mind, Inspector, even one-thousandth of a gram can be fatal. We're dealing with a substance here that is a thousand times more poisonous than potassium cyanide."

"Good God! Listen, Doc, are you implying that this stuff crops up in Japanese restaurants?"

"Absolutely! Have I put you off sushi, me-dear?"

Jacob chuckled. He liked and admired Francis Tremethyk. "I was never really *on* it, to be honest, but my sergeant goes to that restaurant from time to time. You might have a chat with *her!*"

The pathologist chortled but hadn't finished instructing his captive audience. "TTX blocks the voltage-gated sodium in nerve membranes by binding to a peptide group at the opening of the channel. Sodium ions can't enter the cell so that the nerves don't fire, and signals cease transmission. Nasty business!"

It was time to be proactive. "Two things spring to mind: first, our killer must be brilliant to know all this; second, it's incredible how a little pufferfish can be so deadly." The inspector looked impressed.

Dr Tremethyk was enjoying himself. Chatting with Vance made a welcome change from slicing corpses and writing reports. "On the latter, the fish is lucky because of a single amino acid mutation, so it has a modified sodium channel and is immune to its own poison. Our helpless little pufferfish has incorporated TTX into its defences."

Vance stared at the examiner. "Going back to our killer, I wonder what sort of preparation she would need to produce her venom? I'd tend to rule out a laboratory unless there's one near London producing synthetic TTX?"

"There are one or two. They are allowed to manufacture under strict licence for research purposes. Somehow, I doubt your killer is a molecular scientist prepared to have her face captured on closed-circuit film. These people are highly paid, but I suppose you have to explore every angle."

"Can you make me a list of these labs, Doc?"

"Humph! As if I've nothing better to do. But to be clear, I believe it's more likely that your killer has a supplier from a Japanese restaurant. Let me explain. Pufferfish—either cooked or served raw as *sashimi*—is a prized Nipponese delicacy. Because the tetrodotoxin molecule is too stable to be destroyed by cooking, the chef has to carefully remove the liver, ovaries, and intestines, all of which contain high toxin concentrations, before preparing the fish. Would you believe fugu chefs face three years' training during which they have to prepare and eat their own fugu before they sit a written and practical examination? Only then are they allowed to serve it to the public."

"That's one way to guarantee they don't make mistakes."

Tremethyk chuckled, but his face then became grim, "Indeed. Despite that, around fifty to a hundred Japanese each year die from TTX poisoning."

"You're kidding! Are you telling me that this *sushumi* is available in London?"

"Sashimi! Yes, but only in the most expensive restaurants. You see, we're not like some oriental customers. In Japan, the best chefs leave just a trace of the toxin in the fish so that their diners can enjoy that delicate tingle to have the thrill of playing Russian roulette, but without risk."

"Sod that for a lark! Those cordon-bleu bods must be confident of their skills."

"Of course, just one slip of the chef's knife, and you die."

"Have you ever eaten sashimi, Doc?"

"On a couple of occasions, I have, and it's delicious."

Vance pursed his lips, tilted his head, and peered at the pathologist from under a lowered brow. "I think I'll give it a skip. But one thing is bothering me."

"Go on?"

"Well, these chefs even in London must be highly paid. Why would they compromise their career by selling our killer fugu liver, ovaries, and what was it, intestines?"

"I'm not a detective, but I haven't met a rich person yet who doesn't want more money. Either that or she has a contact in the kitchen who can smuggle the stuff out. She would still have to prepare her deadly cocktail ready for injection, so your killer must have some chemical knowledge. Even if rudimentary equipment might serve, she'd have to be careful not to poison herself."

"If only! Maybe she works as a cook in a Japanese restaurant. We can begin by checking the kitchen staff in every Japanese restaurant in London and interviewing every chef. Did you say not all of London's Japanese restaurants serve sashimi?"

"I'll bet you can whittle them down to a dozen in London, Inspector."

Jacob leapt up. "Well, thank you, Doc, you've been most accommodating."

"My pleasure." He stood too. "Oh, by the way, Inspector, let me know when you fancy sashimi together—my treat."

"Not likely!" Vance left the office with a grin on his face, rapidly morphing into perplexity, with him wondering whether he'd just idly tossed away an exquisite indulgence at the pathologist's expense.

Upstairs, he discovered that Shepherd had returned from interviewing the couple who had chanced on the body. After hearing her report with nothing helpful, he updated her on the murder weapon and the getaway car.

"I've got something right up your street, Brittany. I'm sending you to the best Japanese restaurants in London to interview the chefs and to check on the kitchen staff."

"Blimey, sir, do you know how many Japanese restaurants there are in London? Hundreds!"

"I think you missed one little word, Sarge. I said *best*. There can't be that many who offer genuine sashimi, surely?"

She frowned and ran the tip of her tongue along her upper lip. "I suppose not. But there must be a dozen in the Mayfair area for starters."

"Well, begin there. You never know, you might find one you fancy."

Shepherd looked doubtful and pulled a face. "A bit beyond a sergeant's pay packet, sir. Anyway, I was going to ask you whether we should try and find a link between the two victims?"

"Get off to Mayfair. You know what to ask the chefs. I'll get Max onto a possible relationship between our two unfortunates."

Max Wright was aware of information that had not reached Jacob. The second victim was a chartered accountant named Martyn Lawson, aged twenty-eight, who worked for a practice close to the Barbican Centre.

"I've managed to find no connection between Martyn and Gillian, sir, at least, not from a professional point of view. He was on the auditing side, but his partners and employers, don't deal with Gillian's estate agency. The company tends to be more upmarket. On the other hand, we can't rule out that the victims may have met socially."

Detective Inspector Vance considered this. "True. I'll get a constable over to the practice and one to Lawson's family. Let's see what we can turn up. Nothing from forensics at Heathrow, yet?" Max shook his head. "I have a pleasant surprise for you, Inspector. One of my contacts came up trumps and sent me the program you wanted. I went straight to the film of Ms Coombs's murder." He clicked on an icon on his desktop. The frames he had chosen to enhance, showed Allenbury Lane in colour. "I adjusted the saturation to compensate for the artificial lighting. This coloration is as close as I can manage. Our killer is a blonde —we knew that—we didn't know that the mudguards were that mustard yellow while the rest of the bike is black."

"Well done, Max. That program might well come in useful in future. Call me as soon as you hear anything from Dr Markham and her squad."

"Will do, sir."

Vance decided that it was time to report to Ridgeway before his superior put pressure on him. Whilst he did so, he would praise Max Wright. The technician was a valuable team member and often displayed initiative. Vance wondered if it might be appropriate to plead for more policemen for what was becoming a complicated case to solve. As he took one step towards the door, to his irritation, the desk phone rang. It was Max.

"Sorry sir, I forgot to tell you, probably because it was so easy to find. That poem by Roisin Kelly? The title is *Oranges*."

In a change of plan, Detective Vance called Ridgeway, instead of passing by his office. He wanted to sound out a newly formulated theory with his superior officer.

"Sir, can you fix an appointment for us both with the commissioner? There's progress to report."

The killer was simultaneously pleased and irritated. Content because the intended murder scene was mere seconds away on foot from the tube station, annoyed because the said location was hard to enter. He stared balefully at the imposing grey iron-railed gate. Over the ornamental entry in large numerals and letters stood out the legend, 78 White Horse Yard.

His planned reconnaissance had transformed unwittingly into a plan of action. The unforeseen difficulty of access made him consider adopting one of the other two sites on his matrix. He dismissed the idea at once because of the convenience of the tube station and its name *Angel* that so amused him. After all, he reasoned, he liked a challenge—working out how to get in and out of the yard, killing a random victim without being seen, leaving the necessary clues on the body, all in extra quick time, was part of a military-style operation that so appealed to him. Without catching anyone's eye, he would examine the shutting mechanism of the gate. As he thought, an electrical impulse governed it. To gain access from outside would require someone pressing an admission button from within the building or the possession of a master key.

He sauntered a few yards along the busy road before coming to a pub. *The Pig and Butcher,* and its name redolent of slaughter appealed to him, so, he decided to enjoy an ale there. The sign on the wall announced hand-pulled craft ales, not that he was a connoisseur, he was more of a prosecco drinker. Still, he ordered a pint in the lounge bar and noticed that the pub offered food. His stomach reminded him that he had only eaten snatched meals of late. Leaving his beer for a moment, he ambled over to the bar, found a menu, and carried it over to his seat. The Paddock Farm Tamworth pork, pickled girolles, apricot, carrot and mustard purée tempted him, so he placed his order with the barman. When his delicious food appeared, aromatic and steaming under his nose, he realised that he had made an excellent decision, and not just for his stomach. Sitting at the next table, where he couldn't help but overhear them, were an estate agent and a prospective client. At the mention of the White Horse Apartments, his interest quickened.

"To be honest, it's somewhat more than I wanted to pay," the client confessed.

"You get what you pay for in this area, sir. We *are* talking about a luxury duplex apartment. Seven hundred and twenty-five pounds a week is well within the average rental bracket for Islington. You have to consider the position and standard of renovation. All the floors are washed oak, and the owners kept the original crystal glass windows—"

"Even so—sorry to have taken your time."

The client knocked back his gin and tonic, stood and made his excuses. The estate agent, looking glum, still had at least half a pint of beer left in his glass.

The interested eavesdropper, his meal almost finished, ate another mouthful, keeping one eye on the vendor to make sure he didn't leave, pushed his plate away, wiped his mouth, and settled back in his chair.

"Good food in this pub," he said to start a conversation.

"Yes, I often come here at weekends. They do a good Sunday dinner."

The killer smiled and considered. "I must try it one weekend. But excuse me, I didn't mean to listen in on your conversation, but are you an estate agent?"

"I am, in fact." He fumbled with his wallet and took out a business card. "Here's my card. As you can see, our offices are nearby. I was trying to interest that gentleman in the flats close by. I don't suppose—"

"Absolutely. I'm in the area because I'm looking for a long-term let. I had noticed those attractive apartments at number 78."

"The very ones. Would you like me to show you around whilst we're here?"

The killer thought it through. He was without his weapon and clues, but it was a way into the property. Maybe he could make a follow-up appointment. After this plausible hesitation, he said, "Let's finish our drinks, then, by all means, give me the tour."

Later, sitting on the rattling underground train, idly watching passengers come and go, he smiled to himself. He had an appointment for the following morning with the friendly agent, what was his name? He took the card from his pocket: *ah, until tomorrow at ten o'clock, Matthew Spinks.* He rolled his neck. The top of his spine ached more than usual. How he wished people wouldn't stare at him. It was so rude.

He did not waste time thinking about his potential victim and the right to life. That would never do. The estate agent was part of an inexorable process—a mere cog in a mechanism.

The corner of Detective Inspector Jacob Vance's mouth twitched fleetingly upwards in response to his immediate superior's solidarity. Ridgeway introduced the conversation with the Commissioner like this: "Ma'am, the Detective Inspector has the sharpest mind among my men and, indeed, he has already formulated a working hypothesis about our killer, haven't you, Jacob?"

"It's like this, ma'am. I'm now convinced we're dealing with a psychopath with a point to prove. The original message this maniac wrote to you suggests she—"

"She?" the commissioner seized on the pronoun.

"The evidence we've gathered points to a female perpetrator. We have the same blonde with long hair captured on film at both scenes. As I was saying, the letter hints at a grudge against the police, for reasons unknown. She has launched an insane challenge based on culture—this much we know. Also, she has adopted other psychotic behaviour with regard to the victims. The penetration of orifices with sharpened paintbrushes is nothing less than manic. The notes she has left as clues to her insane scheme bring me to the one piece of good news. The poem that my sergeant took to be a threat against your person, ma'am, takes on another meaning when you consider the title.

*"Oranges!"* cried the senior officer. It came to me on my drive home last night. "As soon as I remembered Roisin Kelly's title, I confess to a sense of relief, from a selfish point of view."

"Precisely, ma'am," Vance smiled sympathetically, "but that led me to think, if the poem isn't a threat against your person, the only significance it can have for our investigation lies in the title. The colour, orange."

"How does that fit with the first murder?" Ridgeway asked, his tone and expression sceptical, but only for the benefit of his superior officer—he wanted to give Vance every chance to explain his startling theory.

"Perfectly, sir. You see the first poem, the haiku, contained explicit reference to yellow. I believe that this madwoman is *painting* the London E2 district with death. She is designing a work of art in her crazed mind and our task is to identify it."

"Oh my God!" The commissioner sank into her seat, her voice barely audible. "B-but that implies as many murders as the colours her so-called painting portrays."

"Indeed, ma'am."

The commissioner's dark brown eyes seemed to darken further into two pieces of coal. "You must stop her at all costs! She spoke of eight victims—"

"Forgive me, ma'am, actually, *nine*. But soon she'll get over-confident and make her first mistake. Then, we'll have her."

The commissioner's goddess-like countenance crumpled. If he hadn't known better, aware of her reputation for hardness, Vance would have sworn she was about to cry. She was not, but, for a charismatic leader, she was mumbling uncharacteristically. "How many more, how many more?"

Suddenly, her fist came down hard on her desk and the dark eyes bored into his. "Get her, Jake, before she kills again! And you, Mal, see that E2 is swarming with our men."

"I'll put everything into it, ma'am," Jacob managed, with a sinking heart, and he saluted.

# CHAPTER 9

THE DELIVERY MEN WERE NOT DISAPPOINTED BY THE APARTMENT with its view over the Thames. The strange occupant of the property was another matter. He was insignificant and weird, dressed in a monk's habit with the cowl drawn over his head so that his face and body were mostly hidden. More used to delivering to the rich and famous, and hoping to meet a celebrity, the muscular pair of operatives lowered the high-end model of their luxury massage chair to the lounge floor, glad of a chance to regain their breath. Their last delivery, a month before, had been to the stately home of a rock star in the Berkshire countryside and the one previous to that to the mansion of a Premiership footballer in Cheshire. Any hopes of an autograph for the kids faded on the instant at the sight of this weird monk.

"Where would you like it placed, sir?"

"Right where that armchair is," the voice from deep within the cowl said. "There's a convenient socket right there." He pointed.

In a trice, the men hoisted the former favourite seat into the corner of the room indicated by the monk. With somewhat more difficulty, they heaved the massage chair to its position overlooking the river. In their experience, this was the first customer who did not wish to sit in the chair immediately as they ran through their spiel explaining the chair's features. Then again, everything about the odd monk unsettled them, except for the generous tip he pressed onto them.

As they took the lift down to ground level, one turned to the other. "What did you make of that, then, Alf?"

"Takes all sorts, Mickey. Here, do you think he was a real monk? I mean, aren't monks sworn to poverty? The chair alone costs nine thousand quid, mate, not to mention the price of that flat. Did you see the view? Some people have all the luck!"

"Nah, Alf, I reckon he's a weirdo. Probably a writer, or summat like that—"

"Yeah, but bless his heart, that's a handsome tip he gave us. Fifty quid each, and we didn't even get to the explanation of the calf and knee massage rollers."

"Yeah, weird! But he can mug it all up in the manual or phone to headquarters if he can't sort it out."

"Tell you what though, when he's all set up, enjoying the heat therapy and listening to his music from the speakers in the headrest whilst staring at the river traffic, with 4D massage rollers in operation—"

"Yeah, lucky bastard! Give me some of that!" They laughed as they headed out of the Riverside complex in their white delivery van, unaware that their latest customer, divested of his garments worn only to hide his appearance, was already light years ahead of them in his working knowledge of the chair, having studied the manual online for days. Now, he was enjoying the physiological benefits of the invention, blessing every penny he had spent on the luxury item. Aunty Amy would have approved.

An hour later, while the delivery men were swigging their beers at his expense, he was sat at his desk, feeling on top of the world, and laughing hysterically as his fingers sped over the keyboard of his computer. The letter came in the aftermath of his latest conversation with Lord Robert and began:

*Dear Commissioner Aalia Phadkar,*

*Your investigation seems to have stalled; you are making little progress. It is time I gave you a helping hand. Understand that I am just a pawn in Lord Robert's master plan. I shall want immunity after his arrest after due consideration by the courts of my cooperation.*

Luckily, there was no one to hear his manic laughter as he reread the opening three sentences. He must hurry to finish and get the letter in the post because Lord Robert insisted on him fulfilling the third execution as soon as possible. Damn it! He could do without Lord Robert playing around with his head. The man oozed confidence—if only he could be like him! How exactly did you put a peer of the realm in his place?

---

THE FOLLOWING DAY, NEW SCOTLAND YARD

On the first floor of New Scotland Yard, Sergeant Shepherd stood back and admired her handiwork in front of a whiteboard that contained her neat handwriting and photographs of the two victims of what she had headed as the E2 KILLINGS. The board included the colours yellow and orange to illustrate Vance's painting theory. To one side, she had written the three letters TTX in a box from which an arrow led to the words: *Japanese restaurants*. In a few minutes, she would deliver her speech to the assembled detectives, they would include some extra draftees to help with what increasingly appeared to be the activity of a serial killer loose in central London. She was acutely aware that the highest-ranked officers would be in attendance, it made her a little nervous, although she knew every detail of the case so far.

Brittany Shepherd didn't need to worry because her conference was about to be spectacularly derailed. Abruptly thanked and told to sit by Commissioner Phadkar, it instantly became clear that there were new developments. The Press Liaison Officer, Mark Sadler, had been summoned to the meeting and the head of the Metropolitan Police addressed him first.

"Mark, good of you to come along at short notice. What I need from you is your best efforts to drip feed this case to the press in such a way as the two killings appear to be random. At this point, we can exploit any theory *except* the truth. I don't want the public panicking, thinking there's a serial killer stalking the streets of E2. I'm sure that if you bring all your experience to bear, you can oblige us on this one."

"Consider it done, ma'am. Just one question, do you have reason to believe that your killer is about to strike again?"

"Indeed, I have, Mark. I'm holding it in my hand. This morning." She flourished a letter, and the gathering noticed for the first time that she was wearing surgical gloves. All eyes had hitherto been on her charismatic face. She continued, "A letter addressed to me arrived, which brings me," her eyes perceptibly darkened, "to another delicate matter that will become evident as I read:

*Dear Commissioner Aalia Phadkar,*

*Your investigation seems to have stalled; you are making little progress. It is time I gave you a helping hand. Understand that I am just a pawn in Lord Robert's masterplan. I shall want immunity after his arrest after due consideration by the courts of my cooperation. As yet, I dare not supply his full name as I live in fear of his wrath. You must realise that it was his idea to test your cultural preparation, which he retains far inferior to his own. It would help if you investigated that unashamed paedophile infecting the Upper Chamber by his very presence. The longer he is allowed to pervert the course of British justice, the more victims there will be. I refer not only to those hitherto targeted by him in the E2 district but also the innocent children whose lives are daily scarred by unscrupulous adults of his persuasion. Dear Commissioner, I implore you to liberate me from the ever-tightening clutches of this depraved overprivileged assassin. I, too, am his slave, his hapless victim, and have been since girlhood.*

*I have directed your attention to the mastermind. Now it is up to you to put an end to his nefarious machinations.*

*Yours in humility and hope,*
*Lord Robert's plaything.*

At last, she paused for breath, and her noble countenance held them in thrall from the Detective Chief Inspector to the lowliest of constables in the gathering. Each man and woman was hanging on her words and expressions. They were unsure whether her face or the letter was more shocking.

"Ladies and Gentlemen, I hardly need explain that the case has suddenly taken on a different significance. With the House of Lords involved, I dare say that our paymasters in the Home Office will be scrutinising our every move. So," she thundered, "let's make sure that none of our moves is a false one. The utmost delicacy and discretion are called for here. That includes the Press, Mr Sadler."

"Yes, ma'am."

"Any comments, any questions?"

Shepherd timidly raised her hand.

"What is it, Sergeant?"

"Well, ma'am, I wonder if we should open a discussion as to the veracity of the letter. I mean, this could still be the work of a crank. It's the same person that wrote the first one, but she's thrown a different slant on things, settling the blame on a peer of the realm. But what if there is no Lord Robert involved? This communication might be an elaborate red herring."

"If I may, ma'am?" Ridgeway intervened. "We should consider the peril not just of dealing with peers, but also of neglecting a matter sensitive to public susceptibility. Imagine if it ever came out that the Met was unprepared to follow up on accusations of paedophiles in the Lords. I'm afraid, Sergeant Shepherd, that would blow our credibility to smithereens for years to come."

"Nonetheless, the sergeant makes a good point, Detective Chief Inspector. Nothing can be taken at face value in this case. We must explore every avenue whilst treading on eggshells. Sergeant, please now resume the presentation to your colleagues." Aalia Phadkar crossed her arms and stared into the distance.

Brittany Shepherd walked up to the whiteboard, picked up a pointer from the aluminium rack running along its bottom edge, stood to one side of the board, and tapped on one word: *blonde*.

"The only trace our killer has left so far for Doctor Markham and her forensics people was found in the Heathrow hire car. As our Chief so aptly put it"—she glanced at the impassive Phadkar, still with folded arms— *"nothing can be taken at face value in this case.* Our forensics colleagues recovered a single blonde hair, no doubt from our killer, but the thing is, it was not human hair, but synthetic—a wig, then. So, two things spring to mind: first, our killer may not be blonde; second, we have no DNA to work on.

She went on to outline Vance's theory of the killer painting the E2 district with colours. She referred to the two poems and her pointer tapped the locations of the crimes on a rough map that she had drawn earlier, each zone shaded in the appropriate colour.

"Excuse me Sarge," came the harsh voice of a chain-smoking constable, "we'd have to assume that if the killer is inviting us to identify a work of art, by painting with numbers, as it were," he coughed, "sorry. Well, the piece of artwork certainly won't be an Old Master, will it? It's going to be an abstract or," he coughed again, "Pop Art, you know, Andy Warhol, or something similar."

"Good point, Constable Oldham," the commissioner interjected. "Thank you, Sergeant, if that's all, I'd like to call upon the expertise of a profiler and psychologist. Please!" She waved an arm.

A middle-aged woman wearing sensible tweed clothes, pretty and well-coiffured, introduced herself. "For the few who don't know me, I'm Miriam Walker, psychologist or, as some prefer, profiler. Whilst the catchword seems to be to take nothing at face value, which in any case, is a motto of mine, this woman shows signs of psychosis in her letter. She appears to convey classic symptoms of dissociative identity disorder. Whilst Lord Robert may be a real-life peer in the House—I'll come to that in a moment—we cannot dismiss the notion that this Lord is a separate identity of the same killer. Let's say that he controls her behaviour at different times, which might well lead to memory gaps and, or hallucinations. There is a proviso in my mind, however, and it is a strong one. DID is usually the result of sexual or physical abuse in childhood and becomes a way to distance oneself from trauma. It may not be casual that the writer refers to paedophilia." The pleasant, attractive face registered confusion. "So, you see, ladies and gentlemen, sadly, until we have more to work on, it is equally possible that Lord Robert exists, and that he does *not*." She sat down slowly among hissed whispers and gasps of dissatisfaction.

"It looks like we need another murder to make progress," Mal Ridgeway muttered to Vance, standing next to him.

Before the detective replied, the profiler stood again. "I'm sorry, I almost forgot one important detail."

Jacob Vance groaned. He didn't have much time for methods outside traditional policing. She was saying, "It is abundantly clear that our killer is a clever woman. Just consider the level of language she uses in the letter, for example, *nefarious machinations,* which isn't the lexis of your everyday neighbourhood bully. She leaves few leads to follow because she is of far above average intelligence.

"Yeah, bloody Moriarty!" Vance growled loud enough only for Ridgeway to hear.

"Don't worry, Jake, you'll get her." His superior had every confidence in his inspector.

Ridgeway organised detectives to check out past debates in Hansard regarding paedophilia. They were to come to him with any discoveries so that no indiscretions would occur. He trebled patrols in the London E2 district, which proved to be a waste of time. With no further comments or questions, the meeting dispersed.

In the early afternoon, Ridgeway summoned Vance to his office.

"Have you heard, Jake?"

Jacob grimaced for two reasons: he hated being called Jake, and if he had heard anything he wouldn't need his boss to tell him.

"What, Chief?"

"There's been a murder again! Another estate agent killed in the same way as the first two."

"Bloody hell! Where this time?"

"So much for our E2 theory. This time, it's in postal district N1—close to the Islington Angel underground station. The victim is a chap called Matthew Spinks, a well-known estate agent in the area. He was in his early forties. He leaves a wife and two young boys. You'd best get off down the Liverpool Road. It's a place," he consulted a notepad, "by the name of White Horse Yard."

"Is it, indeed?" muttered Vance, thinking about colours. He called Sergeant Shepherd on her mobile, who was busy interviewing another chef in Mayfair, and ordered her to get along to White Horse Yard immediately.

Somehow, although the two officers were equidistant from the murder scene, Brittany Shepherd arrived several minutes before her inspector. He found her already dressed in a protective outfit and talking to the MOE.

"Ah, here you are, sir. No doubt it's the same killer. No sharpened paintbrush this time, though."

"Hold hard, Sergeant, I think you should see this," came the Cornish accent. Dr Tremethyk was probing into the victim's throat with a sizeable pair of tweezers. Carefully extracting a foreign body, lodged post-mortem, according to the medic, deep in the man's throat. It proved to be a half-empty, tightly rolled at the bottom, 37 ml tube of Titanium White oil paint.

"There you are," Vance growled. "No coincidence—*White* Horse Yard and titanium *white*."

"Your theory is gaining momentum, sir," Shepherd admitted.

"There's this, too, Detective Inspector." Tremethyk held out the by now standard plastic envelope. "Another note for you."

Vance clenched his jaw. He detested being toyed with by this maniac and felt no closer to apprehending her.

"There is one thing that's different, Detective," the doctor said. "There's no puncture wound to the throat. Your killer must have struck at another part of the anatomy. I haven't found it yet, boy, but I will. Never fear, I will. By the way, time of death about six hours ago."

"Around nine o'clock this morning, then," Vance calculated.

"That's suggestive, sir," his sergeant said.

"Why, Brit?"

"It suggests to me that the victim had an early morning appointment with the killer. The estate agent would have had the key to one of these properties. The witness, over there, found the body here at a quarter to nine this morning. She knew him. Claims he sold her flat to her two years ago. The murderer couldn't have entered the compound without a key, so Mr Spinks opened the gate and led the way."

"To his death," Vance added in a murmur. He questioned Mrs Brimble, the witness, and combed the scene thoroughly before leaving, managing to add little or nothing to his knowledge of the case.

At the same time that detectives Vance and Shepherd were discussing him, the murderer was staring at the occupant of the other seat, now positioned a couple of yards from his luxury massage chair.

"I got lucky, this time, Lord Robert. It very nearly blew up in my face. *The best-laid plans* etcetera—I was about to strike when he turned around and fought me off. Luckily, I forced the needle under his jacket sleeve and into his forearm. I only had time to push the tube of paint into his throat and leave the poem before that prying neighbour woman came poking around. I managed to hide behind one of those smelly wheelie bins. Ugh!"

He pressed the nape of his neck into the soft headrest of the massage chair and shook his aching head gently from side to side.

"What do you mean? Excuse me!" He glared at the nonchalant peer in the other chair and pinched the bridge of his nose before shrieking, "Goddam it, Lord Robert! I keep telling you, a knife is of no use. How do you think I could have got away from the scene of the killing if I'd been covered in blood? No, sir, you might like a nice gory crime scene for spectacular effect, but as I keep repeating, it's not practical. Haven't I proved it to you already three times? In and out, swift, and clean as a whistle. All right, I almost got caught this time, but I know why. The location was too complicated. No, sir, I won't make that mistake again. Please leave me now. I don't feel well, my head's splitting, and I feel disorientated. Yes, of course. The next one! The day after tomorrow—it's all worked out. Leave it with me and return to the Chamber. I know you're a busy man. Narrowing his eyes, he watched the peer depart the room. His relationship with him was indeed a love-hate affair. Lord Robert had better watch his step. What was the old saying? *Hoisted by his own petard?* Well, one of these days he might become one of the nine victims if he wasn't careful. Oh damn! That reminded him, he'd forgotten to spray **9-3=6** on a wall in White Horse Yard. Would the police even notice the oversight? He doubted that they would. They were such pathetic dullards! It went to show how flustered he had been. He'd make sure that the next murder went as smoothly as clockwork in a much more suitable location.

# CHAPTER 10

## NEW SCOTLAND YARD, LONDON

On one of his rare visits upstairs, Doctor Tremethyk hoped to be the bearer of intriguing news for his friend, Detective Inspector Vance.

"I've brought you the autopsy report, Jacob. I wanted to share my wisdom verbally on this occasion."

"Much appreciated, Doc. Out with it then."

"To begin with," the doctor spoke slowly with hardly a trace of his Cornish accent, "the victim, *ahem,* Matthew Spinks—by the way, the widow came in to identify him. She's a lovely young woman, heart-breaking all round—was right-handed. How do I know? Well, that's the arm he chose to defend himself with. I guess that the assassin was going for the throat as usual when the man suddenly turned and tried to fend away the syringe. Still, in the rapid action, it must have entered under his cuff and plunged into his forearm, about here," he indicated a place halfway between wrist and elbow. "Matthew put up a struggle, judging by the entry and exit wound. The needle actually became bent out of shape."

"What does it tell us about our killer, Doc?"

"We have some scientific certitudes, Detective. Not that they help. You already know the murderer is a woman—"

"That's not true. We *think* the killer is female because we saw her on video. But we now know the subject wore a blonde wig. We can't exclude a male in disguise."

"Well, my findings indicate that the assailant was five foot four or five tall. That makes her petite, or if the person is male, he might have been born prematurely to be so short. I doubt whether a not fully-grown teenager is your killer."

"Mmm. That's helpful. It looks increasingly like our suspect is a petite female," Vance mused. "The fact that she was surprised whilst attacking indicates that her routine was thrown awry."

"What do you mean, Jacob?"

The detective smiled grimly. "There are some anomalies this time. You placed the time of death at around nine o'clock. Have you had reason to revise that opinion?"

"There's always some latitude when assessing the time of death. It could have been up to thirty minutes earlier."

"That would make more sense. The witness, Mrs Brimble maintains she found the body at 8.45. It's even possible that she unknowingly disturbed the assailant, who dashed out of sight. You see, there was no sharpened paintbrush this time. Neither did she spray her homicidal formula on a wall. I guess that her priority was escape without being seen."

"Aye, true. But don't forget," the Cornish accent suggested strong emotion, "she rammed a tube of paint down the victim's throat so hard that it created lacerations to the oropharynx. By the way, me-dear, did you know that your killer is no artist?"

"How did you work that out?"

The doctor smiled and looked slightly embarrassed. "In my student days, I dabbled in oils. You see, the size of the paint? Well, the thirty-seven-millilitre tube is available only in a ten-pack in that particular brand. No self-respecting artist would use those. The killer probably bought them online. Titanium White has strong opacity and tinting strength, while the Zinc is a more transparent white. Titanium naturally dries faster, while the Zinc White takes its time." The doctor, a man of science, knew what he was talking about and revelled in demonstrating his knowledge. "Titanium White is the most common of the whites used for painting. It's bright white, almost bluish, and has excellent opacity and high tinting strength. Zinc White is very transparent and has a tenth of the tinting strength of Titanium White."

"Okay, so, our murderer isn't a serious artist—point taken. You know, Doc, every minor detail, such as this, helps piece together an idea of who we are dealing with. I don't think the paint itself, whether Titanium or Zinc has any importance. Its significance lies in the colour. Our suspect is leaving a trail of colours, first yellow, then orange, now white. Did you read the note, by the way?"

"No, it was rolled tight. I just retrieved it from wedged inside his shoe and bagged it up. Why, what did it say?"

"A poem, like the other two. We have no difficulty finding the titles and the poet with a search engine. Hang on! Here it is. He reached for his copy printed out on A4. It's called SNOW by Edward Thomas. Rather nice if you like that sort of thing. Vance began to read:

*"In the gloom of whiteness,*
*In the great silence of snow,*
*A child was sighing*
*And bitterly saying: "Oh,*
*They have killed a white bird up there on her nest,*
*The down is fluttering from her breast!"*
*And still it fell through that dusky brightness*
*On the child crying for the bird of the snow."*

Detective Inspector Vance cleared his throat and gazed at Tremethyk. "I think the messages of whiteness and death are both evident in those words, don't you?"

"It's a lovely poem, apart from our homicide context. I'm

ashamed to say I'd never heard of Edward Thomas. Our killer is a cultured woman.

"Not necessarily, Doc," said the ever-practical Vance. "Nowadays, all you have to do is Google something like *poems about whiteness,* and hey presto! Up pops your poet talking about snow. The miracles of technology!"

"I guess you're right, Detective. Each to his own job. I'll leave you to yours and return to mine."

"Thanks for the report, Francis. I'll read it now."

He didn't read the dossier at once because he pondered on the significance of the colours over a coffee. With Sergeant Shepherd's map of E2 no longer relevant as a grid for the maniacal *painting,* they would have to extend their canvas. But when and where would their killer strike again?

The murderer had plenty of choice for his next location, for apart from there being different suitable areas of London in terms of street names, the one he had settled on was dense with them. He need not limit himself to streets either because there was a station and a bridge, even a subway bearing the name Blackfriars. Whereas the black interested him, he wasn't enthralled by the friar part. He laughed out loud at how he had dressed as a monk—him! His laugh echoed in the dank underpass. The green mildewed walls caught his fancy and made him think of an underground tomb, but the place, suitable in that respect for death, was unsuitable in every other way. The constantly passing traffic made it too exposed for his activities. He dismissed the notion and hurried out of the tunnel back towards Blackfriars Passage, the narrow road that, so far, he liked best. The low volume of vehicles was constrained to one-way, and the street had various hiding places. Another positive was that solitary pedestrians used it to cut through towards the river from Queen Victoria Street.

Alternatively, there were the two stations, the underground and the mainline. They had the advantage that he could easily inject somebody with poison without being seen amid the confusion of the bustling crowds. Still, the main drawback was that he would be unable to leave his *accoutrements*, as he liked to call the objects he placed on the body. Also, how could he spray his message unseen in a station? The location, therefore, practically chose itself.

He gazed around at Blackfriars Passage. Where it swept around in a tight curve, the pavement was protected by black cast iron bollards standing like soldiers in a row. White caps and a touch of red to pick out the moulded stars and rim attractively topped them. The appeal of the setting to him was that it reminded him of Murder One. There was no similarity except that in Allenbury Lane, he had been able to hide behind a brick column to await the blonde. Here, the enormous concrete V-shaped supports likewise provided a convenient lurking point.

The narrow street had double yellow lines on either side, so parking was unavailable. Walking towards the tube station, he noticed that the attractive bollards continued to delimit a large, paved area at the junction of Blackfriars Passage. A series of bicycle racks were occupied, but each berth was wide enough to hold two machines, not that anyone had doubled up. Ideal! The following morning, he would go to the container terminal, retrieve his motorbike, and park it here for a high-speed getaway. Well, not too fast, he laughed, he didn't want to attract attention. Everything was now in place—all he needed was the victim. He guffawed at his reflection in a plate glass window. The victim—as if that was a minor detail! He had to stop himself laughing hysterically. It was so funny! Be careful, he warned himself, there's no way he should catch the eye of passers-by on the eve of a murder. Forcing himself to become serious, he hurried into the tube station, took out his Oyster Card and headed for the Circle line. His motorbike awaited him. Of course, that meant becoming a she with long blonde hair on the morrow, and that thought pleased him—or rather—her.

Outside of Japan, probably the most famous Japanese chefs in the world resided in London. As soon as her inspector had engaged her to interview the Mayfair chefs, Sergeant Shepherd had mugged up on the pre-eminent ones. She had regarded it as a great privilege even to speak with Chef Chen Morimoto, who had taken a liking to the detective, with her striking 1920s-style prettiness. One day, she would tell her jealous friends how the chef had encouraged her to sample his *wagashi,* which she thought were among the prettiest things she had ever seen. "You must drink green tea with wagashi, Sergeant. There is an ancient Japanese proverb that says that a person has a separate stomach for desserts!" His deep laugh betrayed his wiry frame. Brittany Shepherd blessed the day she decided to join the police as she savoured the gourmet dessert. Like the majority of his fellow countrymen, the chef was exquisitely polite. With patience, he explained the plant-based ingredients that she had never heard of such as mochi and anko. For her part, she resolved to start putting money aside. Her taste buds in overdrive, the sergeant decided that an evening in Chef Morimoto's restaurant would be sheer heaven.

The chef's benign countenance only stopped smiling when Shepherd outlined the nature of her investigations. TTX was the murder weapon, and she described how three people had died. The chef took her through to his kitchen and invited her to watch as he prepared the harmless-looking pufferfish. His razor-sharp knife flew, expertly guided around the anatomy of the creature, removing entrails and organs. At every stage, he explained the procedure. "These parts are deadly. Just such an amount," he showed her a speck of intestine on the tip of his knife, "could kill a two-hundred-pound heavyweight boxer in an instant. So, Sergeant, you see how careful I have to be when I prepare sashimi? I confess that when I did my training as a young chef, I was terrified of eating my very own sashimi dish." His deep rumbling laugh surprised her from such a wiry figure, but everything about him delighted her.

"What do you do with these entrails after you have removed them, Chef?"

With the flat of his blade, he slid them onto a wooden cutting board and carried them across the kitchen to an incinerator. "This model is costly but also most efficient. Whatever the waste, this fish included, that we put in here is reduced in bulk by ninety-nine per cent and then converted into a sterile ash. So, you see, the poison in these organs becomes a neutral powder."

"Excuse me, Chef. I'm obliged to ask this question. Do other cooks in your restaurant prepare sashimi?"

Horrified at the suggestion, his expression told her the answer before he replied, "Oh, no, Detective, that is unthinkable. It would be quite unethical. I am the only person to touch the fugu fish."

"Nobody could misappropriate a small amount before incineration, I suppose?"

"I am a busy chef, but certain things transcend food preparation, Sergeant. I would never leave a deadly poison unattended. Apart from the fact that I can guarantee the character of each of my employees."

"Yes, of course, please do not be offended. That is all very satisfactory, and I'll be sure to dine in your restaurant one of these evenings."

"Please do, Detective Sergeant, and when you come, be sure to tell the waiter to advise Chef Morimoto." He patted his chest with pride and beamed at her. She agreed she would and took her leave of the pleasant Asian gentleman.

Later, in New Scotland Yard, she was able to relate her experience to Vance, but her tone caught his attention when he had decided that her investigation of restaurants was of no interest to him. Years of working with Shepherd had taught him that her instincts should be followed up. She said, "The two chefs are like chalk and cheese. Morimoto is charming, cooperative, and kindness itself. Tatsuo Narisawa, on the other hand, as famous as the former, is evasive, impatient, and, I'd go as far as to say, even *furtive*. It was as if he couldn't wait to get me off his premises, sir.

That chef is hiding something or covering for someone, I'll stake my career on it."

"I'll have to pay Chef Tatsuo Narisawa a visit in person, Brit."

The visit was scheduled for the next morning, but other events would take precedence over Vance's time.

# CHAPTER 11

## THAMESIDE, LONDON

The motorcyclist, hunched over her handlebars, roared across the pedestrian Millennium Bridge, breaking every rule in the Highway Code, heedless of risk to life and limb. Fortunately, the bridge is thirteen feet wide, so terrified tourists were able to hurl themselves aside as the maniac driver hurtled along the centre of the bridge. One outraged Korean tourist, showing laudable presence of mind, flung her trolley at the rider, but although it struck the motorcyclist's thigh, it did little more than produce a wobble before falling harmlessly to the pavement. Reaching the Southwark end of the bridge, the speeding motorcyclist headed straight for an eighty-two-year-old woman. The pensioner, paralysed with fear and hardly nimble, stood like a night-time rabbit transfixed by oncoming headlights on a country lane. Swerving slightly, with a whoop, Bethany thrust out a booted foot, to send the elderly lady crashing to the ground. Later, the aged victim would be treated in hospital for hairline fractures and contusions.

Thundering off the bridge, along another pedestrian route before entering the one-way system on the opposite side of the river from her intended direction, she slowed to a respectful speed as she navigated towards Southwark underground station. Once passed under the low, blue railway bridge, she drove between two steel bollards and parked her motorcycle, knowingly abandoning it, in front of a glass-fronted high-rise building. With a sigh of regret, she carefully laid her black helmet with its smoked-effect visor on the seat. "Ta-ra!" she said wistfully, looked in both directions, checked the wide pavement was empty, snatched off her blonde wig and rammed it in her rucksack. Ruffling her hair, flattened by wig and helmet, she knew that she would pass as a short-haired tough guy in her leather gear. Confident that her aspect had changed sufficiently, she turned her back on the £6000 Harley Davidson. It would end up in a police compound and be sold off for much less in due course. She didn't care. She would buy a new one if the spirit moved her.

A glance at the wall map in the station entrance hall told her that she had to leave the Jubilee line at Westminster after just one stop. There, she could take the District line to Earl's Court and change again for Fulham Broadway. She was still too high on adrenaline to settle into thoughts of what had preceded her madcap dash across the pedestrian bridge. What nerve she had shown! She couldn't imagine a better solution to her predicament than the one she had enacted. Congratulating herself, she mingled anonymously with the hurrying crowd at Westminster, wondering where they, apart from the obvious map-clutching tourists, were all hastening. Speed of movement suited Bethany then; she needed to walk off the hormone-induced buzz of excitement coursing through her veins.

As the train rattled through the tunnel to Earl's Court, she thought back on the series of events that had brought her into this hot, airless compartment along with other fellow sufferers crammed into a small space to move quickly from one part of the city to another. Give her the 883 Harley and fresh air any day!

Everything had gone so smoothly up to and including the killing. Her victim had been young, maybe an Asian student, easy pickings because hampered by pulling a wheeled suitcase with a rucksack balanced on top. The noise of the wheels on the footpath had enabled Bethany to sneak up behind the young woman, select her spot and plunge the needle into her throat. Still with luck on her side, no cars passed at that crucial moment, so she was able to drag the body behind one of the V-shaped supports before slipping back for the suitcase and rucksack. She placed these, hidden from the road, beside the body.

The train pulled up at Earl's Court station, disturbing her reminiscences. Irritated, almost deciding to stay in the carriage wherever it was bound, to finish her recollections, she changed her mind and made it onto the platform before the sliding doors closed behind her. Spotting an arrow for the southbound District Line, she strode along as far as a directions board, which showed Fulham Broadway in black letters, first among the listed destinations. She hurried on, nipping her nostrils together, all too aware of the characteristic stale smell of the underground. A sudden gust of wind, or rather, displaced air, struck her at the opening to her platform. She clicked her tongue in disapproval, having just missed the train for Fulham.

Consulting an electronic overhead timetable, she saw that the next one for her destination would arrive in seven minutes, so she sat on one of the perforated steel seats to wait and continue rerunning her memories. Now, where was she? Ah, yes, standing next to the dead girl. She looked as if she might have been from the Philippines. *Fancy coming from as far away as Southeast Asia to die in Blackfriars—what a shame,* Bethany thought dispassionately. What then? She had sprayed **9-4=5** on the previously unblemished concrete stanchion for the police to find. She smiled with satisfaction, still resenting the interfering woman of Murder Three who had prevented her from leaving her graffito: **9-3=6.** After spraying her latest numbers, she had tucked the second verse of Housman's poem beneath the girl's bra strap and finally, rather than force the tube of black paint into an orifice, given that she was hidden from view and had all the time in the world, she decided to amuse herself.

Disrespectful of the dead girl, she squeezed black paint onto her upper lip and designed a Salvador-Daliesque moustache on her face with her latex-sheathed finger. Laughing hysterically at the time but being careful not to draw attention to herself on this platform, she limited herself to a smile. She remembered how she had wanted the black paint to make an impression, so she had added a small, inverted triangle under the lower lip to represent a short goatee beard. She gave the girl's eyebrows the treatment as a finishing flourish, making them grotesquely large above the staring eyes. The overall effect, she had to admit, with a glow of satisfaction was worthy of a Hitchcock horror film. How she loved those old films!

After leaving the scene of a perfect crime, Bethany strode along Blackfriars Passage to return to her Harley Davidson, parked in a cycle bay. That was when everything went wrong. As chance would have it, as she wheeled it to the kerb, a cruising police car spotted her. She noticed the policeman's eager face and knew that she had to vanish. Racing through the gears, her trusty 883 blasted down Blackfriars Passage and away through the subway before the police driver could react safely. She was under no illusions that the policemen would have radioed to alert every patrol car in the area, so she had to use cunning.

She heard the police siren blaring, so, first, she had to get off the main road. This manoeuvre she achieved by jumping the bike over another kerb and illegally taking a pedestrian walkway parallel to the river, regardless of the dispersing joggers, cyclists and dog walkers and their insults. It brought her to the Millennium Bridge, which triggered her wild impulse of delight. The rest was history—her only regret being the sacrifice of her Harley. But she knew that driving it to Tilbury and its containers would have been tantamount to handing herself over to the police. Her madcap ride had thrown them off the scent.

Even now, they would be combing the Southwark area. She presumed that they might even have found her bike. Even so, their subsequent inquiries would lead them to a dead-end e-Bay sale, and if they discovered the American importer in question, he would only be able to furnish the false name she had provided for the transaction, paid in cash to avoid taxes. What could the police do with the fictitious name Arnold Bissett? She had deliberately driven without insurance and failed to pay road tax since possessing the bike. Good old Arnie!

Here was her train. She rolled her aching neck and forced back her elbows for relief. How she needed her massage chair! Time to go home. At Fulham Broadway Station, she found a payphone. Muttering obscenities at the flysheet publicity displaying the local prostitutes, she called 999 and asked for the police. Maybe she'd become a modern-day Jack the Ripper and rid Fulham of whores when she'd finished Lord Robert's project.

Refusing to give the operator her name, she quickly reported the body of a young woman and its exact location in Blackfriars Passage. She slammed the receiver down almost immediately, thus giving them no time to set up a trace. Bethany, recognising that the body was concealed, needed it found without delay. Such a perfect killing deserved an ideal outcome, after all.

That evening, Vance sat staring silently at his meat pie and two vegetables, his knife and fork poised for action that was not forthcoming. Helena gazed at him with wifely concern. "Do you want to talk about it, Jacob?"

"You know me, darling, I don't usually let cases get under my skin, but this, I reckon, is the worst of my career, to date."

"Because you're not making progress?"

"Not just that, because we're dealing with a severely unbalanced individual."

"A maniac?"

"Well, any serial killer could be described as such, in my opinion, but this one is showing increasingly disturbing signs of insanity."

"Can you tell me? It might help you cope better."

He smiled at his wife of twenty years and sliced into the pie crust. She made an excellent pastry and this meal, with lashings of gravy, was one of his favourites. He cut a sprout in two and savoured its bitterness before resuming the conversation.

"Our killer would seem to be a young woman, which somehow makes her actions more reprehensible to me. How could she not only kill another young woman, but also defile the body?"

Helena, looking shocked but fascinated, asked, "In what way?"

"She's fixated with colours. It's as if she's murdering by numbers—you, know, like painting by numbers—in this case, murder number four is black. She used black oil paint to design a curly Dali moustache and goatee on her victim and give her thick black eyebrows. I swear, when I saw the body, it revolted me. Poor woman! The previous killings, in sequence, were yellow, orange, white, and now, black."

"Do you think she's a deranged artist?"

"Anything's possible. Do you know, my love, she leaves poems linked to the colour? So, today's verse is titled *Now hollow fires burn out to black* by a poet called Alfred Housman.

"The Victorian writer? Wasn't he the *A Shropshire Lad* poet?"

"Apparently. Poetry's not my strong suit. Have you read him?"

"At university. Unusually for the time, he was an atheist, you know, and those poems—there were more than sixty in the anthology—are pessimistic and preoccupied with death."

"Hence his appeal to our serial killer. She left the second verse on the body today. I'll read it to you after I've done justice to your delectable cow pie!"

Talking with Helena, such an understanding listener, had restored his appetite, increasing with every bite. As he mopped up the last traces of gravy, he glanced at Helena's gratified expression and smiling, said, "Delicious as always. Thank you."

"Why don't you relax in the armchair with a whisky?"

"Great idea, I might try that new single malt I bought at the supermarket the other day. Do you know, they are expanding their range? They must have a good buyer. I wouldn't mind his job!"

She laughed. "I'll bet he wouldn't swap with yours." She went over to the drinks cabinet and took out the bottle of *Tamdhu*. "Do you know it says here the name's Gaelic for a *little dark hill*?" He grunted as she broke the seal and poured the pale amber liquid into a cut crystal glass, adding, "It also says on the label that Tamdhu is the only Speyside distillery to malt all its own barley on site."

"Knowing that won't add to the flavour," he grumbled, still thinking about his murderess. But he was quick to admit, "It's fresh and fruity with a mellow finish. I think it's worth buying again at that price."

"Good." She settled into another chair. "They have one satisfied customer, then. Now, weren't you going to read me that verse?"

"I am." He pulled out a crumpled sheet of paper from his trouser pocket and smoothed it on his lap. He read:

*"Oh never fear, man, nought's to dread,*
*Look not left nor right:*
*In all the endless road you tread*
*There's nothing but the night."*

He let the words sink in, raised an eyebrow for a reaction.

She twirled her shoulder-length brown hair around a finger, considered, and said, "There's nothing remarkable about those lines. Did you say it was the second verse? Maybe the first has more relevance to the crime. How does that go?"

He read:

*"Now hollow fires burn out to black,*
*And lights are guttering low:*
*Square your shoulders, lift your pack,*
*And leave your friends and go."*

"The only significance, in my opinion," he said, "is in the last word of the first line. She wants us to notice *black*. It's part of her mad design."

"Unless the last line is meant as a threat to the police."

"Mmm, it could be, I suppose." He rose to pour another drink. "Do you know what she did today? To escape a patrol car, she drove at full speed across the Millennium Bridge."

"Isn't that pedestrian only?"

"Exactly! It shows what kind of psychopath we're dealing with. She knocked over a poor old lady. Luckily, the hospital has found only hairline fractures, but she could easily have killed her. What it tells me is that she's a quick thinker who'll stop at nothing. She also had the gall to call us with the location of the body."

"Oh, my! I can see why this case is getting to you, Jacob. Why don't you come up to bed and relieve some of that tension?"

He grinned. "First, you ply me with alcohol, then you seduce me, is that it?"

"Who bought the whisky?" she asked archly.

The following morning, he bumped into Sergeant Shepherd outside his office. She grinned at him and said, "You look like you had a good night's sleep, boss."

"It must have been that new single malt," he said bashfully, but she knew him too well.

"I reckon that was just the aperitif before your sleep remedy, sir."

"Shut up, Brit! It's too early for your malarkey! What's that you're clutching in your hot little hand?"

She beamed at him. "I had a bit of a think, sir. Look here, she held up the paper with its streaks of yellow, orange, white and black. What do you think if we give this to Max? I've positioned the colours in relation to the districts the bodies were found. He might be able to get a hit with a piece of abstract art."

"I know it's my pet theory, but if you want my opinion, I believe that the work of art in question contains nine colours, which means that until we get the others, it'll be confoundedly difficult to get any hits from the computer."

Shepherd grimaced. "But if we did, we might be able to anticipate our killer's next move. Say, for example, it's blue. We might predict the name of the street and perhaps even set a trap."

"Don't talk nonsense. What colour does Allenbury Lane imply, for instance?"

Shepherd looked disturbingly triumphant for her inspector's liking.

"What are you holding back, Brit?"

"You know me too well, sir," she smirked. "It was Max who had the idea. Since the last two murders were in White Horse Yard and Blackfriars Passage, he got to wondering why the perpetrator had chosen Allenbury Lane and Satchwell Road."

"And?"

"Here's the thing, sir. Many streets have changed their names from Victorian times to today. Like Allenbury Lane, formerly Primrose Street and Satchwell Road, as was Orange Street."

"Well, blow me down! Our killer has done her homework! Primrose is a shade of yellow."

"Yes, sir, and it goes to prove that your theory was right from the start, plus the bloody poems she keeps leaving, each tied to the same colour."

"Okay, tell Max to try feeding the colour data for matches with the artwork. I still think we'll need more colours."

"But that means—"

"I know very well what it means, thank you, Sergeant!"

She quailed before his glare and hurried away to give Max Wright his instructions. Meanwhile, Vance's frustration was increased by the umpteenth report from forensics, leaving them without any clues on the motorcycle. That it was *her* vehicle, he had no doubt, and he smiled sadistically at the thought that the police patrol had scared her sufficiently to make her abandon a costly bike that he'd give his eye teeth to possess. Not only was the killer smart, but it appeared she was also well-off. He rang DC Mark Allen. "Any news on that number plate, Constable?"

"Yes, sir. The bike's last recorded owner is an American importer in Birmingham, who deals in Harley Davidsons in particular. He specifically remembers this one because of it being all black except for the mustard splash guards. It seems that he hooked our killer through eBay about six months ago. He's in trouble with our lads in Birmingham because he took cash without issuing a receipt. So, we have no trace of the buyer. He remembers the purchaser's name, though, sir, because it's unusual. He says the fellow is called Arnold Bissett."

"Hang on! So, you're saying the buyer was a man?"

"It seems so, sir."

"Hmm. There's nothing straightforward in this case. Have you been on to the DVLA Constable Allen?"

"Yes, sir, but the vehicle remains in the name of the American seller. When I questioned him, he said that Arnold Bissett had agreed to take care of everything and bear the complete expense of owner registration. It's fishy. Especially when you consider that I've been on to every important insurance company I could think of, and nobody has a match with the number plates, except one firm, who still have the American on their books—temporary dealer coverage, sir."

"This all points to our killer covering her tracks either by using a male accomplice or her being a man disguised as a woman. Judging by her build, though, I'd tend to favour the former."

"Yes, sir."

Vance stared at the receiver. He'd forgotten that he was still on the phone, and he was thinking aloud. More dead ends were doing nothing for his mood. They needed a breakthrough in this case. He couldn't see where it was coming from, but then he remembered Chef Tatsuo Narisawa. It was time to consider Japanese cuisine. He opened his door. "Shepherd!" he bellowed.

When his flustered sergeant emerged from behind DS Wright's computer, he called, "We're going to a restaurant, Sarge." He'd let her think they were going out for a meal. Her disappointment would wipe the smirk off her pretty face.

She didn't give him the satisfaction, the sapphire eyes locked with his. "By any chance, Japanese cuisine, boss? Chef Narisawa, is it?"

He scowled and agreed that it was. He should be pleased that his sergeant was brilliant, but he wanted to get one over on her for some infantile reason.

# CHAPTER 12

## MAYFAIR, LONDON

It took Vance longer to absorb the restaurant's elegant décor with its slender cranes amid swirling reeds than to understand the state of mind of Chef Tatsuo Narisawa. It was no mean achievement for a Cockney-bred police officer to enter so quickly into the Asiatic psyche of the chef. A testament to years of getting to grips with human deviation lay behind the Detective Inspector's rapid insights. The first of these was to recognise the accuracy of his sergeant's intuition. Before him, without doubt, stood a man with something to hide. This something, being overlaid by centuries of Japanese culture, made his task that much more complicated.

The beads of sweat on the man's brow, despite the efficient air-conditioning of the premises, spoke volumes to Vance's trained eye. Since the police officers had arrived while the restaurant was closed, the chef's eagerness to return to his kitchen with the excuse that he needed to prepare for the evening clientele cut no ice. He was as elusive and furtive as Shepherd had forewarned. So, correctly estimating the man's code of honour, Vance hit him hard where it hurt.

"Chef Narisawa, if you refuse to cooperate in a murder inquiry, we shall be forced to ask you to accompany us to New

Scotland Yard. What that will mean in terms of your business and reputation, I'll leave to your judgement. Wouldn't it be better to tell us in these pleasant surroundings, here and now, what it is that is troubling you?"

Vance, who was aware of the stereotype of the inscrutable oriental face, watched the opposite in action as a series of emotions: fear, calculation, and at last determination, crossed the lined face of the chef. Most of his wrinkles were of the positive type, smile lines around the eyes and the mouth, but today, his furrowed brow told another story. Shepherd also scrutinised the chef's countenance and, from her feminine point of view, she saw an attractive, rugged visage that would appeal to many women. Of course, as a policewoman, she was searching for other things, such as duplicity, but at the moment, found none. Instead, she felt as much as saw the sincerity emanate.

"Officer, you are quite right that I should tell you everything openly, here and now. May I start at the beginning?"

Trying to put the man at his ease as much as possible under the circumstances, Vance said, "In my experience, that is the best place for a complete understanding, Chef."

"Very well, Detective, my story begins in my hometown of Osaka, a busy port on the island of Honshu. My father was a postal worker and an honourable man, and my mother a housewife and a marvellous cook. Of course, I grew up eating fish as my staple diet and developed a love of cookery from an early age. More importantly, my father raised me with a code of honour and behaviour passed down from father to son through the generations." The chef paused, and his handsome face mirrored his inner turmoil. "My father would have died of shame to see his son interrogated by police officers investigating a murder."

"Murders, plural, Chef. Four of them to be exact." Shepherd twisted the knife, much to her superior's intense but hidden pleasure.

Tatsuo's face revealed how appalling this revelation was to

him, and so, he hurried on with his confession. "I am a man with old-fashioned values, Detective, but I am only human. I have my domestic altars and try to follow the codes of Shinto to honour the spirits of my ancestors. This belief is probably all very strange to you, officers." He looked anxiously from one to the other.

Vance weighed up what might be the best reply because he felt that the chef was on the verge of a divulgence that might represent a breakthrough in their case. Again, it was Shepherd who helped him out.

"Not at all, Chef." She smiled sweetly, trying to gain his confidence. "You know, one of the most influential books I've ever read was written by a Jesuit priest working in Japan in the last century. If I remember correctly, its title was *Zen Christianity*, and among the many teachings at the beginning was a reference to the Japanese practice of Shinto alongside Buddhism. That was what first attracted me to the wonderful culture of your homeland. One day, I hope to come to your restaurant to sample your dishes."

The barriers were down. Tatsuo Narisawa grinned from ear to ear. "If you come to my humble establishment, Madam Officer, I will treat you as my guest of honour." Then his face crumpled as he realised the gravity of his situation. "That is if you don't arrest me for complicity in murder."

Grateful for his sergeant's skilful intervention, Vance decided to take the initiative.

"I think it would help, Chef, if you could explain step by step why you think we should take such serious action. Take your time. Leave nothing out. All I can promise is that we will look benevolently on anything you tell us, as long as you are frank."

The chef leant forward and rested his forehead gently on his open fingers, and he remained silently in that position while he gathered his thoughts. As the moments ticked by, Shepherd shot an anxious glance at her superior, who almost imperceptibly shook his head to warn her to remain silent.

Suddenly, Narisawa removed his hand, raised his head, and said, "You should know, Detectives, that I am a lucky man. I have this successful restaurant with many regular and wealthy customers. From my humble beginnings in Osaka, I can now boast a luxury home in Kingston-on-Thames and a Maserati car. But my most priceless possession is my beloved wife, Hikaru. Have you heard of Hikaru Aikawa, officers?" He gazed at the puzzled faces. "No, of course not, why would you? *Haute couture.* She is the leading designer of clothes in sumptuous, printed silk. Apart from her abilities, she is the most beautiful of women. We are so very much in love. If my dear old father were still alive to see everything his sacrifices to put me through the best chef's school in Japan have brought me, he would be so proud. His lower lip trembled, and the startled policemen watched as one large teardrop spilt down his cheek.

He wiped away the tear angrily with an anguished expression. "And yet, with what I have done, Detective Inspector, I have thrown it all away."

"Tell us what that is, Chef," Brittany Shepherd said, gently encouraging him.

He gave her a weak smile, seemed to pluck up the courage and said, "About six months ago, I met Akina Aoyama, and, to my eternal shame, I fell head over heels in love with her. If you see her, you will understand why. She is a Japanese goddess, and I am such a fool! I should have known that someone so beautiful would not give herself to me unless she had some deeper purpose. I know now that Akina is a shameless high-class escort, willing to sell her services to the highest bidder." He thumped the heel of his hand against his brow. "I foolishly believed her honeyed words about my culinary prowess and failed to resist when she pressed against me and kissed me passionately." He blushed and could not meet Shepherd's eyes, preferring to look at the male detective for masculine solidarity. Vance contented him with a meaningful wise nod of the head.

"She was very clever, Detective," he now addressed Vance

exclusively, "she played me like a fish on a hook for three months. To get to the point, at the end of that period, she produced a set of compromising photographs. Frankly, I had been unable to resist her charms—I'm only flesh and blood, like any other man. Who took the photos and how they did it without my knowing is a mystery."

"Mmm. Nowadays, there's so much microtechnology available, Chef, if you'll permit me, much of the best comes from your esteemed country."

"Ah, yes, I suppose it does. Anyway, Detective, she blackmailed me. If I didn't cooperate, she threatened to send the photos to my beloved Hikaru and the tabloid press. Imagine that! It would have ruined me. The shame would have destroyed me, Detectives." At last, he met the sapphire gaze of the young woman detective. "I would most certainly have to end my life in those circumstances—the only honourable thing to do. Anyway, I asked her how much money she wanted. She sneered and said, not cash but—"

"Let me guess, Vance interrupted, fugu entrails, by any chance?"

The chef looked stricken. "Don't tell me that the four murders you are investigating were victims of TTX poisoning."

"You are very quick on the uptake, Chef. We have information that leads us to believe, I'm afraid to say, the same killer intends to strike again multiple times, and shortly."

"This is all my fault! Of course, I knew how deadly the pufferfish toxin is—all Japanese chefs do. We have a scrupulous code of preparation and disposal. But can you understand, Detective? I could not allow Akina to distribute those photographs. I asked her what she intended to do with the entrails, but she replied by threatening me again."

"So, you gave her the viscera of a fugu."

"Yes, but that's enough to kill a thousand people. I foolishly believed that Akina would use it once on some persecutor, a pimp, or similar. I told myself so many tales to salve my conscience, Detective."

Vance leant back in his chair. "This is what we are going to do, Chef. You will carry on running your restaurant as though nothing has happened. In exchange, you will provide me with Akina Aoyama's contact numbers. Also, you will surrender your passport to my safekeeping and agree not to leave Greater London on any account. How does that sound?"

In a surprising gesture, Tatsuo Narisawa reached across the table, took Vance's hand and, clinging onto it, said, "Detective, I swear to do that! Do you think you will be able to save my reputation and my marriage?"

Vance shook off the hand and looked severely at the chef. "That will not be for me to decide, Chef. What you did was a criminal act that has indirectly led to the deaths of four young people. What about their marriages, eh? Think about that." He modified his tone and said, "What I can do is draw my superior's attention to your voluntary cooperation, which will weigh in your favour. Also, you have mitigating circumstances that should help. Finally, it would be a shame to lose a talented chef who contributes to enriching our cosmopolitan society."

Narisawa stood. "With your permission, I will bring the things you asked for." Again, he surprised Vance by bowing before turning to fetch his passport. He returned with that, a pen, and a small black notebook. He ripped out a page from the back of the latter where he wrote *Akina Aoyama* followed by a telephone number. Vance pocketed the scrap of paper and the passport, saying, "This document will be restored to you, sir, when the case is officially closed."

Shepherd lingered a moment as her senior officer headed for the door. She warned, "From now on, Chef, be faithful to your Hikaru. We may yet get you out of this mess."

The chef said something rapidly in Japanese and bowed to the detective. "Honour me with your presence in my restaurant, Detective. I will keep a table for you and your chosen companion." He bowed again. "On the house, of course," he added to her retreating back.

Vance was in a buoyant mood when his sergeant got into the police car. "At last, Brittany, a breakthrough! I've never had to wait this long in a murder inquiry to turn up something worthwhile."

"It just seems that way, sir. We still have one or two cold cases on our books."

"Trust you to spoil our moment of triumph!"

"But it *is* a breakthrough, boss. Are you going to arrest this Akina?"

"Of course, I will. We'll have to break her down. She's the only person who can lead us to the killer. As I see it, this murderer has the advantage of disposing of vast sums of money. He must have spent a small fortune to get a high-class escort to work for him."

"So, do you think it's a man now, sir?"

"I honestly don't know. I guess I thought that a man might employ an escort more easily than a woman."

"Tosh! Money talks. Our perpetrator would only have to promise a tempting sum to this escort. Escort is only a posh name for a whore, sir. Do you know how many whores bed females?"

"Unlike you, I've never worked in the Vice Squad, Brit."

"Well take my word for it. Our blonde killer could easily have persuaded the Japanese tart to do anything by producing a wad of money."

"I'm sure you're right. Let's get back to headquarters and share our news with the team."

As they drove through the London traffic, Vance suddenly said, "*It would be a shame to lose a talented chef who contributes to enriching our cosmopolitan society.* I can't believe I said that about a man who feeds you *raw fish!*" He snorted, watching Shepherd's facial reaction from the corner of his eye, and smiling to himself. Lost in thought, he elaborated a plan for his next moves, and they involved the unpleasant task of meeting up with a Japanese beauty.

To that end, his first port of call was Max Wright's computer station. He scribbled Akina Aoyama on a piece of paper and handed it to the sergeant. "When you find anything, give me a bell, Max. Five minutes passed before his desk phone rang. It was Max. "I think you'd better see this, sir."

Vance hurried back and gazed at the computer screen. It was difficult for him not to gape or smile stupidly at the image. Akina was a beauty, right enough. Pale skinned, with double eyelids and a perfect oval face with charming rosebud lips and a turned-up nose, the whole surrounded by lush wavy black hair. This perfection capped a slender hourglass figure vaunting long, shapely legs.

That's why our chef called her a goddess," Vance muttered.

"Sir?"

"Nothing. What have you got on her?"

"No criminal record. I brought this image up from the pages of a society magazine, sir."

"Do you have an address for this lady?"

"Blimey, I wish I had! But no, you have to consider privacy laws nowadays. The best I can do for you is say that she lives in Chelsea, and I got that from a magazine article featuring her. As far as I can gather, she's a bit of a high society playgirl."

A lightbulb lit up for Vance. "Wouldn't the Japanese Embassy have an address for her, Max?"

"Probably, but they're unlikely to divulge it if I say she's a suspect in a murder inquiry."

"So, don't say that. Invent something that might be to her advantage

The sergeant looked shocked. "A lie, sir?"

"Come on, Sergeant, this is a homicide!"

The technician winced, frowned, then smiled. "Leave it with me, boss."

A quarter of an hour later, Max knocked on his door with a

flamboyant rap that might ordinarily have earned him a ticking off.

"This had better be good, young fellow," Vance grumbled.

The computer specialist waved a piece of paper triumphantly. "I'm not just a geek. You see, I have other accomplishments—like lying."

"Did you spin them a yarn, then?"

"Too right, I persuaded the man in the embassy that a sugar daddy had left her a briefcase stuffed with jewels in our safekeeping. I think Miss Aoyama's reputation was sufficient to convince him. Add to that New Scotland Yard's infallible record of unswerving honesty, sir."

"Sullied today by a lying geek! Well done, Max! Let's be having that address."

"I think you should go with at least five female officers," he said with a cheeky grin before handing over the address in Chelsea. "She's a cracker, all right," he said as he disappeared from the room.

Jacob Vance stared at the neat handwriting, and murmured, "Mmm, Burnaby Street, very nice! That would be somewhere between King's Road and the river if I recall rightly." He then spent some minutes wondering whether he could justify visiting the ravishing beauty alone. Dismissing the unwise thought, he opened his door and yelled, "Sergeant Shepherd, let's be having you!"

# CHAPTER 13

## FULHAM AND MAYFAIR, LONDON

Bethany grabbed the remote and turned up the music volume. She bounced up and down to the rhythm despite the pain in her back. She loved the words to this part of the song:

*"For there's a guard and there's a sad, old padre*
*On and on, we'll walk at daybreak*
*Again, I'll touch the green, green grass of home"*

and she belted it out with Tom Jones. The song ended: *'Neath the green, green grass of home.* And she sighed dramatically in the sudden silence, imagining the grave in *the shade of that old oak tree,* and wondering what horrible murder the songwriter had committed to be hanged by the neck until dead.

Her laughter, wild and high-pitched, startled even her, so she sighed again, flung herself in her massage chair and set it in motion. She found that she could think better when the roller pads eased the pain in her upper spine. Now, she dwelt on her splendid choice of location for Murder Five. The exquisite irony of it tickled her. What a pity that the old coaching inn no longer existed, but she had the consolation of its name perpetuated to this day. In Victorian times, by all accounts, whores gathered in its doorway touting for trade until Jack put a scarlet damper on their unwholesome activities. Oh yes, thought Bethany, Whitechapel Road, Jack the Ripper's old stamping ground! She would re-tread his unhallowed steps. If only she could guarantee herself a whore for Murder Five. But could she? There must be a way!

"Of course, there is! Don't be such a dullard," the suave voice of Lord Robert cut across her thoughts. With a gasp, she stared at the previously empty armchair. *Where did he come from? What's he saying?* She squeezed her eyes tightly closed and pressed her hands to her aching head. She was getting these splitting headaches more often of late. Maybe she should have a check-up, but she didn't want complications at such a critical time.

"Why all this prevarication? Are you going to give me the satisfaction of number five or not?" Lord Robert pressed.

"I told you, I can't afford to make the same mistake as with the White Horse Yard. This enclosure is a similar situation—all fenced off. You can't be too careful nowadays. You never know, there are all sorts of maniacs stalking our streets." She burst into hysterical laughter once more.

"Get a grip! Pull yourself together. You're making an exhibition of yourself," the refined aristocratic voice reproached, calming her instantly, but causing her to clutch her head again.

"What is the matter with you? Are you unwell? I sincerely hope that you are capable of fulfilling the task I have charged you with. If your choice of location is problematic, why not change it? As you so diligently discovered, there are many alternative places with the correct colour in their name."

"No! I beg you, leave me alone!" She pressed both hands to her forehead and held her breath. Peeping under a lowered brow, she sighed with relief when she saw the armchair empty. Raising her head slowly and painfully, staring past the flashing silver stars, she made sure that he had gone. "Why are you never satisfied?" she shrieked at the vacant seat. "You always seem to catch me when I'm not feeling well. I'll show you what I can do! Just leave me in peace to work things out."

Bethany sank back in her massage chair and let it do its work. Blissfully untroubled by the demanding peer of the realm, she gazed down upon a Thames barge chugging upstream. She loved the evening reflections of coloured lights in the river. As the red portside light slid past her window, she wondered who had first decided on a green light for starboard? By association of ideas with the colour green, her mind wandered back to Whitechapel, and, at last, she hit upon the solution to her knotty problem. All she needed now was to pinpoint the nearest underground station. If she remembered correctly, it was Aldgate East. She rose unsteadily, clutched her head again as if to stop it spinning and staggered to her desk. With difficulty, she extracted the street map of London and found her chosen Murder Scene Five, tracing her finger along Old Montague Street. Ah! She could hurry down this narrow road after she fulfilled her mission, turn right, and walk along Whitechapel Road—*oh, the blessed irony, or should that be the damned Ripper irony?* —and enter the underground to take the Hammersmith & City line.

Everything was falling into place, but she'd have to feel better than at present to execute her plan to perfection. *Execute*—ha! She cackled like a witch, then rolled her head to relieve the pressure. A good night's sleep should make all the difference.

The following morning, Vance and his trusted sergeant headed for Chelsea. Born in the 1970s, Jacob had to rely on film clips to relive the swinging sixties. He would have enjoyed the experience of Carnaby Street, and all, he mused.

Shepherd glanced at the sat-nav and roused him from his reverie, "It's the next turning on the left, sir."

Vance grunted by way of reply and studied the buildings, all neatly maintained, suggestive of an upmarket residential area. He prepared himself psychologically for an encounter with a high-class escort. Unsure of what to expect, he decided to display only nonchalance.

Admitted to the flat by an electronic signal in response to the video entry phone, his resolution was tested to the extreme by the vision that welcomed him into her residence. She glided across the room, and he couldn't help but think of a swan. Contributing to the image were her white satin morning robe and luxuriant hair tied up in a traditional *icho-gaeshi* to reveal a long, elegant neck. Despite his earlier decision, he had to fight the urge to gawp and grin inanely. Indeed, this was the most beautiful woman he had ever set eyes on. His professional persona won through by force of will. "Sergeant, caution Ms Aoyama, if you will."

Shepherd, who had sensed the effect of the exotic beauty on her senior officer recited the standard caution with relish. Even she, a professional hardened to every type of criminal, could scarcely take her admiring eyes off the ravishing creature. As she moved, her black hair seemed to catch the light in natural purplish reflections. She received the news of her serious position with unflappable calm, so much so that Vance was moved to say, "I'm not sure you understand the gravity of your situation Ms Aoyama. Involvement as an accomplice in four murders, and the number increasing daily, could mean a very long prison term. I suggest that you consider your position very carefully."

"Thank you, Inspector." She flashed a smile of immaculately white and even teeth. "I'm afraid that I can say nothing without the advice of my lawyer." Her English, too, was perfect, although there was a charming lilt to her accent, especially when pronouncing the letter 'r'.

Vance glanced at his sergeant, as if for confirmation, although he needed none. Sometimes, being a police officer requires acting skills.

"You are permitted one telephone call, miss. I should advise you that you are under arrest, charged with conspiracy to murder." He nodded at Shepherd, who recited the proper caution as stipulated by the law.

She called her lawyer and surrendered her passport as

requested, then changed into more suitable daytime clothing before they drove her to New Scotland Yard. Vance decided to consign her to a holding cell to give her time to reflect on the reality of her situation. Similarly, he opted to keep her lawyer waiting more than necessary, to establish a minor but practical advantage. The sombre, official nature of the building itself could be relied on to induce the right mood.

When, finally, he and Shepherd sat down in front of the accused escort and her lawyer, they adhered to the letter of correct procedure. Vance was aware that Ridgeway was watching through the one-way glass above them and was determined that he would not veer minimally from the law's straight and narrow path.

Reassured by the presence of her costly lawyer, Akina Aoyama was too relaxed for the taste of her interrogators. Tired of playing the good cop, Shepherd snapped, "Ms Aoyama, we have a sworn witness in the shape of Chef Tatsuo Narisawa, who is prepared to testify in court that you blackmailed him with compromising photographs to procure a lethal poison that you supplied to a person or persons unknown for financial gain. You realise that we can obtain a warrant to search your premises for these photographs at the drop of a hat." She turned her attention to the lawyer, a dapper gentleman dressed in the obligatory grey pin-striped three-piece suit with a sober, plain blue silk tie. "Sir, perhaps you might advise your client on the merits of cooperation with the police at this stage of our inquiries. I am sure that, as an experienced lawyer, you are fully aware of the serious circumstances in which Ms Aoyama finds herself."

The lawyer nodded and smiled tightly. He turned to Vance. "Detective Inspector," he said formally and correctly, "would you consider suspending the interview for fifteen minutes to give me time to speak privately with my client?"

"Of course." Vance addressed the microphone to announce the suspension of proceedings at nine fifty-four am precisely. Over coffee in his room, he told Shepherd, "Well done, Brit, you chose the right psychological moment and weapon to shift the balance in our favour. We'll give them the full fifteen minutes, and I think we'll get the breakthrough we've been seeking. This time, leave the good cop to me. Be as bad as you like but stick to the rules. This lawyer is at the top of his profession, and I have no doubt he's explaining right now how best to reduce his client's inevitably long sentence."

When the interrogation resumed, Shepherd, feeling every inch the bad cop, gazed with satisfaction at the escort's red-rimmed eyes and ruined mascara. The lawyer had made Ms Aoyama realise the implications of her position. Now, she was ready to tell the police what they needed to know. Vance began the recording and the questioning.

"Ms Aoyama, do you still deny your role in supplying TTX poison to a third party."

The beauty shook her head. The inspector said patiently, "I'm sorry, Ms Aoyama, this conversation is being recorded. I need you to vocalise your reply if you would be so kind."

"I do not deny it."

"Ah, can you tell me to whom you supplied the poison?"

"I do not know, Officer."

"But surely, you had contact with this person. You received money to become involved with Chef Narisawa."

She looked worried, frowned, and shuffled in her seat, but replied, "That is true, but at first, instructions came by telephone. I received an envelope in my mailbox that contained a key to a safe box in Blackfriars station. When I opened the box, another larger envelope stuffed with a generous amount of money encouraged me to continue. When the person on the phone told me to seduce the chef, I objected because I am not a sex worker, Inspector."

"But you did have sex with Tatsuo, did you not? Sergeant Shepherd's tone was cutting.

The escort looked dismayed. "Well, yes, you know, in the end, he's a good-looking man and very charming."

"And I expect you were well paid," Brittany tried hard not to sneer.

"I was, yes." Aoyama asked for her handbag, withdrew a handkerchief, and blew her nose in impossibly elegant fashion. Shepherd reminded herself to copy the gesture the next time she had a sniffle. "I received another fat envelope, you see, each time it was more money than the time before."

"Can you say whether the voice on the phone was male or female?"

"Male, Inspector, quite a deep voice. It was an intimidating voice. I was afraid to disobey." She lowered her head, looking ashamed. "Then I got the photographs," she said the word with such a pronounced accent that it was all Shepherd could do not to laugh. But the escort's face crumpled, and she began to cry. Her lawyer offered her a crisply pressed handkerchief from his suit pocket, which she clutched and pressed to her face.

"Take your time, Ms Aoyama, would you like a glass of water?" Vance asked gently.

She nodded and smiled weakly through her tears.

*What has happened to the queenly swan of earlier?* He asked himself as he rose to pour her mineral water from a glass bottle. She took the proffered drink and said, "I'm so ashamed. They are disgusting. I still don't know how he took them."

"Are you still in possession of these photographs, Ms Aoyama?"

She nodded. Vance looked meaningfully at the recorder, but she understood and addressed the microphone.

"Yes, I am. Not the printed ones. Tatsuo destroyed those—he burnt them in front of me, but the originals are still on my computer. I didn't delete them because I was afraid of *him*."

"Did you ever meet this individual?" Vance asked sharply.

"Just once, outside Euston station there's a pub in a converted gatehouse with a beer garden. It's trendy because they serve craft ales. He told me to take a plastic box with the chef's stuff and on no account to open the container. He was very threatening about that, and he ordered me to sit on the low wall outside the gatehouse. I would know him because he would swap a large yellow envelope for my plastic bag. We were to do that without drawing attention to ourselves. Modesty apart, Inspector that is very difficult for a woman of my appearance."

"Yes, I can see that," Vance said gallantly.

Shepherd grunted and glared at the escort. "Describe the man."

"Well, it was all so fast and happened by surprise. I felt someone tug at the plastic bag, and at the same time, he thrust the envelope into my hand. You know, it was one of those large yellow ones."

"The *man*, Ms Aoyama," Vance said patiently.

"Ah, he wasn't what I expected. It was all so rapid that I didn't get a good look. I think he didn't want me to see him because he was wearing a black hoodie over his head. So, I never saw his face. But—"

"Yes?"

"Well, after the phone calls, I was expecting a big man to match the deep voice. But this was a squirt." She said the word so curiously that Shepherd smiled and corrected the pronunciation.

"A squirt?"

"Yes. I mean, he wasn't tall. I'd guess about five-foot three, and there was something strange about the way he walked away, not that I could study him. He soon vanished into the crowd. It's busy there, Inspector."

"I know. That's why he chose the place. But what was peculiar about the way he walked?"

"Like he was disabled or something, kind of hunched over. I can't explain unless he was trying to remain as unnoticeable as possible."

Vance had heard enough, and he doubted they would gain any more information from the Japanese escort. So, he brought proceedings officially to an end.

Turning to the lawyer, he said, "Mr Stevenson, the Met will oppose bail. We have reason to believe Ms Aoyama's life is in danger, so she will be safer in our custody."

"But surely, Inspector, in that case a safe house can be provided. My client is not used to the spartan conditions of a police cell. I assume that you will be officially charging her with a crime, Inspector?"

"Of course, sir, probably of more than one. First, I must speak with my superiors, as this is a very delicate matter."

"I understand, but I'd press you to make Ms Aoyama as comfortable as possible. I will come here tomorrow morning at ten o'clock to verify her situation. Is that convenient?"

"I'll expect you at that time, Mr Stevenson."

A woman constable came to lead the prisoner to her cell. Alone, at last, Shepherd and Vance exchanged glances. "Not as much as you hoped, eh, boss?"

"We'll get her mobile to the tech boys, but I don't hold out much hope. This killer is far too savvy to have used anything other than a disposable phone or a public phone booth. I had hoped for a description, but the height of her contact makes me think that our famous blonde motorcyclist isn't a woman, but this geezer dressed up as one."

"A trans?"

"That's what I think, Brit. Maybe we should look at our footage from the first and second murders again. Our bobby-dazzler said something very interesting—"

"Our *what*, sir?"

"Oh blimey, Brit, come on, between colleagues, you have to admit that's one beautiful woman."

"True, sir, this poor old policewoman Plod would give a king's ransom to look like her!"

"You know what, Brittany, I wouldn't change a thing about you."

"Oh, get off! You know the first thing you'd alter would be my tongue!"

Their banter continued as far as Ridgeway's room where a dissatisfied chief awaited them. Their grins faded as Vance knocked on the door since the elusiveness of their killer foreshadowed a problematic session with him.

"I've just had the commissioner on the phone, Jake. You've got just one week to crack this case, or she's pulling you off it."

"Strange time to get her knickers in a twist, Mal, right when we've made progress."

"You and I know what a good job you're doing, Jake, but you have to admit, your so-called breakthrough got you no nearer to arresting the killer."

"Look, sir, if we've only got a week left, I'd better get downstairs and work on the leads the latest development has thrown up."

"Leads, what leads? Did I miss something when I listened in?"

"Call it instinct, sir. If it pays off, you'll be the first to know. Now, we should get on."

Ridgeway held up a hand to halt Vance in his tracks.

"I hope you know I'm rooting for you, old boy. I told Her Ladyship there's no better detective available to solve this one."

"Thank you, sir."

Malcolm Ridgeway smiled at Brittany Shepherd. "Oh, and Sergeant, excellent interrogation technique downstairs."

Her face pink with pleasure, Shepherd thanked him.

Outside the room, Vance turned to his colleague. "He's not a bad sort. He was a fine detective back in the day. I was his sergeant once, you know. But it's always the same, as soon as they get behind a desk, they feel the pressure from above and forget that we're doing our damnedest to bring this maniac to justice."

"What did you mean about the leads, sir? Did I miss something, too?"

Jacob smiled. It was his *touché* moment. "Probably because you were too busy picking up on my appreciation of our splendid escort. Among my words, I did say maybe we should look at our footage from the first and second murders again."

"Oh yeah, so you did! Come on then, sir, let's do that."

Max Wright had the footage available in seconds. "Freeze it there a second, Max!" Vance peered at the colour-enhanced image and weighed up the motorcycle's size and the rider's height. He stood up straight after craning over the screen. "Let's assume the handlebars of the Harley are here from the ground. Look where they arrive against our suspect." He held a hand out flat.

Shepherd understood at once. "Good point, sir, about here on our killer." She chopped at the solar plexus area with the edge of her hand.

"So, that would make the murderer no taller than the five-foot three our Japanese lady described."

"Except she's no *lady*, sir."

Vance ignored the remark and added, "Now, take away the wig. Is there anything that proves it's a woman?"

"Her boobs, sir?"

"Anyone can stuff a bra with old socks, Brit."

"True, what little we can see of the face is pretty androgynous, don't you think?"

The DI considered for a moment. "To be honest, the street lighting doesn't help much. Move it along, Max, would you?" He exhaled air through clenched teeth. "Again, see how much shorter the killer is than the victim."

Nothing captured his interest until after the murderer returned to the motorcycle. "That's interesting," he said.

"What, sir?"

"Look how she—or *he*, bloody hell! —is hunched over the handlebars whilst pushing it along the lane."

"What of it?"

"Didn't our witness say that at Euston she spotted that *he was disabled or something, kind of hunched over?* She mentioned a sensation that she couldn't really explain."

Shepherd remembered. "She did, but look here, sir, a Harley Davidson isn't exactly a baby buggy. Those beasts weigh. I dare say I'd be hunched over, pushing one along, and I don't see any signs of disability there."

"And that's a worthwhile point, Sergeant. Given, as you say, that our perpetrator isn't struggling noticeably to push the bike, we could well be dealing with a man."

"A woman could push a bike in neutral, equally well, sir."

"You're right! Maybe I'm clutching at straws, but I still think we might be looking for a—what did the luscious Akina call him? —a squirt?"

"Yeah, *luscious* now, is it? What next, sir?"

Vance had to think. Whenever a case troubled him, he always fell back on a tried and tested method. "Loads of coffee, Brit, and reread every file on the case, in the event that we might have overlooked a small but important detail."

"He means we're bloody stuck," Shepherd whispered to DS Wright, eliciting a sympathetic grin."

"You probably need more colour in your search for the truth," he replied prophetically.

# CHAPTER 14

## NEW SCOTLAND YARD AND WHITECHAPEL, LONDON

At ten o'clock the following morning, Vance informed satisfied lawyer Stevenson that earlier, Akina Aoyama had been transferred to a police safe house in Barking. The detective gave him the address and explained that the new phone number to contact his client was a further precaution designed to protect her. He promised him that he would be granted access at any time of day.

Soon after the lawyer had left the premises, Vance received a call from the commissioner. Expecting her to chivvy him for lack of progress, he was surprised to discover that she wanted to do the opposite.

"Ah, good morning, Detective Inspector. DCI Ridgeway informs me that you are making gratifying headway on the case. Splendid! Do you think you are close to effecting an arrest?"

*The duplicitous son of a bitch! It's **he**, not the commissioner who's piling on the pressure!*

"Well, ma'am, I've already arrested the procurer of the poison, and we're hard on the heels of the murderer, although I'm afraid we may not be able to prevent another killing in time."

"I'm convinced that you are doing all that's humanly possible, Jake, but that's not why I asked to speak with you."

"No? How can I help, ma'am?"

She looked apologetic, and the sucking in of her lower lip told him that she was troubled.

"You see, I've had a member of the House of Lords on the phone this morning. He was on his high horse and put on quite a show. It was Lord Robert Chisholm, and he was hot under the collar regarding inquiries made by one of your lads. You really must choose carefully, Jake, when it comes to approaches that need discretion. It seems that Lord Robert felt insulted by *outrageous questioning* on his attitude to paedophilia. I had a job to reassure him that nobody doubted his moral integrity. Do you think it is quite necessary to pursue this line of inquiry?"

"I think we are at a stage where we can call off the hounds in the Lords. If one of them is involved, as we suspect, it will come out on the arrest of the murderer. If we accuse a peer of the realm of being the instigator, justice will have to take its course."

"Indeed, it will!" Aalia Phadkar smiled at Vance, relishing the kudos the Metropolitan Police would receive if it came to showing that nobody was above the law. "Well, then, Detective, I think that is everything. I'll rely on you to remove the constables from the Lords as soon as possible."

"Consider it done, ma'am."

"Excellent. Keep up the good work, Jake. Oh, just one last thing, how is Shepherd shaping up on this case?"

"Brittany? Indispensable, as ever. Her interrogation technique gained us our first breakthrough—just another of Shepherd's splendid intuitions, ma'am."

"That's what I thought. I've been considering promoting her to Inspector for some time. I think it would be nice if you broke the news to her. But let's hold fire till this case is solved. You wouldn't want to be without her support at this time."

"I won't pretend that I'm not displeased to lose my best

sergeant, ma'am, but I'm delighted for Brittany. If anyone deserves a promotion, she's that person."

"Good. Let's proceed like this: the day you arrest this psychopath will be the day you break the news to Shepherd, alright?"

"Absolutely, ma'am! We'll get the pervert, no worries."

"Good man! I think that's everything."

He left the commissioner's office in a much better mood than when he entered, which said a lot about his new-found respect for Aalia Phadkar, MBE.

At much the same time as Vance exited the commissioner's office, the occupant of a splendid Riverside apartment took a break from studying the London A-to-Z street atlas. Vance, of whose existence the avid researcher was unaware, would have been dismayed to know that his quarry had identified the location of Murder Eight, which would stretch his *canvas* as far as West Drayton. *Not bad,* the figure hunched over the atlas told himself, *number eight already set up, and I haven't done in five yet. But don't worry. That'll be this evening.* He laughed hysterically and began speaking aloud to his female persona as if she were standing in front of him. "Bethany, you'll be taking the evening off. This one's not for you, my sweet. You wouldn't want to sully your luscious lips with a filthy prossie, would you? Don't fret, my little angel of death, I promise you the blue one—every girl loves a sailor, doesn't she? What do you mean? No, the blue'll be Number Six. Have you lost count, my sweet?" He began to chortle uncontrollably despite it making the pain at the base of his neck worse.

That was the factor that decided him to make a cup of vanilla tea, his favourite infusion. Once the kettle had boiled, and the tea brewed, he would settle into his massage chair to ease the aching and tension. When he was thoroughly relaxed, he would run over the plan for Murder Five. "Henceforth M5, Bethany," he told his other self and cackled. "Now there's an idea! What about a series of motorway killings? But no, not even my genius can stretch as far as M62, eh, Bethany?" His maniacal laughter arrived in the kitchen where he settled down to the simple task of making tea.

Entrenched in his massage chair, he ran over M5 in his mind. First, he'd take the tube from Fulham Broadway. By a sublime twist of irony, he could stay on the *green* line, the District line as far as Aldgate East. He had thought he would need to take the Hammersmith & City line, but why bother changing when he could keep it simple?

"Yes, I know, Bethany, you'd love to take the *pink* line! Never mind, sweetie, we might be able to arrange that for another time. This operation will be a swift in and out job. No more trouble with wild bike riding. Fun, wasn't it?" His uncontainable laughter caused him to slop his vanilla tea into his lap and to launch a stream of vulgar expletives. "Sorry about that, my dear girl, but I've just scalded my unmentionables. What do you mean, you'll kiss them better? We'll have none of that, thank you! Ours is an establishment with high standards, saucy little minx! You know I didn't bring you up to be like that. Go to your room and leave me to think things through."

Having dealt with Bethany, he sipped his vanilla tea and watched the river traffic sail by. There was one of those tourist vessels. *I'll bet it's crammed with Korean and Japanese travellers. They love London. But there won't be one as lovely as the Asiatic escort I found to get my poison. She was gorgeous. Oh yes, that was money well spent.*

He worried for a while about the escort. As far as he could judge, she was the only weak link in his indestructible chain.

*No, she didn't see my face at Euston, she was too busy gloating over her money the mercenary hussy! No need to get rid of her then. Just as well, it would be a shame to snuff out someone so gorgeous.*

He tut-tutted, annoyed with his straying mind. Where was he up to? Ah, yes. Aldgate East. Then he'd walk along the

Whitechapel Road, turn left and at the end, left again until he came to the pharmacy. He would have to be outside it for an eleven pm appointment. But there was a problem. He still hadn't set up the rendezvous. *I'll rustle up a brunch of bacon and beans, then set off on a trial run as far as Aldgate, find my target, and ring her. Time to eat!*

At two o'clock, he walked along Whitechapel Road, feeling somewhat disappointed. It was not as seedy as it used to be in the Victorian era. His spirits rose when he saw an old-fashioned telephone booth. When he opened the heavy door, he wrinkled his nose at the foul stench of urine assailing him. Often people were disgusting, he thought. But he would be able to resist staying inside the fetid atmosphere long enough to choose his postcard. Provocative photographs of breasts, thighs and behinds taped up above the phone flaunted prostitutes' wares. He was spoilt for choice among Luscious Lucy, Randy Mandy, Simone-the French Maid, and Baby Doll Belinda. He pulled Randy Mandy off the kiosk wall and forced his way, almost choking, out of the squalid enclosed space.

He hadn't rung Mandy yet. His call needed to come from a public phone. He kicked himself for not taking another couple of postcards in case Mandy was unavailable, but he couldn't face going back into that cloying smell. Walking on, looking for his left turning, he found it and crossed the road at a pedestrian crossing. The long narrow road took him five minutes to reach the end; he timed it for his evening post-M5 retreat. Irritated by the absence of a public phone on that street, he turned into Old Montague Street, where he was more fortunate. A wall-mounted phone, covered by a semi-circular Perspex hood, offered him the chance to make his call in the fresh air. Maybe open-air rather than fresh air was a more accurate description because traffic fumes hung unseen on Old Montague Street. He hoped there would be fewer vehicles passing in the late evening.

He dug in his pocket and pulled out a handful of silver coins he had saved for making calls. Punching in the number on the sexy postcard, he heard the ring tone and pressed three coins into the slot. "Hello, Mandy? Oh, just a punter. I saw your card in a phone box. Yeah, straight sex. I'm no Adonis, a bit on the short side, but I can satisfy a girl. Do you know the pharmacy on Old Montague Street? Near the Health Centre—that's the one. Meet me by the black gates of Green Dragon Yard—" even pronouncing the name gave him a frisson of excitement—at eleven o'clock; my name's Arnie. All right, sweetie. See you there." He slammed the receiver down. It was as easy as he'd imagined, as simple as buying a bag of crisps. Good old Arnie! One thing was for sure, he wouldn't risk a dose of the clap. She had it coming to her, filthy obliging whore.

He strolled farther along the street, arriving at the black railings that sealed the entrance to Green Dragon Yard. The name was fixed to the wall on high in a white plate with black lettering. Lovely! Green was the colour of the day! Pressing against the gate, he tried to judge how much of it could be seen from a passing car—too much! He didn't want the body, sprawled on the pavement, caught in sweeping headlights. He could do without some nosy driver catching him red-handed. His jaundiced eye returned to the iron bars, and he had a sudden inspiration. He knew how to get around the problem. Brilliant! These damned enclosed complexes, burglar-proof, did they think? *If I were a burglar, I'd see that I had a skeleton key to open that lock. I'll sort the problem at eleven o'clock—you can't keep a good Arnie down!*

Now, he would simulate his post-M5 retreat. He checked his watch and launched into a vigorous stride, turning down the narrow street on the right, reaching it in two minutes. Five minutes later, he was on the Whitechapel Road and hurrying towards Aldgate East. Eleven minutes in all it had taken him. Sitting on a bench near the station to regain his breath, he calculated for the evening ahead. Even in the worst-case scenario, at least five minutes would pass before anyone realised the whore was dead and, by then, he'd be almost as far as this main road.

With better luck, no pedestrian would chance upon the prostitute for ages. The police might not be alerted until he was safely home. What an ingenious idea he'd dreamt up, but then, he was a genius!

He glanced at his watch again, just eight hours and thirty-five minutes to Murder Five. He would put them to good use relaxing. Oh, just one thing to do, a visit to a greengrocer's or the vegetable department of a supermarket—also, he knew what time to set off this evening to be on time for his appointment with Randy Mandy.

On his way home, he entered a supermarket known to him, intending to buy *green* peppers. With that in mind, he wandered the store over to the colourful display of fruit and vegetables. His eye was caught by the green, red, and yellow bell peppers. They were no use to him because they were too big. Then, he saw the round green chilli peppers, and he had already slipped on the obligatory plastic glove and opened a bag to put them in when his eye was caught by the unusually shaped lobed peppers next to them. Also, suitably green, he read the name of this variety, provenance Bolivia and had to repress hysterical laughter. To do so, he thrust his fist into his mouth and bit on his knuckles. It would never do to attract attention to himself in a busy supermarket. Even so, he had to wipe away tears of mirth. This little prank would give the police *food for thought.* He sniggered aloud at his pun and selected five of the small, green peppers.

*(Old Montague Street, eight hours later)*

Good old Arnie watched the black gateway from a little farther down the road. He had been there seven minutes when the prostitute arrived. Whilst he waited, he titillated his imagination by reconstructing the façade of the Green Dragon Inn in Victorian times. He populated it with whores and imagined a courteous Jack the Ripper approaching one of the unsuspecting girls dressed in a long skirt, her breasts bulging over a tight bodice.

Mandy didn't disappoint him in that respect. Also, she was

punctual, he'd give her that. There was no mistaking her profession from her red stiletto-heeled shoes, black fishnet stockings, leather microskirt of the same colour and a red halter top hugging her braless breasts. This vision was topped by bouffant peroxided hair.

"Hi, I'm Arnie," he greeted her. "Mandy?"

"Yeah. Blimey, you were telling the truth. You are a shortarse, ain't you?" The heavy red lipstick over her mouth broke into a wide grin.

The killer had planned for this greeting. "Just right to snuggle into those tits." He smiled, stepping forward to bury his head into her ample bosom. It was done so naturally that Mandy didn't see the latex-gloved hand shoot up to her throat to pierce it with a steel needle. Instant death pumped into her bloodstream, and within a moment, her body went limp against his. The syringe returned to his pocket. He rapidly unbuckled the extra-sturdy belt he had strapped around his waist. Now, he passed it behind Mandy's body and the railings, bringing it round to buckle it tight under her breasts. Stepping back a few inches, holding his breath, he watched her head loll onto her chest, and her body sag against the thick leather belt but remain in place—a semblance of standing, as he had hoped. Now she just looked like a whore who was the worse for gin.

No time to lose, he thrust the usual prepared note into her ample cleavage. She had brought a large white handbag with her. Into this, he transferred all but one of the curiously shaped, green peppers from his pocket before clipping it shut. The prostitute's jaw had sagged, leaving her mouth open, into it he popped the remaining pepper. In his opinion, it gave a splendid wholesome touch of *green* to that gaping red slash of a filthy mouth. He glanced along the street. There were no pedestrians, perhaps because nowadays there was no pub in the vicinity, which helped his cause. A car flashed past, and he was sure that he just looked like a punter with a drunken whore. Still, he didn't have time to waste, for his black spray was on standby. He sprayed: **9-5=4** on the pharmacy shutter. Sniggering, he glanced back at the corpse and knew that even the police would be bright enough to know that *he* had planted the green peppers in her handbag, now that he'd had the inspiration to pop one into her mouth. Checking his watch, he set off at the pace he had adopted in the afternoon. As he hurried along, each time a car drove past, he half-turned to make sure that none of them slowed down as they approached the dead whore.

As soon as he turned the corner into the long, narrow street, it didn't matter anymore. *I've done it, Bethany baby! I'll be back home in no time. Straight in and out, just as I told you.*

The river slid somnolently past his window as he gazed down onto the coloured lights. Their sparkling reflections hurt his eyes because he was experiencing another of his splitting headaches. He knew it! Wasn't it just to be expected? Precisely what he didn't want—that suave voice criticizing him again.

"My dear boy, you have let your very respectable standards slip after such high-class victims until today. Whatever possessed you to lure a prostitute to her death? That's hardly going to make the headlines, is it?" The voice dripped sarcasm, and he couldn't bear it. He pressed his hands over his ears, but he could still hear him. "And in that respect, dear boy, you are a profound disappointment to me. Five deaths, all with the same *modus operandi,* and no mention in the gutter press of a serial killer loose on the streets of London. I think you must make an effort to give these so-called journalists something to write about, don't you? Why don't you kill one of them, dear boy? Ha-ha! Yes, why not? That would make them sit up and pay attention, wouldn't it?"

"Leave me alone!" he shrieked. "Can't you see that I'm ill? I need my rest. Go away, Lord Robert. I promise to think about what you said. I promise I will." He pressed the heels of his hands into his eye sockets. When he took them away after a few moments, the armchair was empty. He saw flashing silver zigzags. "Have you gone?" He hardly dared hope. He would have to take two or three paracetamols. Lately, he needed them more and more to take the terrible headaches away. Why did Lord Robert torment him every time he had a pounding head? And how did he come and go so easily in his apartment—it was a mystery.

# CHAPTER 15
## NEW SCOTLAND YARD, LONDON

The Cornish accent of Francis Tremethyk came vigorously into Vance's ear, "So, I thought you'd be interested in this detail. Your killer has moved on from mutilating her corpses with sharpened paintbrushes to a more decorative approach. What do I mean? Well, this time, she's placed a green pepper into her victim's mouth. Yes, a green pepper, but wait for it! It's a Bolivian or Peruvian variety known as the *Mad Hatter* pepper, owing to its shape." Now, Dr Tremethyk's accent strengthened. "Do you think our witty assassin is toying with the police, Jacob, me-dear?

"I've about had enough of this one, Doc. I'll have a job to keep my hands off his throat when we arrest him. Hang on. I'll come straight down to have a look at this latest fatality. I'm on my way."

Face to face with the medical examiner, Vance found himself interrogated, not the questioner.

"I couldn't help but notice, me-dear, that you referred to the murderer with a masculine pronoun. Have you changed your mind? I thought you were looking for a woman."

"I'll confess, Doc, I'm torn between the sexes. One day I think it's a man, the next, I'm back to thinking the killer's a woman."

"In my opinion, for what it's worth, these little extra touches have something devious and thoroughly feminine about them." He looked guilty. "Good job your sergeant didn't hear me say that!" He chuckled.

"And, of course, there's the chosen method of killing, generally associated with the fair sex," Vance put in.

"Talking about which, there's nothing so fair about Mandy on the slab over there, poor cow." The examiner jerked his head in the direction of the corpse. "A prostitute from the Whitechapel area. She had the usual postcards in her handbag—the titillating sort you can find stuck inside phone booths. She plied her trade as Randy Mandy, from her documents, née Amanda Bridges, forty-one years old. The characteristic findings in these cases: evidence of multiple abortions, previous STDs, and inner elbow scarring from past drug abuse. An unfortunate case, our Amanda, me-dear. But she didn't deserve to end up here like this, though, eh, boy?"

"No, Doc, she didn't. We'll get the perpetrator soon. I'm sure of that. But what can you tell me about the cause of death?"

"TTX, just like the others. This time, I'd say that your killer was in an embrace with Mandy. The angle of needle penetration suggests directly upwards at close quarters."

"So, it is a man, then!"

"Good God, me-dear, you are an old-fashioned copper! You can't rule out two women in a passionate clinch, now can you? And what's more, the killer was shorter than her victim, and I still say it would have to be a particularly short male."

Vance looked crestfallen. "You're right, Doc. This case is really getting to me, and I no longer know whether I'm coming or going."

"Maybe you should show this to your psychologist lady." He dropped the Mad Hatter pepper into Vance's hand. The strangely shaped fruit, with its elongated lobes, indeed, looked like a miniature hat. "The message is green rather than the vegetable itself, as we know from the note."

"*Fruit*, Doc, the pepper is botanically a fruit, not a vegetable."

"I know that! I just didn't want to surprise an old-fashioned copper. *Touché,* me-dear!"

They laughed to break the tension of their traumatic surroundings, at least, Jacob chortled for that reason. Putting on his serious face, Vance returned to business. "A note, you say? Another poem?"

"Not this time, our psychopath lassie is enjoying herself. She's lightened up. It's a song this time. You're old enough to remember Tom Jones's *Green, Green Grass of Home* I take it?"

"Even if I weren't, it's a standard. Surely, everyone knows it. The subject of the song is a murderer on Death Row. She didn't want us to miss the reference to green. The murder was at the Green Dragon Yard, too. This maniac is playing with us. I'll bet Her Ladyship, the commissioner, wishes she'd never insulted the intelligence of the criminal classes. Her ill-judged remark has cost five lives—and counting—"

*"Nils desperandum, me-dear, illegitimi non carborundum"*

Vance smiled grimly. "That's just it, Doc, this bastard *is* grinding me down!"

"Congratulations on your knowledge of mock Latin and fruit, Detective Inspector."

"Bollocks, Doc! See you later." He left the mortuary in the despairing frame of mind Tremethyk had warned against, little knowing that upstairs his mood would improve.

Sergeant Max Wright, as cheerful as usual, was the source of the improvement. Spotting the inspector passing his workstation, he called, "Sir, I might have something for you!"

"Might? Max—*mights* aren't good enough!"

"I've developed an original seeker program—all my own work. Now that we have five colours, I was able to do it. I've limited the parameters to modern paintings. Old Masters, that's too wide a field, and somehow, although we can't rule out traditional art, I feel that our killer would use something more graphic—"

"Is there a point to this, Max? I'm a busy man."

"Yes, sir, there is. I'm getting to it. But first, I need to explain the limitations. We have only five of the nine colours in the artwork. Also, we don't know the range of the future killings, so, our canvas might expand at any time, let's say if she strikes well south of the Thames, for arguments sake," Vance nodded impatiently, "but one parameter would stay constant—that is, the distribution of the five known victims. They will remain in the same relationship, with their respective colours, whatever the size of the canvas. Sorry, sir, I'm getting there. You see, I've had a hit! Just one out of thousands, so the likelihood of it being our murderer's choice is extremely high. I've printed you off a copy." He handed a colourful A4 sheet to the detective.

"Blue, sky blue, and red," Vance muttered to himself, naming the three colours the killer hadn't employed so far. "It's charming. What a shame we have to associate it with murder. Who's the artist? Does it have a title?

"The artist was French, a man called Charles Lapique." He consulted a notepad. "Born 1898 and died 1988. He painted this work in 1962."

"Did he? Title? It might be important."

The sergeant flipped a page. "Um, yeah, here it is. A French title: *Jean sans Peur*."

"John the Fearless," Vance translated. "It kind of rings a bell. Some historic figure?"

"I checked him out, Inspector. He was the Duke of Burgundy. Let's see." He referred back to his scribbled notes. "Not that I can see a direct connection myself. He lived in the early fifteenth century and ruled France on behalf of the mad king, Charles VI. He was famous because he murdered the king's brother, the Duke of Orléans." Max Wright looked sheepish.

"What is it, Max?"

"Nothing, sir, just a wild idea of mine. See, that murder started a civil war, and this Jean justified his action by pointing to the dissolute lifestyle of the victim. He said he got his just desserts—and I quote— for *taking his pleasure with whores, harlots, incest, and adultery with a knight's wife*. Well, I thought, with our latest stiff being a prostitute but, no, the first four victims don't fit, do they?"

"At the moment, I don't feel as if I can dismiss anything, Max. I can't remember a case as intractable as this. But well done! Listen here, when I look at this, the blue strikes my eye most. Assuming that we're working on the same scale as the previous murders for our framework, which part of London would this area be?" He pointed to the blue area, one of four, to the right of the picture.

"Funny you should choose that one, Inspector. It's the one that fits best with her other movements, besides, I should add that the area is known as *the Blue* in local parlance. It's the SE1 district, sir, traversed by Blue Anchor Lane. There was once a public house there called the Blue Anchor."

"Knowing where she plans to strike next would give us an advantage," Vance paused and frowned, but we don't, do we? She could choose among the several red or sky-blue areas next, and I can't enter her crazy head. Or she might opt for one of the other three blue zones, Max."

"That's right, unfortunately, but maybe we could spare a plain-clothed officer to patrol Blue Anchor Lane for a few days."

"What about the title, *Jean sans Peur?* Do you think it is a random choice? I don't."

"Is it a declaration that our killer is fearless? Better still, might she be called Jean? As in the English pronunciation. A murderess who's boasting that she's *sans souci*."

"Do you speak French, Max?"

"Schoolboy level, sir. But there was a lager, *Sans Souci*, a few years ago, and I checked out the meaning."

"Bold or carefree, isn't it? But knowing our killer's first name isn't going to be much help at the moment. I think I should have a word with the commissioner, maybe we can bring this series of murders to an end now that we know the artwork."

With this in mind, he phoned Aalia Phadkar from his office. As ever, the commissioner was receptive and invited him upstairs at once.

She welcomed him into her office with a dazzling smile.

"Progress, Detective Inspector?" she greeted him.

"Yes, ma'am, we have solid confirmation of my artwork theory." He went on to explain.

She looked impressed. "Have you discussed this with Malcolm Ridgeway?"

"No, I haven't. I thought, under the circumstances, it's up to you."

The lovely face clouded into a wrathful expression. "In what way, Jacob?"

There it was, the formal name. She was angry with him, otherwise, she would have called him Jake. In any case, he didn't mean to ask her to issue an apology, so he'd better clear the matter up."

"I'm not suggesting an apology, ma'am, no way. But referring back to that damned letter, our assassin wrote." He unbuttoned his breast pocket, took a slim black notebook out, opened it and cited: *the dire consequences will assume the form of a series of executions—eight, to be precise, which will only cease if the Metropolitan Police has the wit and cultural preparation to explain the theme underlying the killings in the minutest detail.* I thought maybe we could issue a statement to the press explaining each poem and the Lapique painting underlying them. Perhaps, in that way, the killer will keep her word and stop at the fifth execution, as she calls her murders.

There is something positively intimidating about a beautiful face that contorts with rage, and the commissioner's was no exception. A less stalwart police officer would have trembled, but with sinking heart, Vance held her ferocious stare.

"Don't provoke me, Detective Inspector," she hissed. "You can't expect me to take the word of a serial killer. When a psychopath gets a taste for murder, nothing will stop them except capture. Concentrate your efforts on that and that alone. Good day to you, Jacob!"

"That went well," he muttered to himself in the seclusion of the lift. Gloomily, he realised that no statement would be forthcoming. "We'd better prepare ourselves for another death," he told his reflection in the mirror, running his hand through his hair to adjust a wayward lock or two. Was that a grey hair? He took it between finger and thumb and pulled it from his scalp. Exiting the lift, he bumped into Shepherd, who caught him examining it.

"Evidence in our case, sir?" she asked sincerely.

"Yep, evidence that it's turning my hair grey, Sergeant." He dropped the offending hair to the floor. "Have you got a minute? There are developments."

She listened intently over a coffee as he brought her up to date. When she agreed with the commissioner about Vance's request for a statement, he snorted and dismissed it as female solidarity.

"I thought it was worth at least trying to save four lives, even without a guarantee of the assassin stopping."

"But, don't you see, it would be admitting to the world and his dog that there's a serial killer on our streets and that we are no nearer to capturing her? You'd be creating panic for no gain, and the commissioner saw that straightaway."

"You're probably both right, but dammit, Brittany, this case is making me doubt my abilities as a detective."

"Don't be daft, boss! You're the best we have!"

"Thanks for your loyalty, Sarge, but I doubt that very much as things stand."

"Do you know what I think?"

"No, but I'd like to."

"I think you should call our resident psychologist to get her opinion. This psychopath is exposing more and more traits for our consideration. And on that score, there can't be all that many supermarkets or greengrocers that sell Mad Hatter peppers, and

I'm going to pinpoint those that do. I'm pretty handy in the kitchen and didn't even know of the existence of that variety of pepper."

"Me neither. Good idea, we might discover our killer's area. We could do house to house calls and find the blonde with a Harley Davidson if we knew that. You see, we're stymied, we can't get the press to make appeals to the public whilst the commissioner keeps the case under wraps. It's like working with my hands tied," he said, and his sergeant couldn't fail to detect the desperation in his voice.

"Right, I'm off," she said. "I'll limit my search to that part of London where our murders all intersect." She showed him a zigzag design scribbled on paper and a ring incorporating all five termini. Our killer is based inside this circle, on either side of the river. Do you want to place a quid or two on it?"

Vance grinned. Thank goodness his sergeant was still on the ball. She was as confident and cheerful as he was unsure and depressed. He wouldn't show her his mood, though. "Good thinking, Brit. We're closing in on the maniac, and we'll arrest her within a matter of days." He hoped rather than believed it, but his tone was sanguine for her benefit.

At that precise moment, another confident individual was conducting a recce on Blue Anchor Lane. He wasn't at all pleased with his findings. Most of the long street was nondescript and offered no real opportunity to him until he reached the far end, where the railway passed over a steel bridge, creating a long tunnel on St James' Road. Just before the junction, still on Blue Anchor Lane, viaduct arches contained the remnants of the disused Spa Road station, the first of the two stations of that name. The killer had researched the station well; it was the original terminus of London's first railway—the London & Greenwich Railway opened in 1836. Thanks to his illustrious predecessor, Jack the Ripper, his hero, anything redolent of Victorian times tended to inspire and excite him.

The viaduct arches were closed off by ramshackle feeble-looking doors, painted blue down to about three feet from the ground, where inexplicably they became white. The various decrepit doors looked easy to push open, and they were covered in such warning signs as Safety equipment must be worn on this site; Keep out; or, Construction sites are dangerous to children. He chuckled to himself. "And not only to children," he murmured. Then he shook the interlinking steel barriers erected for perimeter security. *Damn! I have to get past this one;* he chose the last one, the nearest to the underpass, placed next to the last viaduct arch. He studied the tamperproof interlocking steel connection and came to a rapid decision. He needed a hardware shop. *Hardware,* pah! Modern jargon! What was wrong with the good old-fashioned Victorian name? *Ironmongers.*

He knew what he wanted, but also knew that he would waste a great deal of time idly wandering this area, searching in vain. In his previous incarnation, prior to dear Aunty Amy's legacy, he had done DIY work on his flat. He thought back with horror to the hovel he used to live in before Lady Luck embraced him by opening Aunty Amy's door to the Grim Reaper. A large tool store on the Old Kent Road came to mind. They would have what he needed. They had just about everything. He looked around, getting his bearings, and calculated that he could reach the store on foot. A brisk walk of twenty minutes would take him there. Far better to rely on his legs than waste time working out where to find a taxi rank or taking public transport.

He congratulated himself on his memory because when he had walked the length of St James' Road, it brought him straight to the junction with the Old Kent Road. Now, he still had to walk to the store. The road was a major artery and very long, but he remembered that the tool store was near the Post Office, so he turned right and plodded on.

The store assistant looked askance at him when he asked for a heavy-duty bolt cutter. He could see why when he laid a twenty-four-inch Tolsen cutter on the counter.

"It's for the gaffer. He's got arms like a gorilla," he said, which seemed to satisfy the spotty oik. Happily paying almost £20, he strolled out of the shop carrying the tool wrapped in newspaper and bound with brown packing tape. He hadn't walked too far before he realised that the weight of his purchase and his earlier stiff march had tired him too much. He had watched several buses pass him when he strode down St James' Road, so he could wait for one to take him as far as Blue Anchor Lane. Every six minutes, the timetable said. He smiled. Most convenient! He had his Oyster Card to cover the fare, not that money was a problem like in the bad old days. Even with the slow-paced traffic and several stops before alighting, he was back in Blue Anchor Lane within a quarter of an hour.

Trying to keep inconspicuous, he unwrapped the bolt cutter right next to the underpass. Cringing against the wall, he sidled up to the steel barricade, used his jacket to cover as much of the bright, yellow-handled tool as possible, clamped the tungsten-edged cutting blades on the half-inch steel bar and forced the long arms of the cutter together. He had considered himself too weak to manage. The bus ride had been one long worry of what-ifs. But the newness of the device and what strength he possessed combined to succeed. It was easier to cut the bottom bar because he could exert more force on the inverted tool. In moments, the barricade was detached from its neighbour.

The murderer looked around furtively, considered that he hadn't been observed, tried to cover some of the cutter with his jacket and, forcing the barricade backwards, slipped between the two, replacing it, so nothing appeared unusual. His impression of the wooden door was correct; it was rickety; he forced his way inside. Sufficient light glimmered in through the open crack of the ramshackle door. This place had not been visited for years, so it was ideal for his purpose. It would be easy to conceal a body in here, on what had once been a busy railway platform, now no more than an access point for maintenance work on the overhead viaduct that, he knew, carried multiple lines across Bermondsey. He could distinguish piles of scaffolding bars complete with heaps of clamps, planks, and discarded beer bottles in the gloom. He remembered to wipe the cutter handles clean of fingerprints before hiding the tool amid the metal bars.

"Sorry, sweetie," he murmured to Bethany. "You'd better wear sensible shoes if you're coming in here tomorrow evening. What? Yeah, your punk boots will be perfect and dressed in your leather jacket will keep you well hidden in the dark. Clever girl, Bethany, I knew I could rely on you." His conversation with his other persona over, he slipped out of the viaduct and, gratified that the coast was clear, even in the daytime, passed swiftly through the barricade, readjusted it ready for Bethany the following evening, and went off to call the newspaper.

Lord Robert had given him a splendid idea. Although not exactly orders, he felt obliged to obey the peer. Thus, a tabloid journalist would be his next victim. Those ignoramuses deserved to die! They couldn't string one grammatically correct sentence next to another to save their lives—and there would be no question of saving this particular life!

# CHAPTER 16

THE MURDERER RANG THE *LONDON EVENING PENNANT* AND ASKED to speak to the chief crime reporter. She chose the *Pennant* rather than a daily tabloid on the basis that a local newspaper with a vast circulation in the capital should be, in principle, more interested in a serial killer stalking its streets. Fobbed off with a junior reporter, the assassin calculated, as she later explained to her other persona,

"I decided that it matters little which of the rag's hacks we snuff out. The paper will make just as big a fuss over a junior, and he might be easier to deceive than an old pro."

The outcome of the phone call was an appointment the following evening at 10 p.m. by the viaduct arch next to the St James' Road underpass.

The lies that she had told the journalist were that she was a young woman called Bethany, not the killer, but a person who worked for a psychopath, who happened to be eminent in political circles. She promised him the scoop of the century, telling him to check out the five deaths so far. In her high-pitched voice, she spoke of a police conspiracy designed to keep Londoners in the dark about the serial killer, to avoid panic. "But is it right," she asked, "that people, who might otherwise stay indoors, or indeed, help with the inquiries, are deliberately kept uninformed? Isn't it the duty of the *London Evening Pennant* to notify Londoners of everything that concerns the wellbeing of its citizens?"

They continued their conversation with the journalist probing until Bethany said, "Look, Andy, I'll tell you everything you need to know tomorrow evening. No, I can't come sooner. I need to be off work, as I can't have him being suspicious—don't piss me off! You'll get his name, and I'll bring all the proof you need. Okay, you'll know me by my long blonde hair and black leathers, right? I'm not very tall, so don't confuse me for a girl, Andy. I'm all woman! See you tomorrow at ten, Blue Anchor Lane—don't be late!"

*You mustn't keep Death waiting, Andy Harris.*

"Well, that went well, didn't it?" She referred everything to her other persona, sat in his massage chair. He chuckled at how she had conned the reporter, calling her *sweetie*, which she loved, and other endearing names. They both agreed that Lord Robert would be delighted when he called around after an arduous day in the House of Lords.

"Now, I have to do a spot of research," he said, gazing down on a Royal Navy frigate whose horns were whooping either a salute or a warning. "Wicked!" He grinned as he looked down upon the anti-aircraft gun turret. "I'd love to fire one of those and bring down an aeroplane." He gazed raptly at the sleek warship for several minutes. "Now, where was I?" he said aloud as if Bethany were still in the room. *She's probably enjoying a bubble bath, the little minx!*

He went to his CD rack and selected Joni Mitchell's album, *Blue*. He chose the title track and began to sing along:

*"Songs are like tattoos*
*You know I've been to sea before*
*Crown and anchor me*
*Or let me sail away*

*Hey Blue."*

He had thought of copying the lyrics, but it would never do. He mustn't sink into laziness and take the easy option. He'd done that with green, after all, but the Tom Jones lyrics contained the essential element of murder. Mitchell's *Blue* was altogether different. True, there was an appropriate reference to *anchor,* but this was about love, not death. It was a lovely song but entirely wrong for his purposes. No, more research was called for—let it begin!

After an hour of rejecting a series of poems on his chosen theme, he was torn between two. Both were by female poets and captured the essence of his message to perfection. *Blue Moles,* written by the famous Sylvia Plath, began exceptionally, referring to *two moles dead in the pebbled rut.* Wasn't that quite magnificent? And so appropriate! He guffawed aloud at the words, but when it came down to the choice, he decided to make the police's work harder by citing an excerpt from a largely unknown young poet, who used the pen name SerenWise whose lines were just as relevant. He re-read them and chortled. His laughter became almost hysterical when he dreamt up the latest outrage Bethany could inflict on the corpse of the journalist. He wondered what the reporter was doing right now? Probably typing a boring report about domestic violence or petty theft in Lambeth. How could he conceive that his death would be a more outstanding contribution than anything he had achieved in life? Thinking about the reporter, he hoped that he wouldn't be built like a rugby prop. Poor Bethany would be intimidated and have physical problems.

He needed to slip out to procure the necessary item to complete work on the corpse tomorrow evening. Any supermarket would have what he wanted. Bethany would have to take her black rucksack to carry this purchase and other odds and ends. Regarding Bethany, he wandered into the bathroom to reassure her that however muscular Andy Harris proved to be, he would be no match for the contents of the syringe. The knack, as they had both demonstrated so far, consisted in total surprise. From amid the froth of the white bubble bath, Bethany told him not to worry. She would be able to deal with this Harris fellow. She was more worried about dragging his body into the abandoned railway property. She hoped he wouldn't be too heavy because she would need to act fast. Rather like M5, M6 ran the risk of exposure by passing car headlights.

---

As synchronicity, or warped irony, would have it, the killer and Shepherd entered the same supermarket within moments of each other. The murderer could thank his lack of height and no need for fruit and vegetables for remaining out of sight of the detective because she was dressed in plain clothes, a somewhat formal power suit with pinstripes. The tall shelves of goods made an excellent screen. He would not have identified her, but she might have noticed him since she was on red alert after finding that this supermarket, alone among those she had checked so far, stocked Mad Hatter peppers. She had left the store, writing its name and location in her notebook, and got into her car—which might have alerted the murderer by its local plates, the cluster of antennas, and dark tinted windows—by the time he had studied the conserves and cookery section and selected his ideal purchase. Carrying his shopping away in an eco-friendly bag, he returned home, oblivious to his close encounter with his nemesis.

Fate, however, is full of curious combinations and twists. In one unfortunate turn of events, Vance chose two detectives to patrol Blue Anchor Lane in shifts. He gave the evening shift of the following day to a young Welsh constable, Bryn Williams, telling him to be on the lookout for a petite blonde behaving suspiciously.

The other detective met DC Williams on location at seven in

the evening the next day and truthfully reported that he had wasted the last eight hours on pointless observation for the suspect. He warned Williams that *the Blue* was infamous as a hotspot for race crime and youth disorder, especially as night drew on. "Mind you, it's not as bad now as it was in the noughties," he said encouragingly when the young Welshman looked worried. "Radio in, Bryn, if you feel under threat, but I think the biggest danger is likely to be boredom." He grinned.

Bethany was vaguely uneasy that evening but couldn't quite put her finger on why. She had prepared her rucksack and slipped the weapon into her jacket pocket so she could whip it out when needed. Still, she couldn't settle. Even the river traffic, her usual source of relaxation, couldn't calm her, so she set off early for Blue Anchor Lane, reasoning that if she arrived before Andy Harris, she'd be able to study him from a darkened alcove and determine whether he would be too heavy for her to drag his body. In that case, she decided, she'd abort the operation and risk Lord Robert's wrath. There were other zones and other victims, after all. For example, a schoolgirl wouldn't pose this type of problem.

For this reason, she found herself on Blue Anchor Lane, standing in a shadow where the lamppost cast no light, one viaduct arch farther down the lane from the meeting point. It was lurking there that DC Williams spotted her. Since her straight blonde hair hung over the collar of her black leather jacket and she was undoubtedly petite, she perfectly fitted the description that Inspector Vance had furnished. Heart beating quickly, in his inexperience and enthusiasm, he committed a grave error. He should have radioed to headquarters that he was in the presence of a suspect, but breaching the rules, thinking that taking the exclusive credit for the arrest and seeing that the suspect was a mere slip of a girl, he approached her.

"Excuse me, miss. Police." He flashed his warrant card.

"Get off," the blonde replied. "It's dark. I can't see that. Bring it over to the light, she stepped into the brighter arc cast by the streetlamp. "Let me see. You can't be harassing innocent pedestrians, you know."

"I'm not harassing," he said, his accent from the Welsh valleys, drawing closer with no apparent reason to fear her. Bethany pretended to crane forward to read the warrant card. "Oh, Metropolitan Police are you, boyo?" She feigned a Welsh accent and he grinned. She stepped closer as he replaced the warrant in his pocket. She lunged, and her needle plunged into his throat. Unsuspecting, he was defenceless. The TTX, as she knew, required only moments to do its deadly work. As his knees buckled and he crashed to the ground, she looked along the street, where, to her relief, no vehicles approached. Instead, St James' Road was much busier where cars flashed past, just emerging from the underpass, or entering it. The drivers had no reason to take their eyes off the road ahead at a dangerous junction, so she felt unexposed. Although reasonably tall, the policeman was no giant. She grabbed his ankles and began to drag him along the lane as far as the last barricade. More efficiently than she had supposed, she reached the last barrier and noted with pleasure that the streetlight did not illuminate it.

Shoving back the steel obstruction, she hauled the body towards the dilapidated wooden door. It opened precariously, and as a car flooded the road with light, in the nick of time, she was able to close it enough to conceal her movements. Without shutting it completely, she used the torch on her smartphone to check the time. Twenty to ten, so she had twenty minutes before her appointment. That gave her a quarter of an hour or less to conclude here. First, she nipped outside and replaced the barrier so that nothing looked suspicious and dashed back inside. Using her torch, she took out a jar of bilberry jam—or *blue*berry as she preferred to call it—a spoon and opened the lid. She dipped the spoon into the conserve and transferred it to her mouth. "Mmm, delicious, my favourite!"

Next, she began to smear the jam over the dead copper's face. Only when she had finished the whole jar and flung it into the dark depths of the space around her, did she shine the torch on her grotesque handiwork. "Beautiful irony!" she chirped. "A Welshman, therefore, a Briton! The ancient Brits daubed their faces with woad and here's a poem with the title *Woad*. She rolled the prepared sheet of verse tightly and slid it up the dead man's sleeve. "All done here," she said, glancing at the time. "It only took seven minutes. I'd better go before Harris gets here—he doesn't know it, but he's one fortunate young fellow!"

She slipped through the narrow gap and stared hard towards the road, hoping against hope that the journalist hadn't come early. There was probably enough TTX to eliminate him, too, but she didn't want to alter the plan of murdering one victim at a time. It would transform her sprayed nine minus formula, and that would never do! Since she couldn't see anyone, she reached into her rucksack, took out the black paint spray and bent down to squirt it onto the white area at the bottom of the door: **9-6=3** about two-foot six from the ground.

As soon as that was done, she hurried to the barricade, saw a double-decker bus farther down the road, too far away for the driver to see her, so she pushed the barrier aside, dashed through, replaced it, adjusted her backpack, and strode around the corner into the underpass, helpfully illuminated by oncoming headlights. If she could reach The Elephant & Castle tube station, she would be safely away from the scene of the crime. She should have destroyed the copper's radio, she tut-tutted, annoyed with herself. Going back to remedy the oversight was out of the question—too risky. *Mind you, they'll probably find the body thanks to the device, so I won't have to phone in.*

This kind of worry set her to thinking more clearly. She stopped, withdrew into the blackness of a shop doorway, pulled off her wig, stuffed it into the rucksack and ruffled her hair into shape. "Better to be less noticeable," she muttered.

It was a stiff march as far as the tube station, as it was well beyond the Old Kent Road Post Office, but once there, she could take the Bakerloo line to Embankment, change onto her District line to reach Fulham Broadway. Maybe killing the cop and not the journalist had spooked her because now that she was on Old Kent Road, only atrocious luck, such as a random stop and search, could devastate her plans *and that,* she comforted herself, *ain't gonna happen.*

Sitting regally in her massage chair, Bethany reached an arm behind her head and rubbed at the nape of her neck. As often happened when she relaxed after a severe bout of stress, she felt a migraine coming on. To prevent it, she switched on the massager and closed her eyes. She dozed and let the tension seep out of her tortured body. She definitely didn't need the debonair voice from the armchair, heavy with reproval. "My dear girl, what on earth possessed you to kill a policeman? I thought we'd agreed on a journalist?"

"Lord Robert, won't this keep till tomorrow? Can't you see that the whole business has taken its toll? I have a migraine. I beg you, let's talk about this tomorrow. Since there was no reply, Bethany found the courage to open her eyes, focused with difficulty and, to her relief, saw that the armchair and its surroundings were empty. Again, Lord Robert had left the apartment as silently and ghostlike as he had entered. She wondered how he managed that.

*(The following morning, New Scotland Yard)*

Sergeant Shepherd's expression alerted Vance. At a glance, he saw that something was seriously amiss.

"What is it, Sarge? Has our serial killer struck again?"

"I'm afraid so, sir! The fact is, DC Williams hasn't reported in, and it's not like him. As a rule, he's so precise."

"He's the young fellow I put on *the Blue* for the evening shift," Vance said, more to order his thoughts than to converse.

"I've tried radioing him, but no luck," Shepherd said, biting her lower lip. "Do you think we should get over to Blue Anchor Lane, Inspector?"

"Let's go, Brit. I don't like the feel of this, one little bit.

As they cruised along the lane, Vance was unimpressed by

the normality of the surroundings. The occasional shop and a kebab house at the start of the lane. The monotonous two-storey buildings. Parking bays delineated in white interspersing the restrictive double yellow lines. The sporadic roadside tree. Until heading towards the end of the lane, he spotted a viaduct. Counting five visible arches, he ordered Shepherd to pull over into the last white bay which was fortuitously vacant.

Getting out of the car, Vance called to his sergeant. "Over there! There's an underpass, and the viaduct seems to have been converted into a kind of storage depot." His local knowledge didn't extend to railway history. "Ten to one Williams will have kept his eye on this precise area." His policing instincts were on red alert as they approached the viaduct.

Shepherd looked with distaste at the decrepit blue and white painted doors with their warning signs. "You can see why they've barricaded it off." She was a couple of steps ahead of her inspector, so having seen nothing unremarkable so far, she continued up to the last arch.

"Sir!" she hissed, pointing at the last door. There it was, unmissable, in black: **9-6=3.** "Our murderer was here."

"Yes, and, oh, my God, I fear her victim was Williams. Look here!" Vance heaved the metal barrier backwards. "It's severed, so the killer must have sawn through the steel."

"No, sir, look. It's a clean cut, so she must have used a proper bolt cutter on it."

"Would that slip of a bitch have had the strength?" Vance sounded doubtful.

"I reckon I could do it with a professional tool."

"You might be right," he conceded. "Let's go in, but we'll stick to crime scene protocol, he reminded her. They went back to the car, opened the boot, and took out latex gloves which they each pulled on. Shepherd selected a heavy-duty LED torch and looked at Vance questioningly.

"I think that's everything, Brit. Pity we haven't got SOC

protective gear with us, but if we tread carefully and little—" he left the rest unsaid.

Slightly before they reached the door, the sergeant's keen eye spotted something, and she hauled Vance to a halt. "Look at the fresh scuffing on the ground. It seems that someone has dragged the door open more than once recently."

"Some of it may be due to railway maintenance workers, but the spray suggests otherwise."

"So does the ground in front of the other doors." She pointed to the undisturbed weeds and gravel.

"Knowing that the killer entered here doesn't change anything," the inspector whispered. "Do you have your gun?"

Shepherd nodded and passed him the torch, drawing out her service pistol and flicking off the safety catch.

"Should we call for back-up, sir?"

"Not yet, Brit. Going by her previous killings, she won't be here, and I'm more worried that DC Williams *will* be. We're going in." He hauled on the dilapidated door, holding his breath, lest the rotten wood detached from its hinges. It didn't, so he stepped into the gloomy interior, where he heard the buzzing of flies."

Directing the powerful beam of silver light towards the droning murmur, it caught the bluebottles whirring over the face of a corpse.

"Jesus Christ! It's Bryn. But what's that on his face?" Shepherd gasped.

"Blue! It looks like jam, hence the flies." Vance snapped into command mode. "Outside, now! Call headquarters. I want forensics and Tremethyk here ASAP!"

He followed his sergeant back to the roadside, where she, green around the gills, was communicating with Scotland Yard in urgent tones. He gestured silently, indicating that he was going back to the car. Moments later, as she adjusted the barricade, he handed her a reel of crime scene tape, taken from the car boot. They wound it around the steel barricade and tied off the end.

"All we can do is wait until the experts to get here, Brit."

"Let's hope that our murderer has made her first mistake this time."

Although he desperately shared this sentiment, Vance ignored it, saying instead, "Was he married?"

That concentrated her attention marvellously. "Bryn? No, sir, he had a fiancée, I believe. If I recall, she manages a boutique in Wandsworth or thereabouts."

"Radio in and get a policewoman on it, Brit. The sooner she finds out from us, the better. This story will hit the media, bigtime."

Vance could not know that the press was already sniffing around thanks to Andy Harris. Not long after the scientists arrived on the scene, Harris himself sought out Vance since they had indicated the detective inspector as the man in charge of the investigation. Overly wary of the Press, by nature, nonetheless, the detective was deeply interested in what the youthful reporter had to tell him.

Having listened carefully to the journalist's account, he looked him in the eye. He said, "To my mind, you were the intended victim, Mr Harris. You've had a lucky escape and can thank my poor constable in there," he jerked his thumb, "for deviating the killer from her objective. I'm going to ask you to come to Scotland Yard and give a formal statement, sir. Meanwhile, try to remember even the smallest detail of what our psychopath told you, however insignificant it might seem to you.

"Crikey, it's better than winning the National Lottery!" the journalist murmured.

"We'll do our best to keep you safe, sir. One never knows when dealing with a maniac, it's better not to run any risks."

# CHAPTER 17

## THE BLUE AND NEW SCOTLAND YARD, LONDON

Doctor Tremethyk was the first expert to rejoin Vance back at the roadside. His marked Cornish accent indicated his state of mind. "Your psycho has excelled herself this time, me-dear. Such a waste! A young constable with his career ahead of him and defiled in a shocking and pointless way!"

"Come on, Doc!" Vance put an arm around the bowed shoulders. "From the medical point of view, what can you tell me?"

Not far from retirement, Francis Tremethyk gave him a grateful look and snapped back into professional mode. "The same as most of the others, me-dear, a single puncture wound to the throat. It's odds on that it's the same serial killer. I'm stating the obvious, I know. It's certain to be TTX, and if it's any consolation, I'd say that the poor lad was dead before he knew it."

The doctor glanced back at the viaduct. "I suppose that I should leave this to the remarkable Dr Markham, but you know her, she insisted on snaffling the note before I could get it to you. Quite right, too! Although I'm no expert on poetry, at a rapid reading, I'd say it was a poem—about woad. I'd stake my intellectual reputation on that. Not that there was a title. But consider, Jacob, that poor boy's face was lathered in blue jam. So, your signal is blue, but it's also a sure message about woad, for some reason. You will know, I'm sure, that bilberries are known by many names, including whortleberries, but as our transatlantic cousins might say, give me good old *blue*berries any day.

"The killer wouldn't have known in time to plan her jam exploit that Bryn was a Welshman. It's got to be mere coincidence," Vance said more to himself rather than to the Cornishman, another Briton. And what's more, I've never met anyone more English than Harris, the intended target. I don't care for coincidences, but, no, this *is* one."

The short monologue left the doctor bewildered, but what the onrushing, white-garbed Sergeant Shepherd had to say, he did understand.

"Sir!" she cried exuberantly, "our murderer has made her first mistake!"

"Don't tell me we've got a lead, at last, Brit."

"I think so. Dr Markham's team retrieved the jam jar our assassin tossed away. Maybe she was distracted or in a hurry because it's not like her."

"Are you saying there are dabs all over the jar?"

"I don't know about that," she said. "We can but hope, but what I *do* know is this, the brand was the supermarket's own. And listen up, it's the same supermarket as sold the Mad Hatter pepper. With your permission, I'm going to stake it out across its opening hours until I've got the bitch! She does her shopping there."

"Good thinking, Sarge. You've got it! I'll keep you informed of any developments."

"Oh, and sir, another thing. She hid the bolt cutter among some old scaffolding. Since they are brand new heavy-duty cutters, there can't be many places hereabouts that sell them."

"I'm on to it, Brit. Good work!"

The cutters were, indeed, to provide Vance with a minor lead and a major insight. As soon as he returned to New Scotland Yard, he went to forensics and asked Dr Markham about them.

"What can you tell me about the bolt cutters, Sabrina?"

"Quite a lot, actually, Jacob." She smiled at him. "They have a whole story to tell. First, the killer wiped her prints off them before leaving them hidden among the scaffolding. Secondly, she may have cleaned off the prints, but she forgot to remove the price sticker—and that, Detective, was a bad slip because it tells us where she bought them. I'd say very recently, too, since they're brand new. It's all quite suggestive if you add the discard jar to this."

"What does it suggest to you, Doctor Markham?" The formal title suggested how highly he valued her deductions.

"Overlooking the price sticker suggests she was working in poor light. Doctor Tremethyk puts the time of death around ten o'clock, and it must have been pitch black in there. Tossing the jam jar indicates she was in a hurry. I mean, she could easily have taken such a small object away with her. The bolt cutters, a relatively expensive tool left behind, makes me think that they were too heavy for her, confirming her known slightness of build."

"It's all logical thinking, Sabrina. We're lucky to have you on our side." He grinned.

"Good grief, Jake, what other side would you have me on?"

They laughed together, and Jacob wondered, not for the first time, why this captivating woman was still single. Thrusting aside his distraction, he asked sharply, "So where did she buy the bolt cutters?"

"There's a big hardware store on Old Kent Road near the Post Office. Your delightful Sergeant Wright supplied me the address. Here it is." She handed him a scrap of paper with the scribbled whereabouts.

In the absence of his sergeant to ferry him, Vance requisitioned a vehicle and drove himself to the store. An elderly assistant shook his grey head perplexed but helpfully went to his colleagues and returned with a youth suffering from acne. The lad told the inspector that he had sold a pair of heavy-duty cutters the previous day. "I remember, like, 'cause the geezer didn't look strong enough to cut anyfink. What he said was that his gaffer had arms like a gorilla's, I recall that."

Vance was on red alert, and he smiled encouragingly at the assistant. "You are a big help, young fellow. Just think for a second, can you describe this fellow to me? Any particular details will be of assistance."

"Well, yeah. Like I said, he was a weedy type, 'bout this tall." He held a hand out flat at about his chin height. "Short, mousy-coloured hair and he walked strange."

"Strange? How do you mean?"

"Well, kind of hunched over. Like this," the assistant rounded his shoulders, hunched over and mimicked a walk.

This performance triggered something, but he couldn't quite put his finger on it.

*I'll read through our reports back at base.*

"Thank you, mate, you've been a great help to our investigation." He handed over a visiting card. "If the geezer turns up again, ring me at once, but don't let him hear you. He's a danger to the public." Suitably impressed, the lad tucked the card in his overalls pocket and said, "Yeah, I'll do that."

Driving back to New Scotland Yard, Vance tried in vain to remember. Annoyingly, the word *hunched* had triggered something, and he couldn't quite place it. He sighed at the prospect of ploughing through pages of reports. His visit to the hardware store had been productive because it confirmed an earlier suspicion that the killer was male. The long blonde hair had been a disguise to throw them off the correct trail from the start. This stratagem explained why *she* had exposed herself to the CCTV camera in Allenbury Lane. Brittany had remarked that it was suspicious at the time, and his sergeant's intuitions were never wrong. He smiled sadly, knowing that soon he would lose her valuable support. Still, if he could persuade the commissioner, he had a constable in mind for promotion, who might have the attributes to replace Brit. Yes, DC Mark Allen deserved upgrading, no two ways about it.

In his office, Vance took out the thick file of witness statements and began with those regarding the murder of the blonde estate agent. As it happened, what he was searching for was not among murder witness reports, but when he saw the name Akina Aoyama, it jogged his memory. Frantically, he flicked through to the escort's statement, and there it was:

*I mean, he wasn't tall. I'd guess about five-foot three, and there was something strange about the way he walked away, not that I could study him. He soon vanished into the crowd: it's busy there. Like he was disabled or something, kind of hunched over. I can't explain unless he was trying to remain as unnoticeable as possible.*

"That's it!" Vance cried out aloud in his empty office, "and what if he wasn't hunched over to look unnoticeable? What if the murdering bastard's a hunchback? If that's the case, it'll make it much easier to capture him. Hang on, though! Better not get carried away. Maybe he's bloody cunning and putting on an act like when he was a blonde woman. Anyway, I'll give Brittany a bell."

He considered for a moment whether to call his sergeant on her radio or ring her on her mobile, and the thought that their suspect was a cunning devil made him opt for the latter. Criminals often tuned into the police shortwave band, and he didn't want to alert the killer.

A couple of rings, and Brittany's voice came through. "Have you got anything for me, boss?"

Rapidly, he briefed her on his findings, concluding, "So you're looking for a male with a peculiar, hunched walk, but a short male with or without the hunching should warn you. It seems that our assassin is an inveterate actor."

"In which case, I'll still look out for the petite blonde. We can't be sure how he, she, or it will turn up!" The sergeant made light of the demanding task, knowing that it was their only lead after six murders.

Almost as soon as Vance had finished on the phone with his sergeant, Dr Markham knocked on his door. The forensic report was ready, but as Sabrina Markham succinctly put it, "Not much use to you, Jacob, no dabs. In that respect, our murderer is diligent. It'll be damned difficult getting a conviction without evidence, old pal."

The sour expression on Vance's face changed at the endearment. He was fond of the scientist and wanted to be positive.

"Thanks to your sharp eyes, Doc, we now know from the hardware store that our assassin is a male and a consummate actor."

"Is that so? He also has a penchant for poetry. I passed on the note found on the body to Max." She smiled and hesitated, then blushing as she spoke, "Do you know, Jacob, Max asked me out to dinner?"

"Did he, by Jove! And did you accept?"

She looked pleased with herself. "Not that I'm seeking your approval, Jacob, but he's quite a charmer."

"So, that's a yes, then."

She smiled coyly. "Don't you go sticking your oar in, DI Vance!"

"Wouldn't dream of it. But I need to see Max about the note."

"I'll come along to keep an eye on you, Jacob."

He grunted, and they left his office the short distance to Wright's computer.

"Oh, hi Sab—*er*—Dr Markham, Inspector."

"What do you have for me, Max? Vance asked shortly.

DS Wright scrabbled around among his papers and produced the poem in its evidence bag and another sheet that he handed to the detective with the complete poem.

"Our murderer planted the verse without its title, sir, which is *Woad*."

"Ah, so Dr Tremethyk was right about that. Can we conclude anything from the words?"

Max Wright took up the transparent evidence envelope and said, "It's a lovely poem by a lady poet who goes by the name of

SerenWise, I'd say she deserves greater appreciation. Anyway," he read:

*"This blue is what I am—*
*Used once by warriors strong,*
*To paint their bodies*
*For war and to belong.*
*Find me there;*
*In that pigment from another time,*
*Find me in the soft blue prose,*
*In the lonely indigo rhyme."*

Vance followed the reading on the printed sheet and then re-read it. True, he liked the poem, too, very much. Max was saying, "The murderer wanted to underline blue, and we were one step ahead when we identified Blue Anchor Lane, unfortunately, as it turned out for Bryn. We know that the killer's next move will be red, sir. But this poem also clearly states *paint their bodies for war.* That's why he daubed Bryn's face blue, lest we had any doubts that this *is* a war!"

"His next move will be red, will it?"

"I believe so." He took out the Lapique print and pointed at a red zone. This area will be his likely choice, but what I've done is take all possible red zones and cross-reference all streets whose names contain red. Here's the list, but I don't think we can move on that large a scale, sir.

Vance looked with dismay at the long list and muttered, "We're going to have to rely on Sergeant Shepherd."

The decision not to anticipate the murderer in the probable area that Max had indicated was fortunate because, in his riverside apartment, the assassin was working on a surprise location. He was also laughing at a notion that had come to mind. Unfortunately for Shepherd, he cancelled his original shopping expedition as a wild idea, overtaking the original one to buy goji berries occurred to him. At first, he intended to tuck a goji berry under each eyelid of his next victim, but by an association of thoughts, he moved on to poisonous berries and opted to explore nearby woodland for black bryony berries. His research had informed him that they were available at this time of year and that he could find the plant climbing in hedgerows. A part of the yam family, the plant produced bright red and extremely poisonous berries. He decided to gather some and place them in the victim's mouth. Therefore, today would be dedicated to a trip into the countryside. He could combine it with a survey of the M8 area, which was out in the sticks. "Yes, I know, Bethany, that's the sky-blue area. The next is red and in SW3. I know that! Now, let me concentrate, there's a sweetie," he said to his other persona.

*What a shame I don't have my Harley Davidson. It would have been helpful for this trip, so I'll check whether the tube goes that far.*

A quick search online told him that West Drayton was served by National Rail overland trains, and just inside London Underground Zone 6, to get there using his Oyster Card.

"Excellent, Bethany, sweetie, I'm off hunting for *Tamus communis,* so if Lord Robert turns up, deal with him, my little angel of death, okay?"

That settled, he grabbed a jacket and set off for the nearest tube station.

Stationed in front of the supermarket, Shepherd's achievement that day amounted to offending a petite blonde by asking her to prove that she wasn't wearing a wig. Permission to conduct a simple tug test accorded, Shepherd was profuse in her apologies when, embarrassed by her mistake, she looked a fool. She drove away with gritted teeth ten minutes after the supermarket closed but determined to continue her vigil the following day.

# CHAPTER 18

## WEST DRAYTON, NORTH LONDON, AND NEW SCOTLAND YARD

THE KILLER RATTLED ALONG HAPPILY IN THE TUBE CARRIAGE TO West Ruislip. The farther he travelled, the more his mood improved at the thought that the police would not expect a murder so far from the city centre where he had hitherto depicted his *canvas*. The very notion made his heart sing, and the mirth bubbling under the surface threatened to burst out in uncontrollable laughter. Such an attention-drawing performance was unacceptable as it would make other passengers stare and note his already too memorable physique. Stifling his urge to explode into merriment, he got a grip on himself by digging his nails into his palms.

He was sorry that today's expedition was only for a rapid survey designed to collect necessary material for his *red* killing, still, patience was a virtue that he embodied, he told himself smugly.

Exiting the West Ruislip underground station, he confirmed that the U3 bus would take him to Mabey's Meadow, the area and its transport network having been a subject of his careful research. Since he felt the need to stretch his legs, he opted for the eight-minute walk to his destination. He had read online that he would gain magnificent views over the River Colne from the meadow, and, if he was lucky, catch a glimpse of an electric-blue flash: a diving kingfisher. It was a little late in the year to chance upon peacock butterflies, but he spotted three banded demoiselle damselflies to his great satisfaction. His alertness pleased him because Bethany was a Nature-lover, so on his return home, he would report his observations to her, where she would hang on his every word, the sweetie.

Making his way to the fringes of the willow wood, where the undergrowth grew tall, an attentive perusal brought him to a hedgerow where he found what he sought, namely, black bryony. He studied the plant's anti-clockwise upward twining and its heart-shaped glossy leaves with their veins forming a network pattern. Any doubts he might have harboured about identification were dispelled by the shiny, red berries hanging temptingly within reach. Engrossed in his discovery, he did not notice an elderly, blue-rinsed lady in tweed slacks and heavy woollen cardigan observing him. She kept quiet until he extracted a jackknife, severed a bunch of berries and dropped them into a paper bag.

"Hey, young fellow! I hope you know what you're doing."

The murderer spun around and stared at the meddlesome old biddy. "What's your problem?" he snarled.

"A little friendly advice, young man, those berries are highly poisonous. Hereabouts, we call them the *Devil's cherries.*"

The assassin couldn't contain his glee, guffawing so loud and long that the poor elderly lady feared that he was a maniac. This impression increased when he wiped his eyes with a sleeve and tried but failed to get his words out as hysterical laughter racked his slight frame.

"Pardon me, I must go now," the terrified woman said, eyeing the jackknife and longing to be anywhere other than near the madman. The evident terror in her eyes and her arthritic attempt at fleeing brought him to his senses. He swore loudly.

"Hey, wait! Devil's cherries—hee-hee! That's brilliant! Come back. I won't hurt you!" he lied. He had decided to slit her throat before she could blab. But, fortunately for her, she had slipped down a passageway between two houses, and he dared not pursue her as he'd attracted enough attention as it was. He would have to hope that she kept her mouth shut, but he knew she would call the police by the look on her face. That type of busybody was sure to do that. No, he would have to be cunning and give the boys in blue the runaround.

To this end, he decided to vary his route by taking the U1 bus to West Drayton station and, from there, the TfL train to the Paddington terminus. As he rode along, the implications of his encounter with the nosey woman sank home. With any luck, she would call the police to divert their attention for the next murder erroneously to north London instead of his choice in SW3. His assumption was correct in every detail, for the widowed Mrs Marge Winterburn was on the phone to the police as his train glided towards Paddington.

Her statement was somewhat confused since she had been frightened and was short-sighted. Still, she provided sufficient information to tally with the identikit supplied by New Scotland Yard.

"We've had a sighting, Sarge," Vance told Shepherd over the phone. "Our assassin scared an elderly lady witless. She came across him gathering black bryony berries, and when she pointed out that they were highly poisonous, in her own words, 'He flipped and began laughing like someone out of a horror film'."

"Let me guess, black bryony berries are bright red, right?"

"As acute as ever, Brittany!"

"You haven't told me where the sighting occurred."

Vance scratched the hair at the temple. "That's the odd thing. It's well out of his previous range in West Ruislip."

The sergeant frowned. "It might be that the only reason he

was up there was to collect black bryony berries. I mean, you don't find them on the Embankment, do you?"

"But if he wanted to indicate red, he could more easily buy raspberries or strawberries from his local supermarket, couldn't he? That's why you are stationed outside his store of preference." Vance frowned, too. He disliked phone calls and not studying his sergeant's facial reactions. Her voice came through clearly. "You're right, of course, and it suggests that his next killing will be in or near West Ruislip. If I remember correctly, it's the terminus of the Central line. We should have the local bobbies check the station and its CCTV for our suspect. There's no point in my carrying on this vigil today if he's gadding about up there. I'm coming in."

"Good, you can help me identify places in West Ruislip with red in their name. See you soon."

This identification proved much easier said than done. Intense scrutiny of street names for the whole of Hillingdon Borough failed to throw up a single 'Red'. They found an Azalea Walk, but as Shepherd reasonably pointed out, not all azaleas bloom red. "Still, Cherry Lane might fit the bill," Vance said.

"Yeah, true, but that would mark a change in his methods. All the streets have contained the colour word, so far—oh, except for Primrose Street," Shepherd commented, "For that matter, there's a Holly Drive, too."

"Unless—" the detective inspector drummed his fingers on his desk. "You've reminded me of the first two murders. They were committed in streets that subsequently changed their names."

Several minutes later, Max Wright presented him with a list of pre-1912 former street names, twelve containing 'red' but none in the Hillingdon Borough area.

"I know this is a long shot, sir, but—"

"Go on, Max," Vance urged.

"Well, again, it would be a change in the killer's *MO* but since there are no 'red' streets, maybe Catlin's Lane in Eastcote is the answer. The first house on the left was built in 1913. It's a detached house with a red tile roof. Its walls are mostly rendered except for several courses of redbrick at the base, which finish with a decorative triangle pattern. If you like, I can zoom in on it with a satellite image."

"Good thinking, Max, but it seems a little far-fetched even for our creative killer," he watched dismay register in Max's expression, "but I'll tell you what, we'll increase policing in Hillingdon and pay close attention to Catlin's Lane and the other two possibilities."

Meanwhile, the murderer had refined his plans for the next day. Happy that the police would not suspect his target area, he put the final touches to his preparations in place. These preliminaries included a survey of the selected spot. Out of a considerable range of appealing names, he had chosen this one to fit neatly with the previous murder in Blue Anchor Lane. This street was in the Chelsea district, and the symmetry of the name: Red Anchor Close, amused him. When he first searched for it, he walked straight past, along the narrow Old Church Street because it was an almost hidden opening tucked away on the left. Red Anchor Close constituted a modern mews-style gated and part-paved cul-de-sac approached through an entrance under a building on Old Church Street. Since the wrought iron gate was more ornamental than functional, the close was perfect for his purpose. Taking every precaution not to be noticed, he slipped under the iron arch but didn't loiter.

He counted seven properties in the close and no movement even at three o'clock in the afternoon. He presumed that there would be none in the evening, either. The two-storey buildings with brick facades, one or two rendered, were well-maintained with a variety of parapet or flat roof styles. Not lingering, he moved ghostlike back onto the long, narrow street with its double yellow lines on one side and black iron bollards set in the pavement.

*Oh, excellent! A superior area for a killing! Tomorrow evening it is, then.*

As he looked around, satisfied, his eye was caught by a painted sign high on a building a little farther down the road. A pig's head emerging from a white shirt and black bow tie and green jacket, a neatly folded handkerchief tucked in the breast pocket, the head sporting a monocle, pleased him.

He laughed out loud and hastily glanced around to make sure nobody had noticed. Above the image, neat lettering spelt: *The Chelsea Pig.*

"I'll have a drink there, they deserve my custom just for the sign," he murmured. By choosing a table near a window, he was able to view the passers-by. In his imagination, he created a scenario where he dragged each one into the cul-de-sac and murdered them. The decision he made was to inject the poison before the dragging. It would be so much easier and effective. One thought led to another, and he realised that the street would need to be very quiet for his plan to succeed. Not even a single witness must see him haul his victim into the close. Technically, this presented him with some difficulty, but he loved a challenge. Since he had overcome all the hazards thrown up by White Horse Yard, this seventh murder would surely be more straight-forward.

*No, Bethany, not six.* ***Seven.*** *You can't count, silly billy!* He told his other persona, whispering so that the old fellow nodding off over his daily newspaper, his pint half empty, at the next table, wouldn't hear him. Bethany was a darling, but she could be a trial sometimes.

As the murderer quaffed his beer, Shepherd, frustrated at the lack of progress in the case, decided to resume her vigil outside the same supermarket. The more she thought about the absence of street names with red in them in Hillingdon, the more she was convinced that the killer would strike in another area, closer to the previous killings. She pulled out her battered copy of the AZ of London streets from her handbag and ran down the index, in between comings and goings from the supermarket. Next, she cross-checked with the print-off of the abstract painting by Lapique and tried to see some pattern in the six murders. As she placed crosses on the coloured sheet, she could only spot their grouping in the central London area. By joining the crosses, she hoped to reveal a shape, but nothing was forthcoming. Except, wait! Maybe the lines resembled a witch's pointed hat. In that case, to finish the image, the next murder would be in the SW3 district unless it was a coincidence.

Fumbling with her AZ, she discovered just one 'red' in SW3—a cul-de-sac called Red Anchor Close. Not one to keep her thoughts to herself— one never knew when an intuition might be pertinent—she rang her senior officer.

"Sir, I've had a thought…" she went on to explain the idea to Vance.

"A witch's hat! You have to be joking! Talk about clutching at straws. I thought we'd decided that the next killing would be in the UB7 district. So, to be contrary, you look at the area diametrically opposite. Come on, Brit!"

"Sorry, sir, you're probably right, but I keep thinking that the murderer might have gone to West Ruislip solely to gather those damned berries. I reckon he's as mad as the Hatter and will do whatever it takes for his crazy schemes."

"I spoke with Miriam Walker this afternoon, and our psychologist agrees on that. She made a point of reminding me that our subject is always one step ahead of us and has only made two minor mistakes. She seems to think that the extension to UB7 will be a deliberate ploy to catch us off our guard. The killer can't know that the terrified widow phoned us, so that must go down as his third mistake. The least we can do is try to profit from it, Brit. Oh, by the way, our lads in West Ruislip spotted a figure matching our suspect arriving by tube at about ten o'clock this morning, but so far haven't found footage of him returning, so they've set up surveillance in the station on the chance of nabbing him."

"You're quite right about taking advantage, sir. Let's hope they get him. Sooner or later, he's going to need something from this supermarket. I think I'll stay here until closing time, but what do you say if we set up surveillance tomorrow by some of our constables? I'd rather be more active, to tell the truth." That agreed, she settled back to watch and think.

# CHAPTER 19

The murderer held his breath and tensed his muscles, ready to leap forward at the approaching young woman. She deserved to die for the way she was dressed since a cool autumn evening merited more respect. She was wearing a short skirt and a tube top that revealed her navel. Her long legs ended with cork wedge-heeled shoes and black-painted toenails.

She was only ten paces away when his muscles tensed even more, but for an unforeseen reason. A red Nissan pulled up to his left in one of the parking bays on his side of the street. The driver would have a perfect view of the assault if he chose to spring forward. By the time he had decided not to reveal himself, the unsuspecting young woman was safely past, blissfully unaware of how close she had come to leaving this world.

The driver, also a young woman, waited for her companion to get out of the car before locking it. The presence of another person saved her life because the killer was frustrated and intent on retribution. The two young women turned away and followed the first, the intended victim, into the nearby *Chelsea Pig* pub.

Still seething with frustration, the assassin felt in his jacket pocket and took out a key. Walking over to the Nissan, brimming with desire for revenge, he ran the metal along the driver's side, scoring deeply into the paintwork.

"Hey, you! What do you think you're playing at?" came a gruff shout. A tall man in a red baseball cap, worn backwards, multicoloured T-shirt and ripped jeans confronted him. "I saw what you did. You're coming with me to find the owner. I saw her go into that pub." He pointed.

*Where the hell did he spring from? The Devil take me if I'm going with him!*

The killer's hand tightened automatically over the syringe in his pocket. He glanced up and down the street but could see no one else. The vigilante misinterpreted his furtive glances. "And you'd better not try to make a run for it, or I'll belt you into next week."

The smaller man decided to play for time.

"You don't understand. That car is my wife's. She's been unfaithful, and I was boiling with rage. Anyway, it's none of your business."

"Unfaithful? But I saw her with another woman."

"How would you feel if your missus left you for a lesbian?"

The tall stranger bellowed a laugh. "No chance of that, pal! I can understand your old lady, have you looked in a mirror lately?" he sneered. This jibe was his last on this Earth. The murderer's hand shot out and the needle pierced the man's throat near his Adam's apple. His eyes widened as the strange tingling sensation spread through his body, making his fingers feel as thick as bananas. His knees buckled, and he collapsed dead at the shorter man's feet. Heart pounding, the killer made sure nobody was walking or driving along the street. He was in luck. Using every ounce of strength that he possessed, he dragged the hefty fellow through the wrought iron gate, just far enough so that none of the body could be seen from the road.

Hurriedly, he unslung his backpack and took out a paper bag. He panted, and is hand was still shaking from the effort of hauling the body, but he managed to remove the bryony berries to stuff them into the open mouth of the corpse. Out of sheer hatred of the tall man for the aggression he had directed at him, he detached a berry and peeling back an eyelid, forced it between the eyeball and the tight lid as he had initially intended to do with goji berries before he thought of black bryony. He repeated the operation with the other eye. He needed to tuck his red poem somewhere on the body. As venomous as ever he rolled the paper into a slim cylinder and pushed it up a nostril, ensuring it was tightly trapped there. All that remained to do was to leave his classic signature. Looking around, careful to ascertain that none of the residents had heard or seen anything, he took out his black paint spray and, agitating the can, strode over to the brick façade of the nearest house and in wantonly large numbers, sprayed **9-7=2**.

Packing everything away in his rucksack, he slung it over one shoulder and left the mews as swiftly and silently as a Corfu lizard. Clutching his key again, he repeated his earlier gouging of the paintwork, this time, with exaggerated zigzag sweeps. At last, his rage had abated, and lucidity returned. He had known all along that this Chelsea street presented a high-risk factor, but he had overcome all obstacles. True, he'd been forced to improvise, but therein lay his greatness, he chuckled. The imbecile police were no match for him. The Met Commissioner now had seven deaths on her conscience because she was too arrogant to apologise in public for her remarks.

Although he would not admit it, the clash with the man in the red baseball hat had shaken him badly, so he decided to walk off his anxieties. It was a half-hour march to his flat from Old Church Street. At a brisk pace, he was soon out of that road and halfway down Milman's Street before he slowed his stride. A midweek evening by the river would not present him with too many people, besides, the Thames in the darkness exerted a profound attraction for him. Therefore, he walked happily along the waterway as far as Lots Road, absorbing the fascinating lights and reflections in the majestic stream. He barely deigned the Chelsea Academy with a glance, sour that his route had taken him slightly away from his beloved river. He crossed Chelsea Creek and skirted the Harbour of the same name, which brought him back to the riverside walk and then across Imperial Park. He nodded and smiled at a man walking his Alsatian, and before he realised it, he was approaching his Fulham apartment complex.

At home, he would report everything to Bethany and tell her how clever he had been. Then, it would be his pleasant duty to repeat the same spiel to Lord Robert.

---

The following morning, Shepherd drew back her curtains and gazed mournfully at a glorious autumnal morning, the sunlight transforming bronze leaves into sparkling gems. A scarcity of sleep explained her bleak mood, contrasting so strongly with the splendid day. When a case stubbornly refused to fall into place like this one, instead of sleeping, her mind churned over every tiny detail in the files. As she dragged a brush down her short twenties-style hair and gazed critically at her sleep-starved eyes in the mirror, wondering whether she could even mask the devastation with make-up, she decided that she needed to see the Lapique print-off again. Rummaging through her bag, she hissed a colourful curse when she realised that she had left it in the car. Undaunted, she turned to the internet, brought up the image of *Jean sans Peur* and took a screenshot.

At this point, she spotted a vital detail and swore at Max Wright, who had failed to notice that the artwork had *two* distinct titles. After insulting her sergeant colleague with the ripest of dockland language, she calmed and considered that maybe DS Wright had brought up an image with just the one caption. Her mind had gone into overdrive, linking the second title with witness statements, and making a solid connection.

*If only we'd known earlier—oh, Max, Max, we might have saved lives!*

The new title of Lapique's masterpiece opened up a whole new line of inquiry. Reinvigorated, she pulled on her clothes, opting, unusually for her, not to waste time showering. She reckoned that she showered every day, so she could pass this morning in her eagerness to break her news to Vance. His praise would cover her like the water spouting from her shower head, and that would be equally refreshing from a professional point of view.

Autumnal London seemed particularly beautiful to her as she drove to work full of ideas to gain a breakthrough—and all thanks to a one-word title! Dashing to Vance's room, bursting to tell him about her discovery, her face fell at the sight of the inspector's melancholy expression.

"What's up, boss? Don't tell me there's another one?"

Vance gazed at his sergeant with a tight-jawed hangdog face. "I'm a damned fool, and I owe you an apology, Brit. I should never have ignored your intuition. How many years have we worked together? And it's never failed you. Sod me, why didn't I listen to you?"

"Stop beating yourself up, sir, and spit it out! What's going on?"

"What went on, you mean. The fiend has struck again, exactly where you predicted—in Red Anchor Lane. I was waiting for you to come in before shooting over there. Dr Tremethyk is already at the scene. The victim's a tall fellow in his early forties from what I've heard, another to fall foul of the same trademark killing. Damn it! That's seven now, Brit, and we're no nearer to solving this case."

"Oh, is that what you think? Well, I've got news for you, sir! But it'll keep for the car and I'm ready to bet it'll brighten your mood." She twirled and skipped to the door. "I'll get the car, sir. See you on the forecourt in five."

Her chirpy disposition intrigued the detective inspector. He knew her well enough to tell that she was sitting on something of vital importance. *God knows we need a breakthrough!*

In the vehicle, Brittany Shepherd was milking her discovery by dragging out an explanation of how she hadn't slept and the consequences of having left the print-out in the car. Vance, on tenterhooks, snapped, "I hope this is worth the wait, Sarge!"

"Oh yeah, what I'm coming to is that the painting has a *second* title that dear old Max missed."

"Well?"

"It's also called *Quasimodo* as in Victor Hugo."

"*The Hunchback of Notre-Dame*?"

"Exactly, sir! See what that means for our case?"

"Damn it, of course, I do! We have enough testimony about the killer's physical aspect to tally with that deformation."

"Well, sir, I have a hunch if you'll pardon the pun that our murderer's resentment against the commissioner's speech might derive from rejection. Let's say that our Quasimodo wasn't accepted into the force on physical grounds, owing to a deformity. Wouldn't that be motive enough for an unhinged individual to begin his campaign of terror and stick his frustrations up our proverbial arses?"

"Sweetly put, Sarge! I'll phone Miriam Walker right now to see what our criminologist thinks."

There followed a series of grunts and monosyllabic comments that Brittany couldn't piece together, but since they had arrived at the half-hidden crime scene, she accepted with a nod when the inspector said, "I'll explain later, Sarge, we'd better get suited up. But, hey, well done, Brit! This discovery could be the link we've been missing."

When they approached Dr Tremethyk in their protective suits, the Cornishman gave them an anguished greeting, "Ah, here you are me-dears, don't you think it's time you put an end to this maniac's activities?"

"We're doing our best, Doc. What have you got for us?"

"Well, seeing as the remarkable Markham seems to be having

a lie-in this morning, I suppose I can pass this straight to you." He handed Vance a plastic envelope. "The usual colour-associated poetry. No surprise that it refers to red, boy?"

"What else, Francis?"

Tremethyk waved another plastic container, a transparent bag this time. The bright red berries were visible through the material. "*Dioscorea communis,* me-dear or to a mere copper like yourself, black bryony berries."

"The Devil's cherries?" Vance smiled grimly, displaying his general knowledge to the bristly medic.

"Or, as I prefer, *lady's seal,*" the Cornish doctor retaliated.

"Or, black bindweed," Brittany muttered, not to be outdone.

The Chief Medical Examiner looked at her appraisingly and said, "A bright lass like you should be in charge of bringing this pervert to justice. As for you, Jacob, it's about time you hung up your truncheon and retired to spend time with your delightful Helena."

"Come on, Doc, you know as well as I do that you'll retire before me. Maybe your successor will give a boost to my career!"

The doctor scowled and grumbling, said, "You might consider why black bryony berries instead of wasting your mental energy."

"Go on, then, you have a theory, let's hear it!"

The Cornish accent grew more marked. "Not my field—suppositions—but, like you, Jacob, I'm not a believer in coincidences. These berries are highly poisonous, and your maniac must have gone to some trouble to find them when he might just as easily have stuffed raspberries into the poor fellow's mouth. The murder weapon is always a syringe loaded with TTX—a deadly poison—if pressed, I'd say that the assassin is sending a reminder, a mocking memo that he's poisoning at will."

"Not for much longer, Francis. We're on to him."

"I should hope so, me-dear. This maniac is one spiteful individual. Look at what he did to the eyes!"

Both detectives leant forward to peer as the doctor's tweezers revealed the berry under the lid.

Shepherd's quick intake of breath was followed by, "I have an idea that this poor chap disturbed our murderer to his cost, so the killer, full of resentment, showed his rancour like this."

"Quite possibly, me-dear, that would fit. See, we have brains in the Met, Jacob, boy."

But the ill-treated inspector was reading poetry. He broke off to ask, "What else can you deduce here, O wise physician?"

"Point of entry, here, again suggests a shorter person striking upwards with force, see the ring of bruising? I guess the perpetrator would have had his work cut out to drag this gentleman into the mews. That would explain the location of the body, just far enough through the gate not to attract the attention of passing motorists. You will have seen his calling card when you arrived." The doctor pointed to the sprayed formula, **9-7=2**. "Again, the larger size of the numbers compared to previous killings, suggests to me, that our man was enraged."

"Hmm, I tend to agree." The detective inspector would have looked downhearted if the others could have seen past his plastic visor. He knew that the killer would arrive at the ninth murder if they didn't catch him quickly. The damned hunchback was behaving as murderously as Shakespeare's Richard III, but, of course, Vance knew that the much-maligned king's hump was the invention of the Stratford-on-Avon Bard. This Quasimodo was only too real, and he needed to apprehend him before he murdered the eighth victim.

In the car on the drive back to New Scotland Yard, Vance was a mixture of infuriated and optimistic. "Listen to this, Sarge, he read through the plastic envelope that he would have to consign to Sabrina, later:

*"A handful of wolves*
*all cream pelts and sloping shoulders*
*appear with girls in red, jaws*

*snapping like capes;*
*with silver spoons the girls eat the air*
*grow teeth the size of axes."*

"Is it just me, or is our Quasimodo getting more literary? What do you make of that?" He read it aloud once more.

The sergeant pursed her lips, frowned and said, "It's full of aggressive imagery and mentions the colour as usual. I like it. I reckon it's from a longer poem, maybe the first verse? Max Wright will find out in an instant!"

"Yes, Max is going to have plenty to do. I'm going to have him work on all our recruitment rejections over the past fifteen years—well, not all, more specifically, those rejected for physical reasons. That should keep him busy for the day!" He beamed at his sergeant. "Thanks to your sharp brain, Brittany!"

# CHAPTER 20

## NEW SCOTLAND YARD, AND TOWER HAMLETS

A MUCH-CHASTENED DS WRIGHT, SMARTING FROM HIS FAILURE TO spot the second title of the artwork, set to work instantly to please his detective inspector. It required only a moment to bring up and print off the poem for him.

"Sir, it's a poem called *Red* by Anne M. Doe Overstreet from her book, *Delicate Machinery Suspended.* There are two more verses. It's a lovely poem but it doesn't shed any more light on our case. Unless you count the mention of *'parting like the sea before Moses'*—because, of course, it was the *Red* Sea."

Vance read the rest of the poem and had to agree on all counts with the sergeant. It was a splendid poem, but it didn't provide further insight into the killer's warped mind.

"Max, I'm giving you a task of incredible importance. I want you to find anything you can about candidates who have received rejections from the Met on physical grounds in the last fifteen, no, let's say, twenty years. Concentrate on those botched on the musculoskeletal assessment. This research could prove to be our big breakthrough, Sarge, so, make it a painstaking operation."

The pale-skinned sergeant's face blushed to the roots of his hair. In a strangled voice, he said, "It's not like me to miss a single detail, sir. This procedure should be straightforward as we digitalised all our records more than twenty years ago. I'm onto it, boss!"

Repentant, Vance put a reassuring hand on the sergeant's shoulder. "You're the best, Max. Everyone's entitled to an occasional slip." With that, he strolled to his office whistling a tune that had been a hit in the previous century. Max smiled and began typing computer commands.

In an amazingly short time, about forty minutes, Max Wright sat back in his chair with a self-satisfied snigger and rolled his shoulder muscles to ease the accumulated tension that accompanied the work of a computer specialist. He reached for the phone and called Vance's office.

"I think I've got him, no, damn it, I'm *sure* I've got him, sir. If you can spare a minute." The smirk grew as he counted, "one, two, three—"

He'd only got as far as eleven when Vance appeared by his desk.

"Why are you counting, Max?"

"I knew you'd be here before I could get to twelve, sir! We've pinned him down. See?" He brought up a profile, complete with a photograph of a person named Arnold Tibbet. Wright scrolled down and halted the script at *Rejected for kyphosis.* The sergeant's finger tapped the screen over those words. "I've checked it out. The disease means the subject's upper vertebrae are more wedge-shaped, and it often occurs in adolescence. Tibbet was only twenty when he tried to enter the Met. With kyphosis, the sufferer becomes hunchback when severe and only roundback when not. I'm prepared to bet that our killer was in the latter condition at twenty, but our medics picked up on it. And look here, sir, the psychic aptitude test revealed extreme intelligence and no evident psychoses."

"We know he's intelligent, too damned clever by half, but he's had time to develop his psychosis. Print off three copies, and I'll take one to our psychologist lady and one to the commissioner. Hang on! Why is that name ringing alarm bells?"

DS Wright looked so smug that Vance was tempted to clip his ear. "Because, sir, a certain Arnold Bissett bought the Harley Davidson in Birmingham, remember?"

"Bloody hell! That's right, the little creep just played around with his surname and handed over the cash! He's our killer, all right. You know what to do, Max. I want everything you can find on this Arnold Tibbet. Also, make a quality copy of his photograph and circulate it to all stations in Greater London. I want him arrested on sight."

Within an hour, Max Wright and his team of three had discovered a birth certificate registered in the Tower Hamlets borough of East London and a Church of England baptism document, thus, showing that their suspect was now a thirty-two-year-old nominal Anglican. He had two brothers and three sisters and was the fifth child of a divorced mother, now deceased. One of the brothers, Anthony, had a criminal record, serving seven years for the same offence of breaking and entering and manslaughter. The other brother, Andrew, with no record, worked as a forecourt attendant at a petrol station in Lansbury. The sisters, all in relationships, appeared to be model citizens with respectable partners.

Surprisingly, DS Wright could find no vehicle licence for Arnold Tibbet at any age. His last known address, however, was in Fern Street in Tower Hamlets. All this information, he passed on to Vance, who immediately conveyed it to his senior officer, Mal Ridgeway.

"You'd better chase up all these leads, Jake. The siblings might take you to him, but the best place to start, in my opinion, is Fern Street. If you need a search warrant, I'll see to it, but get around there first, and if you find him, bring him in for questioning. Have you spoken to Miriam Walker yet?"

"I have, and she's working on a profile for me. She seemed

pretty enthused about the dossier I provided her and promised to get back to me as soon as possible."

"Good, do you think we can take the constables off the supermarket surveillance?"

"No, sir, I'd like to keep them on until we've actually laid hands on the suspect—if you agree."

Ridgeway frowned. He hated having men tied up twiddling their thumbs, but as it was Shepherd's recommendation, he would go along with it—she was rarely wrong. "All right, we'll leave them on it for a few more days."

Vance breathed a sigh of relief, nodded and said, "I'll call Shepherd, and we'll check out the Tower Hamlets address. If we need a warrant, I'll ring you, sir."

"Fine, good luck, Jake. Oh, and take a firearm with you. This blighter's dangerous."

A short time later, Vance and his sergeant were driving towards the East End of London. When they came to Fern Street, he told his driver, "The even numbers are on this side of the road, there's 114, keep going, Brit. Pull up in front of the yellow building. Our address should be there."

They parked, Vance noting the loiterers on the street, and feeling the reassuring presence of the Glock 17 pistol close to his chest. They knocked at the number that Max Wright had furnished where a pregnant woman with a cheerful, pleasant face answered the door.

"Yeah? Can I help you?"

"Police officers, madam," Shepherd, as agreed, spoke because a female had answered their knock. She showed her warrant card, and the detective inspector did likewise. "We have a few questions, may we come in?"

"Sure, but my Davey's at work."

"What does your husband do?"

"My partner, actually, he's a plumber. He has his own firm, employs three others. They'll be out on calls at this time of day. Can I make a pot of tea for you?"

Brittany Shepherd smiled. "That would be lovely, shall we all sit in the kitchen? It's cosier, I always think."

"Oh, okay, why not? I'll put the kettle on."

"Your first child?" The sergeant smiled and stared pointedly at the baby bump.

"Yeah, it's due in ten weeks. It feels like a ruddy footballer!"

The corners of Vance's eyes crinkled very slightly, with him approving of his sergeant's technique for gaining trust. Brittany asked, "It's a boy, is it?"

"Well, no, but there are a lot of women's teams nowadays. I reckon my girl will play for Chelsea!"

All three laughed, and at last, Vance spoke, "There's a lot of money in women's football for those that make the grade, Ms—er—sorry, we didn't catch the name."

"Cummings, Alison. Everyone calls me Ali, though."

"Well, Alison, let me get to the point. I wonder whether you know anyone called Arnold Tibbett?"

Both officers studied the woman's face for a reaction, and they got it. A strong one. Alison Cummings's face displayed aversion; she almost shuddered.

"You mean the weirdo that had this place before us? Don't look at it as it is now, that's all our work. That Tibbet fellow was renting it. My Davey bought it, we've got a mortgage, because he's got his firm. But honestly, Inspector, the place was a pigsty when we moved in. The neighbours said Tibbet was no trouble, except sometimes he played his music loud, though never at night. I don't think he lifted a finger to improve or clean the place. The funny thing is, unlike some folk, he left all the light bulbs and lampshades. I reckon he must have gone to a fully furnished flat from here. Chairs, bed, and all, he left, but Davey tossed the lot in a skip. You couldn't even flog them, they were so crappy."

"I see." Vance smiled encouragingly. "Well, Alison, you've done the place up real nicely. Now, I don't suppose this Tibbet left a forwarding address, did he?"

"No, nothing like that. And the funny thing is, there's been no mail at all for him. At first, one or two bills addressed to his landlord, the fellow we bought the house off. He's a nice enough bloke, called Stan Meadows. I can give you his address if you like?"

They sipped their tea and discovered that Alison Cummings had never met or even seen Tibbet. She'd only had hearsay to go on, so they took Meadows's address and phone number and decided to chat with Alison's neighbours first. They didn't explain their interest in Tibbet to their host, not wishing to alarm the expectant mother.

Outside her home, Shepherd said, "Nice woman, but no help to us, sir."

"Quite! We'd better try the neighbours, but I doubt they'll have an address for us."

Vance was right on that score, too. They gleaned from a man who claimed he was off work with bronchitis that Tibbet was *a hunchbacked runt of a fellow who kept himself to himself. Wouldn't even pass the time of day with you.*

Stan Meadows was a little more forthcoming.

"You know, apart from his handicap, he wasn't so bad. Funny thing is though, that he was behind four months with his rent, and I was getting a bit uppity about it when he came around here and, just like that, stuffed the lolly into my hands plus the month's penalty for leaving without notice. When I questioned him about it, he said he'd come into an inheritance and didn't have any more money problems."

"That's interesting—an inheritance? Did he leave a forwarding address with you?"

Stan Meadows scratched his head. "Let me see, um, no. But he did say that he was moving upmarket. Going to live by the river, he said. By which I guessed it might be Chelsea or Fulham. He mentioned that he'd have a lovely view of the river from his *luxury* apartment. Fair bragging, he was. I must say," he looked shrewdly from under bushy eyebrows at the detective inspector,

"I wondered if there was a word of truth in it. But the wad of cash he handed over made me think it might be true."

"Thank you, sir. You have no idea how helpful you've been. Have a good day."

"Er, Inspector, might I ask why you're interested in Arnold Tibbet?"

"Sorry, sir, it's an ongoing inquiry, and I'm not at liberty to discuss the matter."

They left a very perplexed property dealer in their wake. Both officers felt very satisfied with the last interview, at least.

"It all ties in, sir," Shepherd said. "If he bought a luxury riverside apartment in Fulham, well, that's near the supermarket we're watching as well as being central to the murder zones."

Vance nodded slowly. "Our next step is to contact all property developers of riverside apartments in the Fulham and Chelsea areas, Brit. They can't have sold or rented too many in the last year and the physical appearance of our suspect will reveal him straight away."

"You're right. Unless, of course, he moved in disguised as a female with long, blonde hair. Either way, we'll get the swine!"

"Max can give us the rundown on the developers, and then we'll be in business."

"Just one thing, sir."

"What?"

"Our killer might strike again before we can arrest him. I have a theory about his next move."

"Come on then, Watson. Let's hear it!"

"Don't go kidding yourself that you're Sherlock Holmes, DI Jacob Vance! But remember where Tibbet was collecting the poisonous berries?"

"I do."

"Well, sir, that's slap bang in the middle of the sky-blue area on the artwork. It's the only colour in *Quasimodo* that he hasn't used yet."

"And you've done your homework, I suppose, Brit?"

"Yes, sir, I'll bet next month's salary that the next killing will be in Skyport Drive in West Drayton."

"That complicates matters."

"How's that, then?"

"I thought we could identify his dwelling and arrest him first, but you could be right. I've learnt not to ignore your intuitions, Sarge. I don't want the eighth victim on my conscience. Let's mobilise our troops to West Drayton. I'll go along with your bet that Tibbet staked out his killing ground on his berry-picking expedition. Let's get back to headquarters, set Max to work and inform Big Mal of our plan."

# CHAPTER 21

## WEST DRAYTON AND NEW SCOTLAND YARD

Detective Sergeant Shepherd was wrong on one important detail, the murderer had not come to Skyport Drive West Drayton to kill but to reconnoitre. His first attempt had been disrupted by the prying elderly lady who had caused his abrupt flight from the area. The previous evening, out of a general sense of dissatisfaction about his choice of killing ground, he had almost aborted the operation. When incidents such as that of the old woman occurred, they created a superstitious unease in him. Secondly, he had not found a street name with the specific wording *sky-blue* in any part of London. The four areas depicted in that colour in *Quasimodo* restricted his choice of location to them, too. He continued with his initial decision out of laziness. With the effort of research into the local transport done and a little knowledge of the area established, he proceeded. Skyport at least contained the keyword sky, but no mention of blue. He had found a wonderful piece by Lord Byron called *Dream,* but the blue-sky reference was tucked away in the long verse, to his annoyance. He needed a shorter poem to stimulate the police minds. Surely they lacked the necessary concentration for Byron. All these minor irritations unsettled him, making him cagier than usual. Now, his long bus journey was coming to an end, for unless he was mistaken, this was the area of the Heathrow Sheraton. The number 350 had brought him to Hatch Lane, and so, he alighted. Disorientated, he looked around, his eardrums buzzing from the traffic thrumming by on the nearby Colnbrook By-Pass. A fifty-fifty choice left him turning right, a mistake he realised when he came to the London Hong Kong Restaurant, which he had noticed on the map when researching the area.

It was a pleasant slip, he thought, enabling him to admire the twin statues of ancient Chinese warriors kitted out in armour and standing menacingly in the forecourt. Having photographed one on his phone, he turned around and headed back past the bus stop, noting the semi-detached suburban nature of the area. He marched beyond Zealand Avenue, another reference point, and gazed at the expected open countryside beyond, smirking at a hedgerow ablaze with bright red bryony berries.

He had reached the place where he needed to cross the road and find an entrance into the complex of wholesalers and retailers that made up a semi-industrial development off Skyport Drive. Finding an open gateway, he wandered in among the white-fronted buildings.

*What a shame they're not painted sky-blue!*

He could not shake off his uncharacteristic negativity. Gazing around, he calculated that this was not by any means the ideal location for murder unless the situation improved in the evening at a late-closing time; maybe he could catch someone tardily locking up. An after-dusk surveillance vigil might be in order, he told himself.

*Damn it! Such a long bus ride for nothing!*

On frustrating days like this, he longed to break the monotony by at least planning a killing—was even that to be denied him? Spotting a sign opposite the corner of the complex announcing *Simple Snacks,* he decided to grab a bite to eat and a coffee. With this in mind, he wandered towards the food van.

His alert brain warned him that there were too many people standing around doing nothing except trying to look inconspicuous for a Wednesday morning in a functioning business complex.

*Cops, damn it! Are they on to me? What can I do? If I turn to run, it would be an invitation to pursuit. Maybe they aren't here for me? I will continue as if there's nothing wrong.*

"Did you see him hesitate and look around, sir? I think he's on to us, but he's not doing anything stupid. I think he's heading for the snack van, see he's about to cross the road."

"You're right, Brit. He's aware police surround him. We'll let him approach the snack bar and then move in. He'll have no escape, but be warned, he's as deadly as a King Cobra," Vance said.

"Yeah, but unlike his poor victims, we'll be ready for the slightest false move. That's why I brought my taser. Just look at the weedy little shit. Look at his hunchback! How can someone like that have killed seven people, to our knowledge?"

"Inside that unfortunate frame dwells a superior intelligence. Let's not forget that in the beginning, the poor blighter had the same motivation as us to join the Met, Brit. How he came to change into a monster isn't our concern, which is to stop him striking again, so be on the alert."

"Let me be the one to cuff him, sir. I'd love an excuse to inflict a little *neuromuscular incapacitation* as the training manual so glibly calls tasering."

"Your wish is granted! Look, he's definitely going towards the food van." He pressed a button and spoke into the radio, "All units on standby, nobody to move unless otherwise instructed, over and out." Gesturing to his sergeant, he said, "Come on, Brit, we're moving in."

A glance at the fixed installation food van, with its bright red lettering *Simple Snacks,* made Vance sigh with relief. Even if the suspect resisted arrest, it would not be as difficult as confronting him in an enclosed space. The two officers saw the diminutive figure with a curvature of the spine reach up to hand money to the friendly assistant inside the van. The killer held a cheeseburger in his left hand, whilst the man was pouring a coffee into a polystyrene cup.

Vance's finger rested lightly on the Glock's trigger, while Shepherd's taser, clutched in her right hand, was hanging parallel to her thigh. The detective inspector nodded to his sergeant without uttering a word. She moved quickly to stand behind Tibbet.

"Arnold Tibbet?" she said. "Metropolitan Police. Don't do anything sudden or foolish as you are in the sights of trained marksmen."

The hunchback, no taller, she judged, than five-foot two, turned slowly to face her.

"Are you talking to me, officer?" he asked, licking mayonnaise from the corner of his mouth ostentatiously. "Here, have you got a paper napkin, mate?" he called up to the astounded assistant who was enthralled by the scene playing out before him. Vance nodded permission to the trader, who handed down three clean napkins. The suspected murderer muttered his thanks and wiped his mouth. "Are you going to let me finish this, copper?" He waved the cheeseburger at the sergeant. "I paid good money for it."

"Yes, but be quick about it," intervened Vance, "then, we'll be taking you to Scotland Yard for questioning."

"Shouldn't you show me some identification? How do I know you're genuine police?"

"Clever little know-all, aren't you?" Shepherd growled. "Don't give me an excuse to use this on you." She raised the taser very slightly.

"A taser, is it? Here, mate, you're a witness to fascist intimidation. Can't a man enjoy a peaceful burger, nowadays?" He took a ravenous bite out of the burger and continued speaking indistinctly with his mouth full.

"Look here, sweetie, I know my rights, and one of them is to see your I.D."

Shepherd fumbled for her warrant card, never taking her eyes off their quarry. Aggressively, she thrust it close to Tibbet's nose.

"Congratulations on being a police officer. I suppose they accept anyone nowadays."

Shepherd seized her opportunity. "Bear a grudge, don't you, Tibbet? Because the Met didn't admit you, right?"

"You ought to know, Miss Plod, that I'm about as misogynist as Noddy, ha-ha."

"And about as tall! Just that this isn't Toyland, it's the real world, Arnold. Here, let me pass you your coffee." She reached up and took the cup from the stainless-steel counter, then, faking a trip, launched the scalding coffee down the front of his pale-green sweatshirt.

"Oh dear, I'm so sorry, how clumsy of me!"

He yelped and tugged the steaming material away from his chest. Vance was smirking, and Shepherd added, I was only trying to help, I mean with you being so short and the counter so high."

"Bitch! I never forgive or forget an insult. Have a care!"

"Threatening a police officer in the execution of her duty?"

"*Execution*, yeah, yeah! I love that term."

"Shut up and throw the remains of your burger in the bin. You won't starve where you're going. Now!" She raised the taser and glared.

Sensing her desire to tase him, Tibbet obeyed, reluctantly, in exaggerated slow motion.

"Kneel on the ground, hands behind your back. That's fine!" In a flash, she had him cuffed and hauled him by the bracelets to his feet. "Start walking that way!" She directed him across the road to a large car park where many employees' vehicles were parked. Vance remained behind a moment to have a quiet word with the *Simple Snacks* employee.

Several other police cars had drawn up close to Shepherd by the time Vance reached them. He gave the drivers a cheerful thumbs up and received grins in return. The Metropolitan Police had their man, or so they thought, on Skyport Drive, that Wednesday morning. A small convoy of police cars returned to New Scotland Yard. Vance had judged the person of Tibbet an insufficient menace to warrant calling for an armoured prison vehicle. Shepherd activated the childproof locking mechanism—as per standard procedure. Since their suspect sat in sullen silence for the whole trip to the Embankment, the inspector's decision proved correct. Besides, as extra security, there were other police cars immediately behind them.

In the controlled surroundings of Interview Room 1, Tibbet was formally cautioned, again, according to procedure, and availed himself of the statutory phone call. He forewent a call to a solicitor, insisting that he wished to speak with his sister, Bethany. Waiving an offer of privacy in front of the two arresting officers, he explained to her the circumstances he found himself in and reassured her that he would soon be at liberty because, as she knew, he had committed no crime. Shepherd and Vance looked on aghast at his audacity, but each, as an experienced police officer, knew that as yet they had no concrete evidence against their suspect. His personal belongings did not produce the murder weapon as they had hoped. Vance had sent out a forensics team to scour the route taken by Tibbet from the moment he had become aware of the police presence. The detective held out little hope that the killer had tossed away the syringe because he had not taken his eyes off him and had seen no such suspicious gesture at the time. But he could not neglect any possibilities.

The official questioning began with the standard recording and Vance following Tibbet's eyes to the opaque glass pane high up in the wall.

"Yes, of course, one-way glass, we're being watched, sir. It's also a guarantee for you that everything is done by the book. Now, please tell us your full name and address."

"You know my name, as you've used it already. Anyway, it's Arnold Tibbet. As for my address, I live with my sister Bethany, but you'll have to find out for yourselves because I don't want you disturbing her sooner than necessary."

"If you refuse to cooperate with our inquiries, Mr Tibbet, it will go into the official police report and may worsen your situation at your trial."

Tibbet laughed. "You aren't too quick on the uptake Detective Inspector. I've already explained that you have arrested the wrong person; I am innocent of the charges."

"Do you deny possession of a Harley Davidson 883 motorcycle?"

"I don't have and never have had a motorcycle, not even a driving licence, Inspector. That should be easy for you to verify. Bethany loves motorcycles, maybe you should ask her."

"Oh, we will as soon as we find her. Do you have other brothers or sisters?"

"You know I do, but I'm cooperating. Let's see, two brothers, Anthony and Andrew, and four sisters, Beryl, Brenda, Beatrice, and Bethany."

Shepherd intervened for the first time, she smiled at Tibbet, and he glared at her. "It's curious that all the male names begin with A and the females with B."

"Curious, copper? It's bloody mad, that's what it is." His face contorted, and his eyes glinted madly. "Our mum was a bloody nutter. She always said she preferred boys and that we were Series A and the girls Series B. What the whore should have said was that she preferred *men*. I had more *uncles* when I was growing up than you've had hot dinners! No wonder our dad upped and scrammed when I was three; he couldn't stand living with the harlot a day longer. I never did find out what happened to him, not that I care. Anthony, Beryl and Brenda were probably his kids. I reckon the rest of us are bastards. Anyway, mustn't speak ill of the dead—good riddance to her—she'll be burning in hell."

Vance couldn't prevent himself from glancing at the opaque glass. To show that he was quick-witted, Tibbet said, "I'll bet you've got a shrink up there analysing my every word. Well, let me tell you, the Met made a bad mistake with me. It's not as if this, he shrugged his shoulders, stops this," he lifted both index fingers and bowed his head towards them, "from working. Your lot turned down a potent brain. I'd have made a better detective than that arrogant piece of skirt you've got as commissioner, I'm telling you."

Vance quickly seized on this statement. "What makes you say our commissioner is arrogant, Mr Tibbet?"

"You must have heard her inaugural speech, Inspector."

"Is that why you sent her that letter?"

"What letter? I don't know what you're talking about."

Vance stood up. "Before I bring this session to a close, and we'll talk again tomorrow, Mr Tibbet, I should warn you that we have enough physical evidence against you to lock you away for the rest of your life. My advice would be for you to think very carefully, this evening. A sincere confession might persuade the judge to reduce your sentence considerably. Think about it, sir."

"I think a lot, Inspector, and I think that you've got nothing on me because I have done nothing. You are barking up the wrong tree. The sad thing is that you've got so near to the truth and yet you can't see it! That's where someone like me on the force would have been such an asset." Again, the contorted features and wild glint in the eyes accompanied his words.

Vance declared the session officially closed and switched off the recorder.

Two burly officers removed the pathetic figure, whom they dwarfed, to a holding cell. Ridgeway came into the interview room.

"Damn it, Jake, you've brought in some kind of poisoned

midget, no pun intended, with a very high opinion of himself. Tomorrow, though, he must have a solicitor in here with him."

"Yes, I confess I stalled over that because despite what I said, we've got very little solid evidence against him. That's why I'm on my way to Max's team. I need two or three key pieces of information. Don't worry, old buddy—sorry, I mean, sir, I *will* hark back to our days together against the massed villainy—we will pin him down. It's only a matter of time. We have to, or else, numbers eight and nine will perish.

# CHAPTER 22

## NEW SCOTLAND YARD AND FULHAM, LONDON

On the orders of Vance, Shepherd paid their prisoner an early morning call.

"Good morning, Tibbet; I hope you slept well?"

"I'd have slept better in my own bed at home, copper."

"And where is your home?"

"Wouldn't you like to know, but my lips are sealed."

With a struggle, Shepherd kept the irritation out of her voice. "There's no point in asking whether you're ready to confess, I suppose?"

"None whatsoever, plod."

She snapped, "As you prefer. You'll stay here to give you time to change your mind. Be seeing you then," she couldn't resist, "Noddy."

She walked away and smiled as his expletives reverberated in his cell.

Upstairs, she went straight to the detective inspector. "No joy, sir, he's less collaborative than yesterday."

"As expected, Brit, but I have news for you. Thanks to Max and his team, we have an address for our detainee."

"We do?"

"Yes, and it all fits nicely, but listen to this, Sarge, the development company behind the Riverside apartments at Fulham, sold a luxury flat to joint owners, Arnold Tibbet and Bethany Tibbet. The company confirms that the deeds contain both signatories."

Shepherd frowned, looked puzzled and said, "But didn't we believe that he was lying about Bethany?"

Vance shrugged. "So we did. But it seems that he's telling the truth, and that he lives with his sister. Anyway, we're going to verify the situation, Brit. I'm waiting on a search warrant, then we'll get around to the Riverside complex, and if Bethany is at home, we'll bring her in for questioning, too."

The sergeant was still simmering from her encounter with Arnold Tibbet. "Those flats must cost a fortune, sir; they're luxury apartments overlooking the river. How can a little creep like Tibbet afford a place like that?"

"It's something we have to find out, Brit. But Max and his lads assured me that the transaction was completely legit. Wrighty says there's no trace of recycled money or anything fishy. God knows how he finds out these things, it's beyond me."

"It's his job, sir. Anything else of interest?"

"Ah, yes, in fact, I had a chat with Miriam, our criminologist. She asked for and obtained Mal's permission to interview Tibbet this morning, after which, she should be in a better position to explain what goes on in that potent brain he claims to have."

"I'd opt for *warped* rather than potent, but it'll be interesting, alright. By the way, sir, when we visit his flat, aren't we bound by procedure to take forensics with us?"

Vance picked up the phone and waved the receiver at his sergeant. "I was just about to phone Sabrina when you knocked. I'll do it now."

A rapid conversation ensued, resulting in Dr Markham agreeing to have her team on standby for a call at short notice.

Whilst awaiting the search warrant, Vance settled to organising all the case notes and writing his report of Tibbet's arrest, which included the vain perusal in the Skyport Drive complex for the murder weapon. The lads from forensics had found two syringes, but the local addicts had used both to shoot heroin into their veins and, as usual, dropped them from senseless fingers to the ground.

In the early afternoon, Vance's desk phone rang, and snatching up the receiver, hopefully, he gained confirmation from his senior officer that a search warrant had been issued for the Tibbets's flat. He immediately called Dr Markham and arranged for a lift with forensics for his sergeant and himself.

Vance chatted with Shepherd, who he sensed correctly, was itching to tell him something in the large people carrier.

"Apart from a few errands, sir, I was at something of a loose end before lunch, so I went over to Max Wright and pestered him about this Bethany Tibbet. The curious thing is that whereas he's been able to compile something of a profile on the other brothers and sisters, he's drawn a blank on Bethany. In his words: *it's like she doesn't exist.* Well, that got me thinking, sir. Remember when we discussed the possibility of Tibbet dressing as a female? Well, I wouldn't put it past the little freak."

"Steady on, Brit. We have to keep an open mind. Think about what he told us about his mother. If all he said was true, there might well be no birth and baptism records for her. It's amazing if she was such a slut that she bothered to obtain them for the others. Didn't Tibbet say or imply that Bethany was the youngest?"

"With Tibbet, nothing's as it seems."

"Indeed, but it appears we've arrived at our destination. You might be staring at Bethany within minutes."

That notion proved wrong because nobody answered the door of the Tibbets's flat. Vance, undaunted, to everyone's surprise, produced the apartment keys. "Among Tibbet's items on arrest," he explained. "No need to break in, lads," he grinned. Dr Markham hauled him back as he was about to enter without protective suiting.

"It's imperative today, Jacob."

"Of course, Doc, I wasn't thinking." Donning the whites, Vance followed the forensics team into the flat. Distracted, the sheer luxury of the dwelling took his breath away, as did the view over the river. The ever-practical Shepherd broke into his appreciation of the apartment.

"You're going to need the keyring again, sir." Her voice came muffled through the plastic visor.

She pointed at the desk, and he understood. The top drawers on either side were locked. They opened with the same unsophisticated key, a two-inch shaft, ending in a plain rectangular bit.

*It would open with any spade-end screwdriver,* Vance thought, before his brain went into overdrive upon finding a treasure trove of evidence. He could feel the electric excitement from Brittany at his side. They bagged up the transparency traced from the Lapique painting, the map of central London with its crosses marking the murder locations from M1 to M9. A small notebook containing the titles of poems and songs familiar to them up to and including M7.

"We've nailed the bastard this time, good and proper, Sarge."

A call from the kitchen had him scurrying in the awkward foot coverings of the all-in-one suit to Dr Markham. She had found a container with suspicious fishy contents.

"We'll have to analyse this in the lab, Jacob, but I'm almost certain that this is the TTX poison. Let's see if we can discover how he extracts it to make an injectable substance."

The following two hours produced a series of revelations, not least among them, another notebook detailing the deadly procedure, a vial full of the liquid and a collection of syringes of various sizes and capacities.

Tibbet's wardrobe provided another surprise. It divulged both male and female clothing and shoes. There were also two wigs, one with long straight blonde hair and the other wavy auburn. The forensics team lifted fingerprints throughout the flat, but the ones Vance was interested in: on the poison container, acetate sheets, map, vial, and syringes, would have to wait until the laboratory examination. Again, they bagged up the evidence for further study at headquarters. The police believed they left with enough material to put Tibbet away for the rest of his life, so they drove away from the apartment in a much happier frame of mind than when they'd arrived.

"No Bethany, eh, sir?"

"No, and the wigs would seem to point to Arnold impersonating, but until we have his fingerprints, we can't be sure."

"Oh, come on, sir, we've got him for sure. I can feel it in my bones."

"You were the one who said with Tibbet *nothing is as it seems*. I hope you're right, Brit. I always err on the side of caution—a trait you still need to acquire, Sarge, if you want to become an inspector."

"Fat chance of that! I'll probably blow my career by tasering the little freak to death!"

Vance decided it was better to leave talk of promotion aside for the moment.

The next few hours, he knew, would be a tortuous wait on forensics. Only fingerprint evidence, at this stage, would nail Tibbet to the crimes. He wrote up the report of the apartment search in the meantime, detailing their findings and referring to the forensic dossier that would be attached. He hadn't quite finished when a knock on the door disturbed him.

The psychologist, Miriam Walker, asked for a few minutes of his time. Vance willingly accommodated her, eager to learn anything about the detained Arnold Tibbet.

"It was like a game of chess, this morning Detective Inspector—"

"Call me, Jacob, Ms Walker, we're on equal terms here."

"Oh, yes, it's Miriam, then. As I was saying, *er*, Jacob, like a chess match with him in the role of a Grand Master. It took me a long time to break through his defences, but if you'll forgive the metaphor, the white queen swept through—"

Vance smiled, appreciating her humorous style, especially a *white queen* for a decidedly black lady psychologist. Her eyes twinkled as if reading his mind. "Well, he had to be the black pieces, Jacob, going by the colour of his heart, but after the last hour with him, I was feeling sorry for the poor man."

"We're talking about a serial killer, Miriam."

"I know. But listen, what he went through in childhood explains but doesn't excuse anything. I believe him when he says his mother was a strumpet. It fits. His father walked out when he was three, and he had no worthwhile male role model. His elder brother was a minor delinquent until he committed his big mistake, involuntarily killing the victim of one of his burglaries. His eldest sister, Beryl, the only sibling to show him affection, upped and left home at sixteen when he was five, unable to stand the strain of substituting her mother and looking after six kids."

"*Six*, are you sure he said six?"

"Yes, why do you ask?"

Vance frowned. "Well, six would mean that Bethany exists."

"Have you a reason to doubt it? Bethany is his favourite sister. If anything, he looks up to her more than Beryl, the eldest. But if you suspect that he suffers from schizophrenia, you'd be right. Most definitely, he hears and communicates with voices in his head. With me, he addressed a Lord Robert as if he were in the room. There's an explanation for it, Jacob."

"Go on." The DI was increasingly fascinated by the character they'd arrested.

"Arnold told me that one of the many stepfathers who passed through had *interfered* with him and with Bethany, and that's why he has a close link with her, certainly protective. When pressed on what interference, he became agitated, and we had to restrain him. He's a deeply disturbed individual, Jacob. He ranted on about paedophiles and can recite chapter and verse from that outrageous organisation that enjoyed a period of public credibility, the Paedophile Information Exchange, how he hates them, Jacob! He's also outraged with the House of Lords and its behaviour regarding the European Court of Human Rights in the case *Z v United Kingdom* in 2001, in which this Lord Robert behaved as Tibbet wished. Since then, it appears that he's made him into a kind of mentor or hero, or both, in his troubled mind. During our interview, it seemed that Lord Robert was advising him not to be so forthcoming. It was almost as if this peer of the realm had a grudge against the police. But, of course, that's part of Tibbet's illness."

"Tell me more about that, Miriam."

"Arnold Tibbet certainly suffers from delusional disorders. There are various types, Inspector *-er-* Jacob, among them, he shows every sign of the grandiose syndrome. The individual displays an over-inflated sense of worth, power, knowledge, or identity. The person might believe he or she has a great talent or has made an important discovery. Then there's the persecutory delusion, with this type of delusional disorder the sufferers convince themselves that they, or someone close to them, are being mistreated or that someone is spying on them or planning to harm them. It's not uncommon for people with this kind of malady to make repeated complaints to legal authorities."

"That's very interesting, Miriam. I think we've seen clear signs of both up to now, but tell me, what triggers this condition?"

"Medical opinion is divided, but evidence suggests that it can be triggered by stress. This theory ties in very neatly with Tibbet's circumstances. Paedophile interference, but also the development of his kyphosis—the hunchback condition—and schizophrenia tend to develop in adolescence."

"Fascinating, but would this necessarily lead to him becoming a serial killer?"

"Not necessarily, but the combination of the grandiose and persecutory delusions *is* somewhat disturbing, Jacob."

"Now, a fundamental question, Miriam, is it possible that this

Bethany is a figment of our killer's imagination, just like Lord Robert?"

"Well, I'm not an authority on schizophrenia, but all my studies to date would suggest not. In every single case I've read, there has only ever been one voice unless you consider those ambiguous cases where demons frequent the head of the sufferer —in those circumstances, some believe you need an exorcist, not a psychiatrist."

"Mmm, and what about genetics? Could another family member display similar delusional behaviour to Arnold? Let's say, Bethany?"

"The fact that delusional disorder is more common in people who have family members with delusional disorder or schizophrenia suggests there might be a genetic factor involved. As with other mental disorders, some believe that a tendency to develop delusional disorder might be passed on from parents to their children. It's a fact that the Tibbet siblings have the same mother. We don't know what she suffered from, but her promiscuity suggests some mental instability. By Arnold's account, we know equally that the husband was not his father and that the mother wasn't too selective about whom she bedded, including at least, one paedophile."

"Miriam, you have been most helpful. Our case against Tibbet would seem to rest on forensic evidence at this point. But if that confirms our suspicions, be sure that you'll be called as a technical witness in court."

The psychologist's very white teeth flashed, and she rose. "My pleasure, Jacob, you're a very attentive listener, by the way. I appreciate that."

"Only when the speaker is worth listening to, Ms Walker. Thanks, once again."

Vance sat back and rubbed his temples in a circular motion. This case had been tricky from the start. And maybe that explained the sensation that nothing was what it seemed with Arnold Tibbet. They were on the verge of solving the case, yet he felt unaccountably pessimistic. However, something was pressing. He called Shepherd and ordered her to go to the Riverside Apartments development company to interview the people who had witnessed the deeds of sale of the Tibbets's flat. He needed to verify the existence of Bethany.

# CHAPTER 23

## FULHAM AND NEW SCOTLAND YARD.

At the real estate developer's office Shepherd's critical eye tore the young receptionist apart. The police officer, something of a stunner according to her colleagues, admitted to herself that she was overharsh. Instinctively, she disliked heavy makeup and, if pressed, would have bet a sizeable sum that those lips were not natural. Finally, she disapproved of tattoos on women unless they were unobtrusive and pretty. The dragon snarling down the girl's left arm met neither criterion.

The receptionist laid her phone back in place and her permanently pouting mouth informed Shepherd, "Ms Wilson will see you now. Please come with me." She sashayed from behind her shining steel and glass desk and clicked the way on perilously high heels along a corridor adorned with large photographs of the modern architecture that the company traded in. Some of the shots featured stunning sunsets over the Thames. Shepherd thought the pictures much more interesting than the swinging rump sheathed in a tight-enough-to-split miniskirt that abruptly came to a halt in front of a mahogany door with a polished brass nameplate at eye-line level. The young woman knocked, waited politely, then opened the door and gestured the sergeant in most correctly, saying, "Ms Wilson, DS Shepherd, Metropolitan Police, to see you." The police officer's opinion of the receptionist went up several notches for her having got her name and rank correct.

"Please take a seat," said a bright and smiling Melanie Wilson. "You won't be offended if I say I love your hairstyle, will you?"

"Thank you. You know, I think it would suit your type of face, too, MS Wilson."

"Oh, please call me Mel—everyone does. Who's your hairdresser?"

Several minutes of chitchat ended with Shepherd giving the estate agent—her correct title was property development manager—her hairdresser's visiting card.

"I'll visit her and tell her that I want a DS Shepherd cut! But, hey! You didn't come here to discuss hairstyles. What can I do for you, Detective Sergeant?"

"It's about the place you sold to Arnold and Bethany Tibbet, one of the Riverside Apartments, some time ago."

"Oh, yes? I remember them. Let me see that would have been towards the back end of last year. Just a moment, I'll get the file." She rose, pulled open a drawer of a filing cabinet, and her forefinger ran along to the letter T. "Here it is." She removed a plain manila folder. "I hope you're not going to tell me there are problems with the money provenance, DS Shepherd?"

"No, nothing like that. The money is legitimate. My inquiries are connected with another matter that doesn't involve your company in any way. My senior officer sent me to check out a couple of matters linked with another case. We thought you might be able to help, Mel."

"Well, anything I can do." She smiled brightly, but her expression grew serious. "They were peculiar, now I come to think of it."

Shepherd latched on to the comment eagerly. "In what way?"

"I remember having difficulty with their appointment to sign the deeds. You see, up to that point, I'd only had dealings with Arnold Tibbet, a curious little man. I'm no giant, Detective, but

I'll swear I'm taller than he. I guess it must be due to the poor fellow's deformity. Am I allowed to call it that? It sounds so politically incorrect. I do apologise."

"Not at all, Mel, facts are facts, and I'm at a loss to supply a better term, I'm afraid. But please go on."

"Well, as I said, he was so polite and sure of himself, and it seemed to me that money was no problem as he accepted even my more extravagant suggestions for extras without hesitation. Frankly, I was delighted with the deal from our point of view. Just that when it came to signing, I fixed an appointment, and for the first time, he created problems."

"Really?"

"Yes, he explained to me that his sister," she opened the folder and checked, "yes, Bethany, was a nurse and with the pandemic, she was run off her feet. He went on at length to explain how the money was his, but that he didn't want Bethany to be left with nothing if anything happened to him." She smiled and met the detective's gaze. "That was thoughtful of him, wasn't it? He appeared to admire his sister, almost as if she were a saint, I suppose."

"When did they fix the appointment to come in together?"

"Oh, but they didn't. He persuaded me that so long as they each signed in front of me, that was legally binding, which is true, of course. So, he signed there and then and fixed an appointment for Bethany the next day."

"Let me get this straight, Mel. Is it correct to say that you never saw them together and haven't since?"

The developer frowned and considered. "Now you mention it, that's true. I've only caught a glimpse of Bethany once since she signed, and I could swear that I saw her drive past once on a large motorcycle."

"A Harley Davidson?"

"Oh, I'm sorry, I don't know a thing about motorbikes." She giggled. "It was big and black, though, if that helps."

"What was your impression of Bethany when she came in to sign?"

Melanie's brow crinkled, and her eyebrows drew together in concentration.

"She was a little odd. She wore a face mask, yet she was still in uniform. Queer, don't you think? I mean, coming from the hospital and still wearing the nurse's hat and cape, but taking the precaution of face covering?"

"Mmm. What can you tell me about her appearance?"

"Let me see. She had attractive long blonde hair, and I was a little surprised that she hadn't tied it up under the bonnet. She must have let it down after work. She wore mascara and grey eyeshadow. Pretty eyes, they reminded me of her brother's. He has nice eyes, too. But his are brown. Hers were a stunning blue colour."

"Are you quite certain of that, Mel?"

"Oh yes. I always take particular notice of details. I love people-watching."

Brittany smiled and took advantage. "What else? Was Bethany tall, short?"

"Medium-height, but she was wearing high heels—another oddity, you'd expect a nurse to wear sensible flat shoes. Like the hair down, I ascribed it to her dressing up a little for our appointment."

"I see. She didn't suffer from the same ailment, the hunch-back, as her brother, then?"

"I don't think so, I'd have noticed, but she was wearing her nurse's cape."

Shepherd nodded thoughtfully. "A couple of things, Mel. Can you show me the two signatures, please?"

"Of course." The manager flipped over some pages, then spun the folder around and pushed it towards the police officer.

Arnold's signature was neat, mature, and confident, with bold crossings and a flourish on the second letter t. Bethany's was altogether more rounded, like a schoolgirl's effort. The two signatures were quite different. "And the last thing, Mel. Is there an optician's near here?"

After obtaining Mel's consent, she took a photograph on her phone of the signatures and memorised directions to the opticians before thanking the property manager fulsomely for her help and taking her leave.

Sometime later, she reported her findings to Vance.

"Tibbet's a crafty sod, boss. As slippery as an eel! Melanie Wilson, the property developer, never saw him and his so-called sister together. That's because Bethany doesn't exist. He even went to the trouble of buying blue contact lenses to cover his brown irises. He was too crafty to do that in the nearest opticians—they'd have remembered his hump. Here, look at the signatures, he's made them look completely different. Also, he wore a nurse's cape—" she related the whole creation of the alibi. "So, you see, sir, Bethany Tibbet only exists in the mind of that warped weirdo."

"Now you're back, Brit, I can ring Dr Markham. She's got our results, and since she described them as *disconcerting*, I told her I'd prefer to wait and have you with me. Two minds being better than one, and all that."

"Yeah, thanks, boss."

"OK, I'll just give her a bell, and we'll go to forensics together."

That done, they set off from Vance's office and took the lift to the basement area where Sabrina Markham had her laboratory. In the confined space, the inspector smiled tightly at his sergeant.

"What?"

"I want you to keep an open mind, Brit."

"Come on, boss, he's as guilty as hell! He's killed seven people and planned two more, and he's taking us for a ride! Well, he doesn't fool me!"

"Is that what you call an open mind, Sarge?"

Before she could reply, the lift juddered to a halt and, by

contrast, the doors slid apart smoothly. She was about to speak when Vance warned her, "Keep quiet and listen. Leave any objections to me, Brit. At least, humour me on that, please?"

"Yeah, OK then."

Dr Markham greeted them with a troubled expression. With a show of concern, she said,

"You're not going to like this, detectives."

"Come on, Sabrina, spit it out!"

The Chief of Forensics looked grim, shook her head and said, "It's an enigma. Arnold Tibbet's fingerprints, as you'd expect, are everywhere inside the flat except where you want them to be, Jacob."

"Do you mean that he's wiped every incriminating item in the apartment clean of prints?"

"It would be easier for you if that were the case, Inspector, but it isn't."

"What are you saying, Doc?"

"I'm saying that there's a second set of prints on every incriminating article—the poison container, by the way, I can confirm it's TTX in the form of pufferfish entrails—and on the syringe and acetate sheet, and so on. Come over here. I'll show you. She switched on and tilted an anglepoise lamp over a set of fingerprints. Look, these are Arnold's taken on arrest the other day, and these are the others on our objects of interest. You can see that they are different and don't correspond to Arnold Tibbet's. I can say though, with certainty, that there's familiarity."

"Hang on, Doc, are you saying that members of the same family have similar fingerprints?"

"Absolutely. It's a scientific fact, Jacob. Pattern types are often genetically inherited, but the individual details that make a fingerprint unique are not. Not even identical twins have the same friction ridge skin and arrangement."

"Bloody hell! So that means that someone else in the family handled the murder weapon, not Arnold."

"It looks that way, I'm afraid. Would you like me to go into more detail?"

"Damned right, I would, Doc. Not that I doubt your professional judgement for a moment."

Brittany Shepherd snorted and glared at the fingerprints bathed in the lamplight.

"There are three major pattern types: a whorl, loop, or arch. The important thing to remember, detectives, is that an individual cannot be identified by pattern type alone. The examiner must look at the next level of detail to make an identification, the specific path of ridges and the breaks or forks in the ridges, known to us as *minutiae*. Creases, incipient ridges, and the shapes of the ridge edges are also useful for identification. Now, detectives, with that information, look carefully again and compare the prints. See, the pattern is familiar, but the ridges and creases do not correspond. On this basis, Arnold Tibbet is in the clear."

Brittany Shepherd remembered her boss's warning and bit her tongue. Instead, Jacob Vance asked, "So, how does the family thing work, Sabrina?"

"Well, the study of FRS—sorry, friction ridge skin—is called *dermatoglyphics* and shows a strong correlation between the inheritance of fingerprint pattern and the overall size, shape and spacing of the ridges. As I said, the identifying ridge features are not inheritable, which is what makes the fingerprint unique. And the answer to why, detectives, lies in the mother's womb. I'll be brief. It's a question of the timing of foetal development, but it's a complex argument. You'll find it in the dossier under *volar pad development*. I can sum up by saying that you are more likely to share pattern type with your family members than an unrelated individual, but your identifying FRS features will always be unique."

"Well, Sabina, thank you for turning our case on its head! It looks like Bethany Tibbet is our chief suspect. But where the hell is she?"

"She doesn't exist!" Shepherd muttered, but Vance caught it.

"Damn it, Brittany, you heard Dr Markham. You've seen the proof with your own eyes. Not even *you* can deny the scientific evidence."

"Nothing's as it seems with Tibbet, sir. I don't know how he did it, but he's taking us for an almighty ride!"

The forensics expert held up a hand. "I'm sorry you've taken it so badly, Brittany, but if I take the stand under oath, I'd have to swear that Arnold Tibbet had never touched the poison or the weapon," Sabrina Markham said.

"Yeah, you're right, of course, Doc," the sergeant said. "It's just that I can't ignore my gut feeling that he's guilty. Besides," she looked challengingly at her senior officer, "why all this palaver with the *Quasimodo* picture and all those poems and songs if it's Bethany who's the killer? He's the one with the hump and the massive grudge against the Met, unless he's brainwashed her. But I beg you not to release him. He's our murderer, sir."

"We can't hold him much longer, Brit. I can probably obtain a few more days custody, but you, *we,* will have to get a confession, or he'll soon fly as free as a bird.

# CHAPTER 24

NOTHING WOULD SHAKE SHEPHERD'S CONVICTION THAT ARNOLD Tibbet was the serial killer and, despite the scientific evidence to the contrary, Vance found he could not cast away years of trusting his sergeant's intuition. With this faith governing his deliberations, he successfully negotiated an extension to Tibbet's detention.

"We can hold onto Tibbet for another ninety-six hours, Sarge," he told Shepherd.

"Four days should be enough to nail him good and proper, boss."

"We have to do everything correctly. That's why I want to eliminate the other siblings before we put the squeeze on Tibbet. I want you to visit the females, take their fingerprints and question them about Bethany. I'll deal with Andrew Tibbet. He'll be at work in Lansbury. Anthony is no problem because he's now five years into his prison sentence and can't have been involved in the murders. Get the women's addresses from Max, Brit. Don't look so miserable, it's part of a plan. Once we've eliminated them, as I hope we will, I think I know what to do with our murderous little hunchback."

"Fair enough, boss, but we need to get a move on if we've only four days. I'd rather be interrogating the freak."

"Be aware that if I didn't think you might be right, Tibbet would be at home now. Big Mal took some convincing. So, let's do this my way. And let's keep our insulting epithets within these walls, for our ears only."

"Very good, sir, I'm on my way." She managed not to scowl at the inspector even if, deep down, she believed she was on a fool's errand.

Later that morning, eyeing a semi-detached house with a well-tended garden from the pavement in Greenwich, Shepherd couldn't help but think that Beryl Tibbet had done well for herself. She walked up the drive towards the garage, turned along the crazy-paved path to the front door and rang the bell. The sergeant waited but got no answer, so tried again with the same result. She glanced at her watch, and it showed ten o'clock, so maybe Beryl had gone shopping.

To make sure nobody was at home, she strolled back to the garage and took the path that ran beside it to the rear of the property. At the end of the garage, there was a trellis fence with a gate. Lifting the latch, Shepherd pushed the gate open and entered the back garden. A washing line stretched from a hook in the back wall to a concrete post set in the ground at the end of the lawn. A woman was bending over a large plastic basin, taking out washing and pegging it to the line.

"Ms Tibbet, if I could have a word with you, please."

"Who the hell are you, creeping up on me? Just a minute, I've nearly finished!"

The woman, in her late forties, Shepherd decided, kept herself in good shape, she noted that as she stretched up to peg a nightdress on the line. A pair of striped pyjamas followed before she picked up the empty blue plastic basin by one handle and marched down the garden.

"What are you selling, then?" The pleasant face belied the aggressive tone.

"Metropolitan Police." Shepherd displayed her warrant card. "I'd like a word with you about your sister if you can spare me a few minutes. Can we go indoors?"

"Yeah, if you like." She led the way into a kitchen with a tiled floor, a table and four chairs in the middle of the room and equipped with various electrical appliances. Above all, everything was tidily in place. Beryl Tibbet appeared to be an exemplary housewife. She hurriedly opened a cupboard and pushed the basin out of sight before indicating a chair and saying, "What's this about? You mentioned my sister. Is one of them in trouble?"

"It's about Bethany. We need to locate her."

"Excuse me, officer, my sisters are Brenda and Beatrice Tibbet. Are you sure you've got the right name?"

"Oh, yeah, certain, and it's your Arnold in trouble. He gave me the name of his younger sister, Bethany."

Shepherd could see that the confusion on Beryl's face was genuine. The woman's eyes widened, and she pursed her lips before shrugging and shaking her head. "You see Detective, that's impossible. Arnie was the youngest of us five. If there'd been another sister, I'd have known because I used to look after my younger brothers and sisters—a proper little mam, I was, until I got fed up and left the old bag to do her duty!"

"Yes, I know all about your childhood, Beryl. Can I call you that?"

The woman smiled. "It's my name, so it's fine by me. Bethany is a pretty name, but I'm sorry, Detective, it sounds like our Arnie's up to something if he's telling pork pies."

Shepherd chuckled at the rhyming slang and said, "Do you have kids of your own, Beryl?"

The round face dimpled and took on a gentle expression. "Two girls. They're at school. One's nine and the other's seven. I'm trying to talk Ben out of buying our Julie a pony because I think she should do a few more years at riding school first."

They chatted about Beryl's partner and his job until Shepherd felt it was time to move on.

"There's just one thing, Beryl, if you don't mind. I have to take your fingerprints. Now, don't worry. It's just to eliminate you from our inquiries—a formality—and I can assure you that we will destroy the prints as soon as your innocence is established. That's standard practice."

"Am I under suspicion, then? And what for?"

There was a limit to what Shepherd could explain, but she managed to reassure Beryl and took the set of prints.

Leaving the pleasant leafy suburbs of Greenwich behind, she drove to Hackney, where Brenda and her family lived. Although not as well off as Beryl, this sister also kept a well-run house and, like her elder sister, expressed no knowledge of a Bethany in the family. She, too, cooperated with the fingerprinting.

Beatrice, the youngest sister, lived only a few streets away from Brenda. Shepherd couldn't help thinking that this sister maybe took after her mother when she saw the lounge floor littered with newspapers, discarded a chocolate box and trainers. The ashtray was sorely in need of emptying and the bookshelves were covered in dust. Cat hairs clung to the sofa, and several empty bottles of beer and their crown caps remained as testimony to the previous evening's activities.

"No, I ain't givin' any prints, copper. I ain't done nuffin'. Besides, my Nigel wouldn't want me doing that."

She took a great deal of persuading, but in the end, Shepherd left with the prints and some relief to be in the fresh air. As she drove away, she considered Beatrice's reaction to the existence of Bethany. Unlike the older sisters, Beatrice held out some possibility of another sister. What she said could not be dismissed entirely because it had a certain logic. Given that when Beatrice was little, she was often, in her words, *farmed out* to obliging aunts—she named two: Amy and Kathleen—she said it might have happened that Bethany had been farmed out on a more permanent basis, not coming and going, like herself. Besides, she pointed out, as the youngest, a mere baby, one of the aunts might have been reluctant to send her back to her slatternly mother.

*A bit rich coming from her!* Shepherd thought as she stopped at yet another red traffic light. How likely, she wondered, was it that Beryl and Brenda hadn't mentioned a baby sister, given that she'd asked specifically about another child. No, she didn't believe that Bethany existed outside the head of the monster in custody. The sooner they could look at these prints, the better. But what if there was a match? That would mean the killer was one of the women she had interviewed this morning. Impossible! Beatrice was slovenly, but the sergeant couldn't conceive of her as a murderer, and the other two seemed model mothers and housewives. She closed her mind to the possibility that Bethany was at large and evading arrest.

Back at New Scotland Yard, she delivered the fingerprints to Dr Markham, who told her that Vance had already consigned Andrew Tibbet's prints. She would have all the results as soon as possible.

She went to Vance's office and knocked. To her surprise, when the inspector called for her to enter, she found the commissioner, who greeted her with a friendly smile.

"Ah, Detective Sergeant, Vance tells me that you are convinced that Arnold Tibbet is the poisoner. But we were just discussing the absence of concrete proof to justify your stance."

"At the moment, we're obliged to release him, Sarge," Vance contributed. "You see, we don't have anything to pin the crimes on him, thanks to the presence of those other prints. Unless we can find and apprehend this Bethany, it looks like whoever committed the crimes will get off scot-free."

"But ma'am," Shepherd objected, "I'm convinced this woman doesn't exist. It's a charade. I don't know how he faked everything, but we've still got ninety-six hours to prove he's the killer."

"I think you'll find it's less than ninety-six, Detective," the commissioner said gloomily. "We certainly can't afford a flood of publicity about a wrongful arrest and seven unsolved crimes. It's been the Devil's own job keeping the press at bay on this case, so far."

"Yes, ma'am, I understand, but if I may—" she went on to detail her morning's findings and concluded, "so, you see, it all points to the *non*-existence of a sixth child."

"Well, the clock's ticking, Detectives. I'll expect a result within the set deadline. If you two can't manage it, no one can."

"Thank you, ma'am, we're on to it!" Vance said.

"He won't slip away, ma'am," Shepherd said through clenched teeth, but in her heart, she didn't feel so confident.

When the commissioner had gone, the inspector made coffee for both and, settling in his chair, put Shepherd's fears into words, pointing out all the pitfalls in their case against Tibbet. "But," he went on, "something Miriam Walker told me gave me an idea of how to get under Tibbet's skin. If we drive him to exasperation, we might break him down, but I want to hold it back for the last few hours and preferably without the presence of a lawyer. We don't want accusations of a confession under duress invalidating our conviction."

"Are you planning to rough him up, boss?" Shepherd looked aghast, although she'd contemplated such aggression in the privacy of her thoughts.

"Of course not, Sarge. What do you take me for? No, it might still be classified as violence, though, which is why I'm holding back in the hope that something turns up in the meantime."

"Um, psychological violence, eh?" The sergeant grinned. "If anyone deserves it, it's that little Moriarty down there."

They ran over the evidence until Vance remembered the most recent acquisition, the notebook with the poems and songs. He sat up as an idea struck him. "Bloody Hell, Brit! Francis Tremethyk is right. It may be time for me to retire, after all. I'm slowing down in my old age. Why didn't I think of this before? At least you had the gumption to take a photograph of the two signatures. Can you get a print from your phone?"

"Max can. Do you need a copy? I'll see to it right now."

Vance smiled. She hadn't asked for what purpose as she rushed out the door. A few minutes later, she returned with a sheet of A4, the two signatures in the centre in black ink.

"They're very different, sir. The crafty sod!"

"Only to the untrained eye, Brit. Forensics have a graphology expert. You see, the science of handwriting analysis is based on the presumption that no two people have identical style. It assumes that because each person's script is unique, it can be matched to an individual by examining subtle details and differences, such as the shapes of letters, the pressure used, and where strokes are begun, ended, or joined."

"So, the expert could prove that Arnold wrote both signatures!"

"Prove, no, not under oath, but he could speak of a high probability. We can add some entries in this damned notebook, too, for his scrutiny. By the way, I never did find a moment to look at the last two planned murders. We suppose that Skyport Drive was the location and listen to this, he read:

*"When I am dead no tears will flow*
*Upon my lonely grave below,*
*But from above the aerial blue*
*Will scatter over me tears of dew."*

He's written a note in the margin. *Superb twin reference.* What do you suppose he means by that? Death and sky-blue would be my guess. Then, below that he's put the poet, *Nikoloz Baratashvili* and the title *Sky-blue.* Give him his due, he loves his poets. The name strikes me as Georgian or something like that. And then underneath he's written, *back to paint.* I wonder what he meant?"

"The warped sod always leaves something on the body, sir. I don't think you'll find sky-blue berries, so it's back to paint. Maybe he was planning to stuff a tube of sky-blue paint in some orifice, the sicko!"

"That's probably it. We'll ask him when we start the interview." Vance glanced up at his colleague. "What about this, then. He's underlined M9, and get this, he'd planned it for the SW6 district. He's written *no colour: the signature.* And then in brackets, he's added *(the big one!)* Look, complete with an exclamation mark. Then, he's written the street name, no colour this time, it's Hugon Road. What do you make of that, Sarge?"

"I'd say that he was planning to go out with a bang. However, what he meant by the big one is anyone's guess. The street name, on the other hand, is as clear as you like."

"It is?" Vance frowned and narrowed his eyes, puzzled.

"Yes, sir. H-u-g-o," she spelt it, omitting the last letter.

"Of course, you're right, clever Brittany! Victor Hugo! The author of *The Hunchback of Notre-Dame.* Hence, he wrote *the signature.* That creature is diabolical. Thank goodness we've got him locked up!" Vance pulled the notebook back towards himself. "Ah, what's this?" He had noticed a piece of paper between the last few unused pages of the notebook. He flicked the pages, coming to it.

"It's a page torn from a book and look he's used a yellow highlighter to pick out a passage. The print is minute, too small for my eyes. It looks like it's from an old volume. You've got sharp vision. Read it to me."

Shepherd began to read and stopped halfway to comment:

*"He therefore turned to mankind only with regret. His cathedral was enough for him. It was peopled with marble figures of kings, saints and bishops who at least did not laugh in his face and looked at him with only tranquillity and benevolence. The other statues, those of monsters and demons, had no hatred for him—he resembled them too closely for that."* "This is Victor Hugo, sir, from the famous book, no doubt about it." She continued reading, *"It was rather the rest of mankind that they jeered at. The saints were his friends and blessed him; the monsters were his friends and kept watch over him. He would sometimes spend whole hours crouched before one of the statues in solitary conversation with it. If anyone came upon him then he would run*

*away like a lover surprised during a serenade."* You know what this means, sir?"

"Go on, Sarge, you always surprise me."

"Well, I can't believe he meant to leave this on the last body. I mean, it's as good as a confession. Unless, of course, he was so cocky that he thought we'd never have worked out that we were after someone with his deformity. That's possible, given his character. He must have been worried we'd get on to him, else why all this pantomime about the sister that doesn't exist and the false set of fingerprints?"

"Do you still believe he's the murderer and that Bethany doesn't exist, despite the evidence? You are as stubborn as a mule, Detective Sergeant Shepherd!"

"Well, if I'd had any slight doubts, sir, that extract from Hugo has settled the matter. I just need to think about how the slimebag got around the problem of the fingerprints. Maybe I'll wake up in the morning with the answer in a sudden epiphany."

"In a *what*, Sarge?"

"It's James Joyce, sir. Our toad isn't the only one with a smattering of culture! It's when you have the electric lightbulb over the head moment, like in the comic strips."

"What, a revelation, an insight?"

Shepherd mock-clapped her hands ironically.

"Oh, I've just had one!"

"What, sir?

"An epiphany! And it's telling me that if you work out the fingerprint conundrum, I'll have you promoted to Detective Inspector."

"Get away, pull the other one!"

"No, honestly. So, you'd better wake up with the answer, young lady."

Shepherd pressed him as to whether he was serious, but he felt like teasing her and became evasive until he said, "Seriously if you could work that out, we'd have him trussed up like a Christmas goose."

"Turkey, sir, nobody eats goose for Christmas anymore."

"I do, Sergeant, and very nice—come in!" he broke off and replied to a knock on the door.

Dr Markham entered, holding a sheet of paper and several pages of fingerprints.

"The Tibbet siblings, Detectives. We have the same clear family pattern in all four individuals, but not one of them matches with the incriminating prints, so none of them is guilty of murder, in my opinion. I'm afraid you are still looking for the missing sibling." She smiled and tossed the paper-clipped bundle onto Vance's desk.

"Just as well then, Sarge, that I issued a description and an arrest-on-sight order to all airports and ports for Bethany Tibbet before you got back from the last of the sisters and talked me out of it. Thank you, Sabrina. Oh, before you go back to your den, or coven or whatever—"

"Careful, Jake, my lad! It's more likely to be a lioness than a witch if you provoke me, but come to think—

"Only joking, Doc. What I was going to ask is whether you can get your handwriting expert to look at these." He handed over Brittany's A4 page with the signatures and the notebook. "I need to know the likelihood of them being by the same hand. Thanks very much, sweet lady."

"I'll sweet lady, you!" The scientist marched out of the room with a toss of her head.

"Jake the Rake fails miserably," Shepherd murmured, but he heard and said, "Listen, fellow witch, get off home and sleep on it. Have your epiphany and ring me if it comes—at any time of day or day!"

She grinned, stood, and said, "Might as well go home. There's nowt else we can do here to nail the toe rag. Have a good evening and my love to the lovely, long-suffering Helena."

"Out!" He chortled as the door closed. Despite the mirth, he was confused and sour about the situation. He hated intractable cases. As he saw it, in this moment of stress, there were three possibilities, each as remote as the other: Brittany's epiphany, he snorted; Bethany's arrest, he sneered; Tibbet's confession, he slammed a fist on the desk. That was the only hope. He, too, would go home, rest, and consider the best way to extract the confession from the-the—he had difficulty choosing from Shepherd's range of Tibbet insults.

# CHAPTER 25

## NEW SCOTLAND YARD, LONDON

Vance got up early and drove into New Scotland Yard because he wanted to test a theory without sticking to protocol. Accordingly, he arranged for a guard to attend with Tibbet in Interview Room 1.

"Here, copper, it's a bit soon in the day for harassing prisoners. Where's my lawyer? Hey you! You're a witness to fascist harassment. What's your name?"

The burly guard did not reply, merely staring hard at the cuffed captive.

"I've brought you here, good and early, so you're fresh and alert, Tibbet," the inspector said. "You should know that the game's up, and we're piecing together the last strands of evidence. I also found your confession." He waved the torn page with the yellow highlighting."

Tibbet sneered, "I've never seen that before in my life. Maybe it's our Bethany's."

"Cut the crap, Tibbet. We know Bethany doesn't exist, except inside your head. I've come here in your best interests. As I said before, a confession will help reduce your sentence, so how about it?"

"No way, Sherlock. You're dealing with your very own Moriarty, in case you've forgotten."

Vance sighed dramatically. The moment had come to test his theory.

"OK, Arnold, I get that you don't want to confess, but how about helping the Met with that potent brain of yours?"

"What are you talking about, my dear Holmes?" Tibbet smirked.

"We've got another difficult case on our hands—he's locked up and refusing to cooperate, too. With your remarkable intelligence, I thought you might be able to eke out a confession if we lock you in with him alone. What do you say?"

Tibbet's voice rose significantly, betraying his anxiety.

"Who is this person? What's he supposed to have done?"

"Oh, nothing much, don't worry, he's only a paedophile."

Tibbet's eyes grew bright, and a horrible sneer curled his lips. "A paedophile?" His voice rose an octave. "Me, alone with a paedophile?" He leapt to his feet, sending his chair toppling over backwards, crashing to the floor. Saliva drooled from the corner of his mouth, Vance thought, *like a rabid hound*. The muscular guard seized him by a shoulder with one hand, raised the seat with another, and thrust the agitated prisoner onto it, holding him down firmly. The captive wriggled and squirmed. "You have to be joking," he spat out, saliva spraying the table. "Alone with a paedo? I'd kill him!"

"So, you admit to murderous instincts, Arnold. How do you suppose you'd do that without your poisoned syringe?"

"You know nothing, copper! There are many ways to kill a man with your bare hands. Don't they teach you anything in cop school?"

"We'll add him to your other seven victims, then. I'm not sure whether you've agreed to my proposal or not?"

"Why should I help the cops get a confession? You're holding an innocent man, *me*, against his will."

Vance feigned a patience-tested voice, "Because, Mr Tibbet,

you are in big trouble, and any cooperation with the police will be looked on favourably by the judge at your trial."

Tibbet glared at the inspector. "Look, I hate to say this about my favourite sister, but our Bethany's landed me in this mess. It's *her* you should arrest, but you can't find her, can you? I'll bet she'll be in Tibet by now."

"I doubt that, Arnold, she'd need a visa to get into China."

"The trouble with you coppers is that you ain't got no sense of humour. *Tibet*—Tibbet, get it?"

"Ha-bloody-ha! So, where do you think she's holed out? That is if she isn't a figment of your warped imagination."

"She isn't!" he spat. "Find my sister, and you've solved your case, Sherlock. She could be in Grimsby for all I know."

Whilst he was distracted, Vance winked at the guard. "Constable, lock him up with the paedophile. Let's see if he's brainy enough to get a confession out of the pervert."

The constable hauled Tibbet to his feet. "Come on," he said in a baritone voice, "Aren't you glad to have some company?"

"No!" The word came out as a prolonged shriek and Tibbet squirmed, wriggled, and kicked frantically.

"Wait!" Vance boomed at the guard. "What's up, Mr Tibbet? Is something upsetting you?" He made his sneer evident. "I'll tell you what, Constable, escort the prisoner back to his cell. We'll give him an hour to decide whether to cooperate with his confession or with that of our paedo friend."

"Yes, sir."

---

Meanwhile, before breakfast in her bedsit, Shepherd was gathering clothes from her linen basket. She carried them into the bathroom, scooped up the pale grey chenille shower rug and the towels to add to the wash load. These, she stuffed into the washing machine, programmed it, added powder, and set it working. She grabbed three different-sized towels from the airing cupboard, each carefully folded, and carried them into the bathroom. The police officer turned on the shower and stripped off her pyjamas. She ducked into the shower, washed her hair, and thoroughly soaped her body with an aloe gel. Refreshed, she stepped out onto the tiled floor and cursed. Of course, she'd forgotten, her comfortable chenille rug was in the washer. She gazed at her wet footprints on the cold tiles, and the epiphany occurred. Drying herself and her hair in a mad rush, she thought about her discovery and the more she dwelt on it, the more she sensed that she was right. She blessed her decision to have a short hairstyle and had it dried and brushed in no time.

*I'll not blurt it out to Jake.*

She rang Sabrina Markham and, after apologising for the early hour of her call—the doctor was still in her nightdress—arranged for a working appointment with the expert, who hadn't belittled her idea in the slightest. They agreed to meet in the laboratory as soon as either could get there.

Brittany Shepherd couldn't recall a time when she had been more eager to get into work. Dr Markham felt the same way because she called Shepherd from several paces behind her at the main entrance. "Come on, Sarge, we need a coffee, then we'll put your notion to the test. I must say, it's a new one on me. While we drink, you can tell me how this theory came to you."

They both laughed at Brittany's fortunate misadventure with the chenille rug. The scientist saying, "Did you know that Guinness and blotting paper were discovered as a result of an accident?"

They chatted happily, enjoying each other's company until they reached the laboratory. Markham tapped in a combination of numbers to open the door. Then, since it was her discovery, Shepherd took control.

"I'll need a latex glove, a scalpel and a flat piece of wood that will fit into the thumb of the glove. Provided with these, Shepherd did not surprise the scientist since she had already explained the procedure. She sliced the thumb from the glove, inserted the wood into the truncated latex digit and carefully cut an oval out of it. Then, she bent down, unlaced her right shoe, pulled it off, tugged off her sock and hopped over to a stool, where she worked the latex thumb over her big toe. "I'm ready, Doc. Now bring me an acetate sheet, a pen and a plastic lid."

The scientist obliged, and Shepherd pressed her sheathed toe onto each surface.

"Over to you, now Sabrina."

The forensics expert hurriedly found a fingerprint kit and took the toeprints after dusting the three objects.

Shepherd pulled her sock on without taking the latex from her toe and grinned at the thought of how she would surprise Vance by wiggling her bare foot at him. However, that would happen only if Dr Markham confirmed her theory, otherwise, she'd only make a fool of herself.

The scientist came over. "That's done, now Brittany, I'll need to take your fingerprints. Now you'll get a taste of how your suspects feel." She took the sergeant's right-hand forefinger and pressed it on an ink pad. She followed suit with the other four digits. "OK, now you are officially on record Shepherd, so you'd better be a good girl!"

They both laughed, but their merriment ceased when Dr Markham got down to the serious business of comparing the prints. After the necessary time for a thorough examination, the expert straightened, grabbed the shocked sergeant, and planted a big kiss on her cheek.

"You've cracked it, Brit! You little genius! That's how the cunning swine created his '*sister's*' fingerprints. Look here, you can see the same familiarity in the toeprint, but the ridges and breaks are entirely different. Let's say, for argument's sake, it's as if your brother had handled the three objects."

"My brother, like Bethany, doesn't exist! I've often wanted a male sibling, but I wouldn't let our Catrin hear me say that."

Dr Markham smiled sympathetically. "I'm coming upstairs to

back you up with Jacob. Besides, I want to see his face after he called us witches yesterday."

In the detective inspector's office, Shepherd crowed, "Watch this, boss!"

Vance gaped as his sergeant bared her right foot and wiggled her toes at him.

"Have you been drinking, Sarge? It's a little early in the day! And what's that on your big toe?"

"When they'd finished giggling, Sabrina Markham explained and produced the evidence.

"Well, blow me down! The crafty little sod! Why didn't we think of that?"

"Either because it's a first, Jacob," said Dr Markham, "or because similar crimes have gone undetected. I'm going to contact the FBI to see whether they've come across such a thing, but because of time lag, that'll have to wait. Are you going to offer the witches a coffee to celebrate?"

"Yeah, it hasn't sunk in yet. We've got Tibbet as soon as we take his toeprint, I reckon."

"You'll need this, sir." Shepherd wriggled off the latex sleeve and handed it to Vance. "It'll be how he did it."

"Thanks. It'll be a joy to see his face when we confront him. But let me tell you about what happened before you two came in to work—I'll tell you over a coffee—" He took three capsules out of a biscuit tin and switched on his coffee machine. As he waited for the device to heat the water, he told them about Tibbet's pathological hatred of paedophiles. "You can't blame him for that, after what he was subjected to, but I'll swear that he became positively homicidal at the prospect of sharing a cell with a paedo. He lost control, and I knew then that I was dealing with a psychopath. Ha! The light's stopped flashing, the machine's ready to make coffee. He inserted a capsule and pressed the button. Moments later, all three were enjoying an excellent espresso.

"What blend do you use, Jacob? It's fabulous," Sabrina said.

"Strange Brew," Vance said, teasing her.

"Listen, mate, I know all of the Cream's songs. Any more of this witch stuff, and I won't answer for *my* homicidal actions."

The inspector tossed her a whole packet of capsules from his cupboard. "You can keep it if you've got a suitable machine.

"Oh, I'll keep it to spite you! We'll see about buying a decent machine to go with this gift. Unless I break into your office on my broomstick one night and filch yours."

They all laughed, then Vance said, I'll ring and have Tibbet taken to Interview Room 1. Sabrina, meet us there with the necessary equipment." He scooped up the latex sleeve from his desk.

In the interview room, as soon as Tibbet entered, he sneered, "What now, copper? Have you dreamed up another bluff to get me to confess? There ain't no paedo down there in the cells, and you know it."

"There are *two,* Tibbet, but we won't be requiring their passive cooperation. We've obtained all the proof we need to put you away for a very long time."

"I told you, it's our Bethany you wan—"

"Shut up, Tibbet! Ah, here's Dr Markham ready to take your prints."

The prisoner looked uneasily at the expert. "What's this? You've already taken them."

Vance smirked, satisfied. "But we haven't got your toe prints, Arnold. You see, we've worked out how you created your red herring."

"You can't do this! There's no law says you can take toe prints."

"Very true, my dear chappie," the inspector said, "but, you see, there's no law that says we can't. You'd better cooperate, I think."

Shepherd, who had been gazing at their suspect without disguising her revulsion, at last, intervened. "Besides, Tibbet, if your sister is guilty, as you claim, you've nothing to fear, have you?"

"That's right, but I ain't going to let you mess around with my feet. I want my lawyer."

"Guard, sit him down, will you? And let's be having his right foot bared," she ordered.

The burly custodian roughly pushed his charge onto the chair and bent to carry out the command.

Suddenly, the prisoner screamed and thrashed his legs to prevent the guard from proceeding.

"No!" bellowed Vance at the guard, "don't strike him, Constable! Dr Markham, did you bring the sedative?"

"You can't do this! I know my rights!" Tibbet shrieked.

Shepherd stepped forward and, bending to stare into his face, noticed the insane glint in his eyes. "You could save yourself a lot of trouble Arnie if you just confessed. In your black heart, you know we've got you."

"Fuck you, copper!"

She kept her thoughts to herself.

*Wouldn't you like to?* She shuddered with disgust. *But where you're going, it's more likely you that'll be penetrated."*

"You're not taking my toe print!" he screeched.

"Very well," said the inspector. "You leave us no choice. Constable, bare his arm. Doctor Markham, you may proceed with the sedative. I hope you didn't mistake the phial with the TTX one we took from Tibbet's apartment," he chuckled malignly: a studied act. "If such an understandable error occurred, it would save the taxpayer a lot of money in years of not keeping Arnold locked up. For one who loves poetry, it would be poetic justice, wouldn't it, Tibbet?"

With sadistic pleasure, Vance gloated at the horror on the captive's face, not knowing if it was death or sedation, as he watched Dr Markham's needle slide into his arm.

# CHAPTER 26

## NEW SCOTLAND YARD, LONDON

Tibbet expected to die of a TTX injection but found himself in dazed numbness, sedated by Dr Markham. Vaguely, he realised that the police had removed his shoe and sock, and he could not combat the lassitude in his limbs to prevent them from proceeding. Dully aware that they were repeating what he had done in his flat by pulling a latex sleeve over his big toe, even in his soporific state, he knew that the Metropolitan Police had outwitted him and that they would have all the proof they needed.

*How did they work it out? Damn them all to hell!*

He felt the pressure on his big toe as the doctor who had jabbed him pressed it onto an ink pad. And that moment signalled to his brain that there was no longer any point in pretence. But his numb mouth prevented him from speaking, for his lips felt like two fused slivers of ice.

Indistinctly he heard the police inspector order the guard to take him back to his cell. He didn't catch the words exactly, but he understood the gist. It would take time to compare the prints. Of course, it would. They would bring him back, and he would tell them what he wanted them to hear. They were in for a shock —*soddin' coppers!*

Whilst Dr Markham took the prints for analysis, Vance put an arm around his sergeant's shoulders. "Brittany, I want to be the first to tell you this—and I shouldn't jump the gun, but I'm confident of the outcome—your insights have cracked this case, and it's not the first time that you've made a breakthrough in a difficult indictment. You're a damned good detective, young lady! What I am about to tell you has been brewing for some time."

She shrugged off his arm and turned to face him squarely. "Do you have any idea of how long-winded you can be, boss?"

His face fell, and he looked at her balefully. "Typical female! You lot always have to spoil the best moments for some reason. I was about to make an important announcement—"

"You've just redefined the expression *about to*, Detective Inspector. Just do it, for God's sake!"

"Undeserving little wench! I was about to say that I'm delighted for your promotion—especially because I won't have to put up with any more of your cheek, Detective Inspector Shepherd."

Her face became a rosy pink. "You aren't joking, I suppose?"

"Far from it, Brittany. I've had permission from the commissioner to tell you myself. Although, to be honest, I was supposed to wait until we'd convicted Tibbet. Still, I'm sure of that now, thanks to you.

"Me, an inspector? I can't believe it. What will I do without you, boss?"

"Soon to be ex-boss, and you'll be fine and can make someone else's hair turn grey. But keep your hands off Constable Allen. I've got him marked down as my new sergeant."

"Great choice, boss—*er*—Jacob, I guess I'll have to find myself a sergeant, too," she gazed at him, moved, "but it won't be the same."

"Of course, it will, but it takes time to build up the rapport. It'll be the same for me with Mark Allen. Now, I suggest that we go to the nearest decent pub to celebrate your promotion. You and me alone, for the moment, then we'll do it properly with everybody when it's official."

"You and *I*," she muttered, luckily too low for him to catch.

When they returned from The Feathers, Brittany fortified by gins and tonics, he by a couple of pints of bitter, they met Sabrina Markham pretending to lurk near his office. In reality, she had spent ten minutes chatting to Max Wright, who had asked her out on a date again after the success of their first evening together. She had heard Brittany giggling on the stairs and nipped across to stand outside Vance's office not to invite wise-cracks from the altogether too smart detectives. So, she greeted them with, "Hi, you guys, I've got three items of news for you in exchange for a coffee. You two look as if you could do with a strong espresso! Some of us have been working so that others can enjoy themselves."

"We've been celebrating Brit's promotion, but hush! It's not official yet."

Sabrina Markham beamed and planted a kiss on the police officer's cheek for the second time in one day. "It's well-deserved and overdue, Brittany. Congratulations."

"I won't believe it until I hear it from Her Ladyship in person."

"You'd better believe it, Brit. You heard it from the greatest living authority on—"

"Aw, shut up and make the coffee!" Shepherd giggled.

"See, Sabrina, I'll be glad to be rid of her!" He switched on the coffee maker and grinned at the two smiling colleagues, but his heart was heavy. How would he ever replace Brittany Shepherd? "Now, Doc, what was it you had to tell us?"

"In increasing order of importance, I have a report from James Horton, our graphologist. In his expert opinion, the two signatures were most likely by the same hand, as were the entries in the notebook. As always, with James, he said he wouldn't swear to it on oath, but the likelihood of them being the same person he described at more than ninety per cent."

"Another nail in Tibbet's coffin," Vance said, more to himself, as he pressed the button for the first espresso.

"I rang the FBI, and our American colleague called me back after a good hour. The Americans haven't any record of such a fingerprint fraud, but he admitted the technique was possible and that a criminal might have gone under the radar, so to speak. He referred me to a Dutch expert who has written scientific articles on the subject, proving that Brittany's intuition was founded on sound practical principles. So, a resounding well done to our neo-inspector."

Brittany took her espresso from Vance and looked pleased with herself but didn't say anything because she was waiting for Sabrina's third announcement on tenterhooks. It wasn't long in coming. "The proof of the pudding is in the eating. I'll get straight to the point." She beamed at the detectives. "Arnold Tibbet's toe print was a perfect match with the prints on the incriminating evidence. Success, detectives! Congratulations, I think we have a watertight case to take to court."

Vance didn't waste a second but reached for his phone. "Bring Tibbet back to Interview Room 1." As soon as he had put the receiver down, he lifted it again to call Tibbet's lawyer. "Yes, I need you present at the next interview. I'm going to charge your client officially with multiple murders. Yes, twenty minutes will be fine." For the third time, he raised the handset. "Hello, sir, in a few minutes, we'll be charging Tibbet. I thought you and the commissioner might like to supervise. We'll be in Interview Room 1. Yes, of course, I've called his lawyer. He's on his way in. Right, fine."

Vance smiled at his colleagues. "We might need your proof and expertise Doc, so you'd better come, too. Brit, Tibbet seems to have taken a personal dislike to you, so you can provoke him to catch him off balance if you get the opportunity. Let's go, then!"

When they entered, Tibbet was seated at the table in the interview room. His first words were, "I want my lawyer present."

"He's on his way, Tibbet, and we'll not start proceedings until he walks into this room. Have you thought about confessing?"

"I've thought about little else. Will I be allowed to consult him before we begin?"

"I believe that is your right, and we'll allow that. Of course, a guard will remain in attendance as prescribed by law."

Tibbet glared at the inspector. "Don't try to tell me that injection that *she* gave me," he scowled at Markham, "was prescribed by law. I don't want any more medication, and I'll tell that to my lawyer."

"If you behave in a civilised manner, it won't be necessary. Besides, I don't see Dr Markham's medical bag this time, do you?"

The lawyer arrived and everyone except the muscular guard left the room so that Tibbet could speak with the legal practitioner. Ten minutes passed before the grey-suited lawyer came out into the corridor.

"Detective Inspector, my client wishes to make a full confession on the understanding that the Metropolitan Police will testify to his cooperation."

"I think you can reassure Mr Tibbet on that point, Mr Prowse."

The police officers, forensics expert and lawyer all returned into the room, where the latter stepped over to his client and spoke quietly to him for a moment.

He moved away, whereas Vance sat at the table opposite Tibbet and switched on a recorder, dictating the date, time and people present. That done, he addressed Arnold Tibbet. "Mr Tibbet, I believe that you wish to make a declaration."

"I do, but forgive me, I need to provide context by quoting Victor Hugo. I have learnt much of his masterpiece by heart and, although this will be brief, bear with me because it's relevant."

"Very well," Vance turned to Shepherd, who was leaning against the wall behind him.

She nodded and said, "I'm all ears."

Tibbet glared at her. "Good, it goes like this: "*We shall not attempt to give the reader an idea of that tetrahedron nose-that horse-shoe mouth-that small left eye over-shadowed by a red bushy brow, while the right eye disappeared entirely under an enormous wart-of those straggling teeth with breaches here and there like the battlements of a fortress-of that horny lip, over which one of those teeth projected like the tusk of an elephant-of that forked chin-and, above all, of the expression diffused over the whole-that mixture of malice, astonishment, and melancholy. Let the reader, if he can, figure to himself this combination.*""

Tibbet puffed out his cheeks as if to underline the difficulty of recalling the Hugo quote, but then, changing his literary voice to the aggrieved tone the officers had become accustomed to, adding, "If you want to understand me and what I've done, think about those words. People don't realise what people like me have to bear. The public consciousness forms the impression that we're all monsters like the Hunchback of Notre-Dame. But look at my face. It's nothing like what that French cretin described. I'm a good-looking little fellow and, apart from this, he shrugged his shoulders. I'm no monster. And as I've been trying to prove to you and your arrogant commissioner, nothing is lacking up here. The cuffs didn't stop him from pointing to his head. I think I've done enough to prove my intelligence is equal, if not superior, to you detectives. I will admit that I unwisely allowed you to find my place of residence. I expected that, though, which was why I made the fake fingerprints." He paused and stared at Vance. "Now, there you did surprise me, Inspector! I never thought you'd work out my little ploy. I didn't expect you to find the picture by Lapique, either, but I will admit, I underestimated you."

"Now, having set the scene, let me confess. Yes, I killed seven people to prove a point to your commissioner. I can't pretend to influence a judge that I'm repentant. I don't care about the people I eliminated or their families. Why should they, or any of you, for that matter," he glared around the room, "have professional careers and a perfect physique, whilst the career I desired, and the body I wanted, were denied to me by this?" He replicated the familiar shrug to evidence his hump. "And, apart from that, I dare say none of you grew up in squalor or was a victim of a damned paedophile."

Vance leant forward and stared into the unnaturally shining eyes, "But none of us has your wealth, Arnold. You have a beautiful apartment overlooking the Thames and a brilliant brain. You could have chosen to use it to work from home. With your potential, you might have proved your genius to the world and done some good for humankind."

"Instead, despicable monster, you chose to employ it in the pursuit of evil," Shepherd put in.

"Shut up, bitch! I'm talking to someone who has some intelligence, not to you."

"Detective Shepherd was the one who worked out the fake prints, Arnold," Vance said gently.

The maniac glared at her so viciously that Vance itched to strike him but controlled himself and even his voice, keeping it calm.

"Arnold, tell me about the murders, begin with the first and take us through the others."

That seemed to massage his ego. "Right, well, the first depended on the colour yellow. I found a street that had once had the name Primrose. It pleased me because it made it more difficult than, say, *Yellow Brick Road*." He laughed at his joke, but nobody smiled. "That woman, she was random. I'd spotted that she walked home late every day when the lane was quiet. I dressed up as Bethany. By the way, my sister *does* exist." The police officers exchanged incredulous glances but said nothing, as he went on to explain the less random nature of the second and third murders, and the difficulties presented by the White Horse Yard killing as they listened with increasing disgust and horror to his confession. With the red murder, he brought them up to date. But now came the most chilling part as he revealed his thwarted intentions. "With sky-blue, as you know, I was going to strike in Skyport Drive, but that went all wrong from the start and led to my arrest. I would have chosen another random victim, someone locking up late, I had thought."

"In your notebook, you wrote that the last one in Hugon Road—Sergeant Shepherd was quick to hit on the Victor Hugo connection—would be *the big one*. What did you mean by that expression?"

Tibbet's sneer made his face light up with evil glee. "Ah, the big one. Well, it wasn't colour connected, I'd have finished *Quasimodo*," he spat out the word, "with sky-blue, no, this was more like the signature on the painting, as it were. I'd studied the commissioner and her family. Oh, yes, I know all about your spinster chief. She has a sister, you know, with three children. The eldest of her nephews and nieces is a student at Imperial College. His name is Farid. He was going to be *the big one*. Then your Aalia Phadkar would have been sorry for provoking the criminal brain."

Vance could not help glancing up at the opaque glass.

Quick as a flash, Tibbet understood. "Is *she* looking at us? Well, *bitch*," he addressed the glass, "I'd have enjoyed snuffing out your nephew. Next time you make a speech, don't forget to show respect for the criminal brain."

"Well, Arnold Tibbet, I think you've said enough. Now I'm going to charge you officially with seven murders and planning two others. We will transcribe the recording and ask you to sign the transcription."

Vance concluded proceedings, turned off the recorder and had Tibbet locked in his cell again.

"I think we can safely conclude that Lord Robert I just another of Tibbet's multiple personalities, Sarge. His muddled head can't distinguish truth from his illness."

The door to the interview room opened, and the commissioner entered. "Congratulations are in order. Well done, all of you. A special word of thanks to you, Inspector," she wasn't looking at Jacob Vance but at Brittany Shepherd. "Your precious insights mean that we shall lock the monster away, as Miriam Walker believes, in a secure psychiatric hospital for the rest of his life. Oh, and not a minor point for me—my darling Farid is safe."

"Excuse me, ma'am, you said *Inspector*," Shepherd said.

"Jacob, haven't you told her?"

"Well, it wasn't official, ma'am."

"It is now! Congratulations Detective Inspector Shepherd." Commissioner Phadkar flashed her a winsome smile.

# EPILOGUE

THE METROPOLITAN POLICE DECIDED TO TAKE NO FURTHER ACTION against Akina Aoyama and Tatsuo Narisawa, although both the escort and the chef were cautioned as to their future conduct. The police maintained that neither person was a threat to the public, and it would serve no purpose to prosecute them. Shepherd persuaded Vance to partner her in a splendid free celebratory meal in Tatsuo's restaurant. Unlike his colleague, for some reason, Jacob would not try the delicious sashimi.

After listening to all the accumulated evidence and the various experts, the Crown Court jury declared Arnold Tibbet guilty on all counts. In his summing up, the judge sentenced him to nine consecutive life sentences to be served in Broadmoor Hospital, a high-security psychiatric hospital in Berkshire.

He had only completed seventeen months of his sentence when he came into contact with the paedophile murderer Edmund McEvoy. The official records reported Tibbet as having attacked McEvoy with a rollerball pen, but his attempt to drive the sharp point into the paedophile's eye failed. Before the prison guards could intervene, McEvoy fatally snapped Tibbet's spine just above the deformity at the base of his neck. Thus, ended the life of the weirdest serial killer that the Met had ever encountered.

Inspectors Vance and Shepherd attended Tibbet's funeral at the East London Cemetery and Crematorium, located in West Ham in the London Borough of Newham. The family opted for cremation, primarily to avoid the likely desecration of the grave.

Outdoors, after the service, Shepherd recognised Arnold's sisters among the few assembled mourners and Vance pointed out Andrew Tibbet to her. "Who's the woman standing apart from the others?" Vance asked, glancing in the opposite direction. Shepherd stared across to the other side of the entrance, where between two headstones, dressed in black, stood a petite young woman with long blonde hair.

"I don't know, but now's a good time to find out."

DI Shepherd headed towards her quarry, but by the time she had scrunched across the gravelled forecourt of the crematorium, the woman had disappeared among the tombstones.

**THE END**

# APPENDIX

For those readers who might feel that the toe print episode and familiarity of prints is a figment of this writer's imagination, I would like to cite two authorities whose articles may be of interest.

I include links to the documents below. I should also remark that any error included in my novel is attributable to me and not to them.

Glenn Langenburg, a Certified Latent Print Examiner at the Minnesota Bureau of Criminal Apprehension, is the author of a fascinating article about what makes fingerprints unique, which appeared in the journal, Scientific American. The document is freely accessible on the Internet at:

https://www.scientificamerican.com/article/are-ones-fingerprints-sim/

Instead, Louis J. van Der Meulen, Commander of the Leyden District of the Netherlands National Police, wrote an amazing article entitled *Fake Fingerprints – A New Aspect* in the Journal of Criminal Law and Criminology. As above, the article is freely accessible on the Internet at:

https://scholarlycommons.law.northwestern.edu/cgi/viewcontent.cgi?article=4355&context=jclc

# ABOUT THE AUTHOR

John Broughton was born in Cleethorpes Lincolnshire UK in 1948: just one of many post-war babies. After attending grammar school and studying to the sound of Bob Dylan, he went to Nottingham University and studied Medieval and Modern History (Archaeology subsidiary). The subsidiary course led to one of his greatest academic achievements: tipping the soil content of a wheelbarrow from the summit of a spoil heap on an old lady hobbling past the dig.

He did many different jobs while living in Radcliffe-on-Trent, Leamington, Glossop, the Scilly Isles, Puglia, and Calabria. They include teaching English and History, managing a Day Care Centre, being a Director of a Trade Institute and teaching university students English. He even tried being a fisherman and a flower picker when he was on St. Agnes island, Scilly. He has lived in Calabria since 1992 where he settled into a long-term job at the University of Calabria, teaching English. No doubt his lovely Calabrian wife Maria stopped him being restless.

His two kids are grown up now, but he wrote books for them when they were little. Hamish Hamilton and then Thomas Nelson published six of these in England in the 1980s. They are now out of print. He's a granddad and, happily, the parents gratifyingly named his grandson Dylan. He decided to take up writing again late in his career. When teaching and working as a translator, you don't really have time for writing. As soon as he stopped the translation work, he resumed writing in 2014.

The fruit of that decision was his first historical novel, *The Purple Thread,* followed by *Wyrd of the Wolf.* Both are set in his favourite Anglo-Saxon period. His third and fourth novels, a two-book set, are *Saints and Sinners* and its sequel *Mixed Blessings,* set on the cusp of the eighth century in Mercia and Lindsey. A fifth, *Sward and Sword,* is about the great Earl Godwine. Creativia Publishing has released *Perfecta Saxonia* and *Ulf's Tale* about King Aethelstan and King Cnut's empire, respectively. In May 2019, they published *In the Name of the Mother,* a sequel to *Wyrd of the Wolf.* Creativia/Next Chapter also published *Angenga,* a time-travel novel linking the ninth century to the twenty-first. This novel inspired John Broughton's next venture, a series of seven novels about psychic investigator Jake Conley, whose retrocognition takes him back to Anglo-Saxon times. In another departure, he published a fantasy novel, *Whirligig,* and now a mystery in the present *The Quasimodo Killings.*

Other historical novels followed including the St Cuthbert Trilogy and the Sceapig Chronicles Trilogy.

In all, he has twenty-three novels published, which can be seen with relative information at the author's website: www.saxonquill.com

---

To learn more about John Broughton and discover more Next Chapter authors, visit our website at www.nextchapter.pub.

The Quasimodo Killings
ISBN: 978-4-82412-289-6

Published by
Next Chapter
1-60-20 Minami-Otsuka
170-0005 Toshima-Ku, Tokyo
+818035793528

10th January 2022

Milton Keynes UK
Ingram Content Group UK Ltd.
UKHW041833221123
432954UK00023B/97